PRAISE F(
THE REGIS

'This is compelling. You won't put it down. Shows how fiction can ...
to reality—almost painfully real.' **Dr Norman Swan**

'In *The Registrar*, Neela Janakiramanan writes with a surgeon's precision and a novelist's sensibility. The result is a visceral and gut-wrenching tale of one doctor's battle to maintain her humanity within a system hell-bent on destroying it. The writing is honest and unflinching and the characters, complex and believable. Like many doctors, I know this story, I've lived this story. Now, thanks to Neela Janakiramanan, the rest of Australia will know it too.' **Dr Melanie Cheng, author of *AUSTRALIA DAY***

'The moving story of a woman, a family and a profession; an insider's view of the good, the bad and the unacceptable in our hospital system that resonates for so many workplaces. A brilliant read from a brilliant woman. Neela Janakiramanan— surgeon, leader, advocate and now talented author.' **Kate Jenkins, Sex Discrimination Commissioner**

'So beautiful. A fitting tribute to our lives and work, and to those who we have lost.' **Dr Ruth Mitchell, neurosurgeon and Nobel Peace Prize laureate**

'Compelling, illuminating and utterly readable. A peek behind the curtain of medicine, quite unlike anything you'd see on *Grey's Anatomy*. A brilliant debut. My brain told me I had to get back to my day job, but my heart wouldn't let me put *The Registrar* down. A fast-paced and fearless novel. *The Registrar* is a wake-up call to the medical establishment. A heroic and high-wire feat of storytelling from inside a world most of us never get to see.' **Jamila Rizvi, author of *NOT JUST LUCKY***

'With knife-like precision, Dr Janakiramanan affords us an intimate view into what may lie behind a surgeon's mask.' **Dr Leah Kaminsky, award-winning author of *THE HOLLOW BONES* and *THE WAITING ROOM***

'Neela has accurately captured the essence of what it is like to work as a doctor in modern Australia. *The Registrar* is an honest portrayal of the cutthroat culture that lurks behind a caring profession. *The Registrar* is a rapid intravenous infusion of caffeine and adrenaline from start to finish.' **Dr Brad McKay, doctor, broadcaster, author of *FAKE MEDICINE***

'A thoughtful insight into the human frailty at the heart of the surgical profession and the way its ingrained traditions fail both its trainees and patients. A poignant glimpse into the fractures at the core of the doctors who are trying to be the best they can be, and have obstacles disguised as words of wisdom that will maintain the status quo placed at every turn.

Every doctor will see themselves in Janakiramanan's tale of surgical training—and it may help every patient see the humanity behind the harried and exhausted demeanours or the arrogance of those that treat them. A must-read for anyone considering or studying medicine.' **Anne Buist, Professor of Women's Mental Health, University of Melbourne**

'Doctors embarking on their final years before officially being called a surgeon are called Registrars. They have jumped endless high hoops to get there to these final years. They are accomplished doctors. Our Registrar in this gripping tale appears to have it all. We expect compassionate competent care. But what are these doctors up against as they aim to provide that and navigate the unseen hurdles, the exam preparation, the effects of a complication, the burnout. Why can't a Registrar be in two places at once? Is that mentorship or sexual attraction? Can it be both . . .

Dr Neela Janakiramanan has crafted a story that rings too true to any surgeon or trainee surgeon. If you want to understand the doctor caring for you, read this. There is a will to improve the system and things are improving. Meanwhile young lives are caught up in lethal or sub-lethal pressures.

A must for a doctor aspiring to become a medical specialist or surgeon.' **Professor Helen O'Connell, AO, MD, FRACS, MMed, MBBS, FAICD, Vice President USANZ**

'*The Registrar* tells the gripping story of a young woman training to become a surgeon in a male-dominated hierarchical world. Whilst it might be fictional, the situations depicted in the novel are all too real for those of us who have worked as junior doctors in the public health system.

I've always questioned people who say things like "a real page turner" but this is one of the few times I've understood what this means. I literally could not put this book down and could relate to the protagonist through all her highs and lows having either experienced them first-hand, or had friends experience them. This novel is relatable for all of us who have ever experienced bullying or prejudice in the healthcare industry or who have been made to feel not good enough. A must-read not just for healthcare workers, but for those in adminis- trative and leadership positions who impact our everyday life and wellbeing. It's time this culture in medicine changes. Whilst it starts with us and our generation fighting for change, we also need those in leadership to understand our struggles, understand that we are people too and that we need supportive and safe working environments or the tragedies described in *The Registrar* will continue to occur in reality, not just in the fictional world. Thank you Neela for telling our story.' **Dr Tahnee Lee Bridson, Founder/President, Hand-n-Hand Peer Support Inc**

'*The Registrar* is excellent but very emotionally challenging. I think this book will be very timely to illustrate the problems of sexual harassment and mental wellbeing/ suicide during surgical training. This is going to be read and discussed widely.

This book illustrates the workload of trainee surgeons, the pressure to perform, lack of support in some institutions, and the major problem of mental health and wellbeing. The disguised nature of sexual harassment by a mentor with power is clearly illustrated. The friendship and support of the trainees and other young doctors is beautifully illustrated as is the reminder to treat the patient as a person with a name.' **Dr Sally Langley, President RACS**

'Loved *The Registrar*. Gritty, humanistic, truthful, hopeful.' **Dr Terry Wu, reconstructive plastic surgeon and arts advocate**

'This debut novel from Neela Janakiramanan presents the very human face (and cost) of a profession we often perceive as utterly clinical. Stirring, complex and powerful, *The Registrar* will bind you till the very end.' **Tarla Lambert, Editor in Chief, *WOMEN'S AGENDA***

'A spellbinding insider's view into a world unseen to most of us. The last few years have shown us that health care workers are the heroes that walk among us. *The Registrar* takes us alongside them to show how they are pushed to the limit. A triumphant debut novel and I hope for many more.' **Dr Kirstin Ferguson, leadership expert, columnist and author**

'Neela takes us into the 24-hour life and mind of a surgical trainee, the good and the bad. It's as if you are living her day as you read—takes me back to my own days as a trainee medical doctor.' **Dr Geoff Toogood, MBBS, FRACP, FCSANZ, MAICD, FHRS, AFRACMA**

In real life Neela Janakiramanan is a reconstructive plastic surgeon with particular expertise in complex hand and wrist surgery. She has wide experience working in the public and private health sector. She is a seasoned public speaker and advocate on issues including health equity, gender equity, and diversity and inclusion. She was also one of the medical leads in the Kids off Nauru campaign, bringing together the Australian medical community and operationalising the Australian Medevac legislation to facilitate medical care for refugees in offshore detention. Neela is a regular contributor to Women's Agenda, and has also written for *The Age*, *Sydney Morning Herald*, *The Saturday Paper*, and often appears on ABC's *The Drum*.

The
Registrar

NEELA
JANAKIRAMANAN

ALLEN&UNWIN
SYDNEY•MELBOURNE•AUCKLAND•LONDON

First published in 2022

Allen & Unwin
83 Alexander Street
Crows Nest NSW 2065
Australia
Phone: (61 2) 8425 0100
Email: info@allenandunwin.com
Web: www.allenandunwin.com

 A catalogue record for this book is available from the National Library of Australia

ISBN 978 1 76106 651 1

Set in 13/19 pt Granjon LT Std by Bookhouse, Sydney
Printed and bound in Australia by Griffin Press, part of Ovato

10 9 8 7 6 5 4 3 2 1

To Brad,

For always giving me a soft place to land

Ars longa,

vita brevis,

occasio praeceps,

experimentum periculosum,

iudicium difficile.

Medice, cura te ipsum.

Chapter One

The child's hand is grey and mottled.

I've crouched down next to the bed to examine it and now I stand up, the urgency of Ngoni's phone call clear. We went to medical school together and he's not often rattled, certainly not by a simple trampoline accident. He's correct, the right forearm definitely has no pulse.

The boy is nine but looks younger, and is much too small for the adult-sized hospital bed crammed into a cubicle painted blue with fish stickers over the wall. He's slumped down, his T-shirt riding up at the back and exposing his belly. The paramedics have strapped up his right arm, and in his other hand, he clutches a small green inhaler that whistles slightly as he takes ragged breaths. His eyes are glazed from the painkillers he's breathing in. His mother hovers, too agitated to sit.

'We took him straight to X-ray,' Ngoni says as he pushes a computer on a trolley into the room. He points at the screen, confirming the severity of the fracture.

Shit.

'What's going on?' the mother asks, her voice shaky, the tear stains on her cheek matching those of her child. She's looking at Ngoni. He waits for me to explain.

'He's broken his arm just above the elbow and the fracture's putting pressure on an artery. But don't worry,' I reassure her, 'as soon as the bone's straight again, the blood flow will return to normal.' I have one eye on the clock above the bed. 'What time did it happen?'

I don't tell her that muscle cells deprived of blood start to die within a couple of hours. I don't tell her that if it takes too long to restore blood flow then the muscles can swell within their tight fibrous coverings and die even hours or days later. In years past, kids with this fracture developed clawed fingers and permanent disability—and the best way of avoiding this is to straighten the bone and unkink the artery as soon as possible. I don't want to tell her that this is a time-critical emergency until I have a plan.

'I think . . .' The mother can't remember how long it's been. She didn't check the time when her son cried out. She didn't look at her watch as she pulled him out of the narrow gap in the trampoline netting and called an ambulance.

Ngoni shuffles some papers and extracts a pink sheet. 'The ambulance arrived at 11.03,' he says.

'They came quite quickly,' the mother adds.

I check the time again. It's already 12.30.

'And when did he last have something to eat or drink?'

'I made him and his sister a strawberry milkshake around ten.'

I sigh. The anaesthetists are going to love that.

'Can you . . . ?' I start, but Ngoni's already nodding. He'll explain what's going on to the mother while I organise an operating theatre. We don't have much time. I tear off some ID stickers with the boy's name, still on their paper backing, and run.

These corridors are familiar to me. Down the hall, up a flight of stairs and then around the corner—the operating theatres are located directly above the Emergency Department. I can plan what to do next while I'm moving.

Mei Ling is the surgeon who's on call. She's the first person I have to tell. I'm just the junior doctor covering for Orthopaedics today. Sure, I've worked on surgical teams for years but I won't even be a trainee surgeon for another three weeks and then it's a further five years to be a surgeon. I'm not allowed—nor qualified—to demand an operating theatre, no matter the urgency of my case. I try four times. Mei Ling doesn't answer her phone.

Shit.

I decide to organise a theatre anyway and then worry about a surgeon. Surely someone will be around.

'Woah, Emma, slow down!' Ibrahim puts his arms out to stop me with a laugh; I've almost bowled straight into him and his team on the stairs. He was my registrar four years ago when I first started working as an intern. I'm still grateful for his patience—medical school teaches us how to perform CPR but not how to treat conjunctivitis.

'Sorry, Ibrahim, I've got a supracondylar with a dying arm,' I say as I rush past.

'Good luck!' he echoes back, a floor away already.

Mei Ling calls me as I burst through the door into the bright hallway that links theatre and intensive care.

'What's up, Emma?' she asks without greeting. After two decades as a surgeon she must know that four missed calls from the hospital mean an emergency.

'Nine-year-old, supracondylar, dominant hand, pulseless arm, heading to two hours post-injury,' I summarise for her.

There's a pause.

'I'm on the other side of town. Can you get started? Tell theatre I've given you permission. At least if you can reduce it and restore blood flow, by then I'll be there to help you pin it.'

I hesitate. Over the last ten years—six as a medical student and four as a doctor—many surgeons have taught me bits and pieces of their craft. But I've never opened an operating theatre on my own before.

'I promise I'll be there, Em. Besides, you're an official trainee in a few weeks. You'll be fine. You've got this.'

'Okay,' I reply, breathless from the sprint up the stairs and the sudden extra surge in adrenaline. I wave my ID tag over the proximity reader and the doors to theatre reception slide open.

'Hi, Em, you look like you've found something urgent,' Chitty, the clerk, observes.

I lean over the desk and search her schedule for the names of the anaesthetist and nurse in charge of theatre today.

'Geoff and Layla,' she says, pointing to the correct rows. 'Give me the patient's details. I'll take it in to Layla and you can call Geoff.'

I scribble a note on the back of the patient's ID sticker with a whispered thanks and find Geoff's phone number in my phone.

'What have you got, Em?' Geoff asks kindly. He's my favourite anaesthetist. He even tried to convince me to specialise in anaesthetics rather than surgery, so I know he'll take me seriously. He also knows that I'm acting up today.

'Supracondylar, dead arm. Unfasted nine-year-old with a belly full of strawberry milkshake.'

'That'll make things fun.' Geoff is dry. 'Lucky timing, most of the morning operating lists have finished and we'll delay someone's start this afternoon. Do you have to wait for a boss?'

'No, Mei Ling said I could start. She's on her way.'

'Are you sure?'

I know Geoff isn't being rude. I *know* that I'm unqualified and it's his job to ask if the operation can be completed before he puts a patient to sleep.

Mei Ling is reliable. If she says she's coming then she means it. But what if there's traffic, what if she has an accident? Then I realise that I know what to do. I know that I can finish this operation. And I realise that Mei Ling, who never accepts a shoddy result, must think I can too, otherwise she wouldn't have given me permission to start.

'Yes,' I say confidently.

'Okay, Em. We'll send for the patient. We'll work around the strawberry milkshake, just don't be a typical registrar and rush us, okay?'

He called me a registrar, I think, and smile. It's the first time.

———

I'm sitting on a stool looking at a satisfyingly pink hand when Mei Ling bustles in still tucking stray hairs under her clean blue balaclava. She inspects the small hand over my shoulder and studies the X-ray I've taken, but doesn't ask for a theatre gown or sterile gloves.

'Good work. Are you going to pin the fracture now, or sit there grinning stupidly?' she asks, a smile in her voice.

One of the nurses hands me the drill with the pin loaded, the tool almost too large for my small hand. I strain to reach the trigger.

Mei Ling's still watching. 'Try your middle finger on the trigger with a big drill like that,' she suggests. 'It's got more reach.'

I set the drill down to reposition and it sits more neatly in my hand.

'Now screen with the X-ray so the pin's at the tip of the elbow, and keep screening with the X-ray as you drive it in.'

The nurses cheer when the pin goes in on my first pass.

———

'Today's your last day here, isn't it, Emma?' Mei Ling asks as we walk to the change room together.

I nod and wave at Layla, the nurse in charge today, and think that I must come back and say goodbye to her. But then, how do I say goodbye to everyone I've ever worked with? I came to this hospital as a medical student, stayed on as an intern, worked my way up. Now, I've been one of the lucky few accepted to the training program to become a surgeon myself, and the College of Surgeons, which oversees our training, will assign me to a new hospital every year so that I can learn from as many different surgeons as possible.

Normally, hospital doctors go up in seniority and change jobs on the same day. I've begged a few weeks leave ahead of this promotion. 'I'm off to Italy on a slightly belated honeymoon before I start at The Mount,' I explain.

She holds the door to the change room open for me and finds the clothes she's messily thrown on a bench in clear haste. *Maybe she didn't have quite that much faith in me after all*, I wonder. Is it too late to turn back, to write to the College of Surgeons and give up my training position, hand in my resignation to The Mount?

But Mei Ling is smiling. She slips off her scrubs and deftly throws her dress over her head. 'Emma, you'll be totally fine,' she says, sitting down to change her shoes. 'Look at you. You just did your first case on your own. Picked the problem and the urgency, organised everything, and then fixed it. You saved that kid's hand. If there's ever a trainee who's going to thrive in surgical training, I'm sure it's you.'

My heart swells.

Chapter Two

The summer pre-dawn light is chasing the shadows from our bedroom. It's my first day as a registrar but I linger in bed, watching Shamsi's back rise and fall, resisting the urge to throw my arm over his shoulder, rub my hand over his closely cropped scalp, kiss the back of his neck. He'd promised to get up with me for my first day. I'm not upset. As a lawyer he works hours that are long enough, and we're both still jet-lagged after flying back from Italy three days ago.

I tiptoe from the room, shower quickly, saving time to dry and straighten my hair, and dress in the skirt and shirt I laid out last night. On reflection I'm not sure that flat shoes look professional enough so I swap them for mid-height heels, not so tall that I'd tower over any of my new bosses.

The person in the mirror isn't someone I easily recognise. Tidy brown hair in a ponytail, pencil skirt over my narrow hips and a collar at my neck are a far cry from the sensible slacks and loose bun I used to wear at my old hospital. With a sigh I pack my bag, filling it with my handwritten notes about this week's cases, and then cram two textbooks on top of them. Still tiptoeing, I escape down the hall and ease the front door closed behind me, pleased to have protected Shamsi's sleep.

————

The nurses' station on Ward 6 East is deserted. A forlorn keening echoes down the corridor, almost words but not quite. Irrationally irritated by a purple carpet square that's been mislaid, breaking the checkerboard pattern with the alternating grey, I drop my bag and lean over the counter to peer at a whiteboard that's been ruled up with tape. There's a column for patients' names, currently covered by a narrow board. Only the column for the medical unit each patient belongs to is visible. I count eighteen rows marked as *Orthopaedic Surgery*, each representing an unknown person who as of three minutes ago is officially under my care.

Where is everyone?

Steve Brown is the other registrar I'm working with this year. We've exchanged emails about meeting on the ward today, but I don't really know him. Surgical training is five years; he's at the start of his fourth year and I'm the baby on day one. We're both new to The Mount. At least our team includes two junior doctors, known as residents, who both worked at The Mount last year. They'll be able to show us where to go.

I wonder if patients know how dangerous it is to be in hospital when this great annual medical migration happens—when whole teams change, and new doctors, who don't know any of them and who don't know where to find anything, suddenly take over their care.

Right now, the ward's empty, even though Steve and I agreed to meet at 7 a.m. and do our first ward round together. I decide to try our office. Rod, the departing registrar, showed me where it was when I came to get a handover yesterday. It was the only useful information he gave me—he wasn't interested in my questions, and Steve didn't turn up at all. Rod handed me a list of the current inpatients, pointed out the registrars' office, then jangled the keys to his BMW before disappearing. I sigh at the memory.

I'm about to punch the code into the office door when it's flung open and someone barges straight into me.

'Oof,' he grunts, grabbing my shoulders to steady us both.

He's about my age and height with short hair that must grow out into ringlets. The rest of him is unremarkable and forgettable. Brown pants, white shirt, a tie knotted imperfectly. I wonder if it's lopsided because of incompetence or a lack of care.

He looks me up and down, lingering slightly too long on my chest. 'Are you Emma?' he asks, stepping back now that neither of us is about to fall over.

I nod, rubbing my side where his elbow's sure to leave a bruise.

'Oh great. I'm Steve. Right. Ward round. Let's go.' With a wave of his hand, he marches towards the main nurses' station.

'Steve, do you know where the residents are?' I call after him, confused. 'And did you get a handover yesterday?'

He pauses and glances over his shoulder at me. 'No, I got back from holidays at midnight. Who needs a handover? Every hospital's the same. Every patient's the same. Right, are you coming?' He's off again.

'There're lots of patients.' Steve observes when I catch up. His brows are furrowed with irritation.

'There were only six yesterday and Rod—'

'Didn't provide any sort of handover, did he?' says a voice from behind us.

I'm startled but Steve doesn't flinch. He turns slowly and offers his hand to a grey-haired woman in a perfectly pressed nurse's uniform, the creases in her slacks so sharp I wonder how she sits comfortably without wrinkling them.

She scrutinises us over glasses that hang precariously on the end of her nose, only friction and the insurance of a golden chain as protection, and frowns.

'I'm Cheryl, and I'm in charge of this ward. You're Steve . . . and Emma?'

Steve draws himself to his full height and grabs her hand to shake it. 'Yes, senior registrar. We need to do a ward round. Now.'

Cheryl raises a single eyebrow at him. The silence lengthens until Cheryl breaks her gaze to lead the way down the corridor. Steve smirks as if he's the victor, though Cheryl hasn't given up anything. She's been in charge of this ward for thirty years and the stories about her are legendary.

There are two identical-looking young men standing in an alcove, one with a laptop on a trolley and the other hugging a pile of patient observation charts. They draw back at the sight of Cheryl.

'Right, let's go,' Steve barks without breaking stride and disappears into the room of bed 1, our first patient.

The two residents start and scramble, tripping over their shoes as the trolley teeters. I sidle up alongside them and introduce myself, and in turn meet Will and Daniel. Despite having the same brown hair, same beard and being dressed identically in blue pants, pale blue striped shirt, pink tie and pointy brown dress shoes, they're unrelated.

Daniel was an intern last year; Will's slightly taller and a year senior to him. Daniel hands me an updated patient list, which indicates our patient in bed 1 is a twenty-three-year-old man with a broken leg.

Steve's inspecting his plaster when we join him in the room. 'You!' he says as we walk in, pointing at Daniel. 'What does the X-ray show?'

Daniel swivels the trolley around so Steve and I can see two broken leg bones glowing across the dim room.

Steve directs his next question at Will. 'Have you assessed his common peroneal nerve?'

Will shakes his head, no.

'Useless,' Steve mutters. 'Emma, make sure you add this patient to the operating list for today. 'Also,' he adds, leaving the room, 'one of you should fix his plaster after the round.'

Cheryl glances at me.

I mouth the word 'sorry' even though I've done nothing wrong.

She nods, almost imperceptibly, and her eyes twinkle briefly. 'You're a bit bigger than when I last saw you, Emma,' she says warmly. I freeze. I've tried to distance myself from my father my whole medical career, and Cheryl's sprung me within moments of entering the corridors he once ruled. With no further explanation, she's gone too.

I'm writing *MBA, ORIF today* neatly on the patient list when I hear a quiet 'Excuse me.' The patient waves me over.

We haven't explained to him what surgery might entail and what his recovery will look like, so I ask in my kindest, doctoriest voice, 'Yes? What can I do for you?' Steve might be a bully and a grump; I can be nice.

'Um, I was wondering when I'd be getting a sponge bath? My mates reckoned the nurses'd be old and rank, but I'd take a sponge bath from a hot nurse like you any day.'

Ah.

I take a deep breath and explain I'm one of the surgical doctors and will be fixing his leg rather than bathing him.

'Oh, you're the surgeon? Well, that's cool too, 'cause you'll be like . . . touching my insides,' he leers.

I mumble something and flee from the room to find Steve squaring off with a colourful woman in a pink and grey fern pattern pouf dress.

'I don't need your permission to see *your* patients. It's part of my job to see the oldies, so you lot don't neglect them to death,' she tells him, one hand on a hip, quietly tapping her foot, the pale pink leather heel waggling. In an institution known for tradition, her outfit is outlandish, and glorious. She holds Steve's eye until his expression starts to fade, much longer than I think I'd ever dare. Then she flashes me a smile and, as if buoyed by an audience, she pokes Steve in the chest. 'Oh, don't be such a cliché!'

Before he can reply, she turns to a doctor largely indistinguishable from Will or Daniel, and cautions him, 'You have to keep an eye on the orthopaedic team.' Adopting a clipped monotone, she adds, 'There is a fracture, I need to fix it.'

Cheryl smirks, Steve releases a sound halfway between an obscenity and a choke, and Will looks perplexed, so I whisper that this line comes from a once-viral video and is often used to remind us that you can't fix broken bones if someone's already dead.

Ignoring Steve, my new hero introduces herself. 'I'm Daphne Ng, the medical registrar. I see every older orthopaedic patient whether *he* wants me to or not. If there's anyone else you're worried about, page me on 117, or my mobile number's on the board at the main nurses' station.' With a nod to Cheryl and a gesture to her resident, she's off into another room, voluminous frock swinging, generous hips sashaying, and pink heels soundless on the thin carpet.

In *our* next room—why do hospitals despise sunlight?—we find a shrunken woman who was the object of the previous conversation. She lies unnaturally rigid, sheets messily tucked in around her. My patient list tells me that Maria's ninety-two, has a long list of medical problems, and lives in a high-level care nursing home. Her next of kin is a niece who lives interstate.

Maria lifts one arm to point at nothing and howls again. 'Oh yo yo yo yo yooooo!' echoes out the door and down the corridor.

Steve's mouth pulls into a disgusted grimace. Cheryl strokes her patient's bony hand and offers her the juice box on the untouched breakfast tray. Maria gazes at her with glassy eyes and takes a loud sip.

Daniel's brought up her X-ray on the computer screen. Before he can speak, Steve cuts him off with a wave. 'She needs her hip fixed. Put her on the operating list, Emma.'

The next five patients are recovering from surgery they had in the last week. They'll be sent home with new hips or new knees, their old worn-out ones replaced with titanium and poly-ethylene. As the nurse in charge of this ward, Cheryl needs patients out to get patients in—we run beyond capacity at the best of times—so facilitating discharges is crucial.

Why am I even here? Steve and Cheryl are arguing, Will and Daniel are writing notes and making things happen. This is, in some ways, the team running as it should. Registrars make decisions and increasingly learn to operate alone, supervised by our bosses, the surgeons; residents enact our decisions and do paperwork. The job demands two registrars, but this morning there doesn't seem to be enough space for both of us.

I'm wondering what I could contribute on these rounds when we walk into the next room. Here the curtains are pulled back and the morning sun illuminates the empty bed. Next to it, a woman named Jacqui Miller sits in a blue vinyl hospital armchair, a half-read novel face down on her lap. There's little to see outside the dirty window—a dingy laneway full of industrial rubbish bins at street level, and the blacked-out windows of the research centre next door. Yet at least there's sunshine, which cuts out completely from level five down.

Jacqui's twenty-nine, like me. Will says she was admitted last night for tests on a lump in her right leg. Normally this would be done as an outpatient, but Jacqui lives in the country so she's come in for a day, notably under the care of Professor 'Bones' Jones, the head of orthopaedic surgery. He's a world leader in rare bone tumours, though Jacqui probably doesn't know this.

'She can go home when the tests are done,' Steve tells Will without a word to Jacqui.

I hesitate while the team leaves. Though we've stood there and spoken *about* her, none of us has spoken *to* her. My eyes catch a small photo on the windowsill, tucked under a bunch of bright gerberas. On a dusty fence two young children in checked dresses and broad-brimmed hats squint into the camera, gum trees swaying in the background. I remember the light on my grandparents' farm, the smell of dust and manure, cicada song on the wind.

I hang back. Kindness can be my contribution on ward rounds.

'How are you feeling?' I start.

'Okay now, I think. Waiting to get here was the worst,' Jacqui replies.

The shiny blue sheet on her bed crinkles under me as I sit, the linen company logo distorted. While searching for the right words I try to smooth the sheet out. 'Are you here on your own?'

'Yes, my husband has to keep the farm going. He'll come if I need surgery . . .' Her voice trails off.

I hope my smile is sympathetic and ask how long she's had symptoms.

'Oh . . . six months?' she muses. 'It's been a bit sore, on and off. And then it got too sore to run, so my GP sent me for an X-ray.' Jacqui looks out the window. She's worried it's cancer and I'm certain it's cancer, otherwise she wouldn't be here, admitted into a precious bed for investigations, under the bed card of a leading bone tumour expert.

To rustle the stillness I point and ask how old the children are.

Jacqui smiles, her first genuine expression. 'Oh, Ruby's two and Maddie's four. We were thinking about one more . . .'

I lean over to pat her on the arm as comfort. She flinches at this awkward touch from a stranger and I realise that I haven't even introduced myself. Here I was being self-congratulatory about my ability to be kind, only to then show such embarrassing ineptitude.

Shit.

I want to tell her that her whole life won't only be full of uncertainties but there's risk in making promises we can't keep. Instead, I assure her that I'll take very good care of her and run for the door.

———

Steve's in the hall, irate. 'We'll be late to orientation. *What* were you doing?'

I open my mouth to answer and realise that he doesn't care.

Will looks from one of us to the other. 'Do you know where it is and how to get there?' he asks, diplomatically shifting the conversation.

Minutes later we're racing down still empty hallways, Steve out of breath and grumbling beside me. 'Why do they always put admin in such hard to find places?'

But truly, Steve doesn't want to know. He's not the sort of person who'd be interested in the history of this hospital, illustrious as it is. Founded in 1845, soon after a deceitful and murderous cattle farmer claimed the land it stands on, The Mount was set up by public subscription so that the wealthy wouldn't have to queue at the Colonial Medical Service. The first physicians who worked here had incomprehensibly left the cobbled lanes and storied halls of London to drink urine and let blood on the other side of the world. Over the years, each generation of doctors selected the next, identical to themselves, a parade of the same names and faces which must hang as portraits in some hallway or meeting room. Even though I tried to avoid it, I've ended up here too, like my own father.

Once hospital care became a public commodity, paid for by government and free for patients, the bureaucracy decided that doctors couldn't be trusted to manage the budget. Old hospitals reluctantly accepted administrators but allocated them the worst spaces, while the professors retained their airy offices. Meanwhile, at the much newer hospital I've just left, planned and built by administrators, they had the nicest wing.

At last, we find the old asbestos-walled administration block where a woman with large hair, red lips and a frown is standing beside a trestle table in a narrow hallway. A black-and-white name badge identifies her as Brenda. I remember seeing her name on my contracts—Brenda Fischer, head of junior medical workforce.

'You're late,' she says coldly.

Beside her, a half-open door leads to a room full of young heads. I drop my voice. 'I'm sorry, we—'

She doesn't let me explain that we've already been here for an hour, seeing patients, working. 'Go in.' She points.

Steve grabs a pile of paper from her table and stalks in.

A similar stack with my name on it is the last on the table. They're printed incorrectly with only one 'n' in my surname, Swann.

Brenda's not interested in my correction. 'Go in, you're late. We can fix that later.' She's so loud the doctors in the back row turn to look.

Tucking the documents under my arm I follow Steve into the room. I'm looking for a seat when my elbow-grip on the sheaf of papers loosens. They spill to the floor, swirling at my feet. Now everyone in the room is looking at me. I feel the heat rise in my cheeks.

The speaker, an elderly doctor who should have retired years ago, stops. He peers over the top of his glasses, head bobbing as he focuses. He leans on the lectern for support, his upper back hunched. The silence lengthens as everyone stares, the projector filling the space with a low buzz, and then he snorts with derision, clacks his dentures and continues with his monotone introduction to The Mount.

One by one the crowd lose interest in me too. I collect my papers and find a folding metal chair at the end of the fourth row. Steve's already found a seat one row ahead and he turns and shakes his head with disapproval. I suppress a desire to stick my tongue out at him.

'. . . and so with that, welcome to everyone, both the punctual and our latecomers, to The Mount,' the old man intones before shuffling from the room.

The infection control nurse is next. She tells us that everything will infect our patients with some deadly microbe. I find an extra hair tie and wrap my ponytail into a bun lest a hospital-appointed hairdresser appear, and wonder if my nails require surgical extraction. We're directed to the hand washing module on the hospital intranet and instructed to complete it by the end of the week, or we won't be paid, and then every six weeks after. Apparently, it's part of our ongoing medical education to stay up to date in rapidly changing fields, such as hand washing. Beside me, a tall doctor writes down how many pumps of soap to use.

The woman from Human Resources is succinct. 'Do *not* ask to be paid overtime, it will *not* be paid. It's an honour to train at The Mount. Any overtime is for your benefit and not that of the hospital.'

Tall doctor scrawls *NO OVERTIME!* on his pad and then underlines it for good measure.

Then it's someone from IT, who tries to teach us how to use the electronic medical records and ends up telling us to ask another staff member already working here. The fire safety officer points out the fire exits on a map, and a representative from the doctors' society pleads with us to join and have eighteen dollars per fortnight deducted from our pay in exchange for occasional pizza and a discounted ticket if they get around to organising a ball.

Everyone's starting to flag when an enthusiastic woman takes the lectern and introduces herself as Professor Brown. She has a short blonde bob with grey roots, crinkles around her eager eyes, and wears a bright patterned silk dress. It's obvious that she's trying to portray herself as different from the rest of the medical hierarchy, but a glinting of rings and bangles and a stern jacket gives her away. Immediately, I don't trust her.

'It's *essential* we treat patients, and each other, as humans first and problems second . . .' Professor Brown puts up cartoons on her PowerPoint and drops some swear words, transparently trying to build rapport.

Tall doctor is writing furiously. I want to snatch the pen from his hand, this is plain common sense.

'. . . vital that you take care of each other, support each other because we must always watch out for doctors' mental health.' Prof Brown lingers over this ominous last phrase before wafting past me and out the back door on a cloud of floral perfume and her own accomplishment.

The room is visibly losing interest—a few people are playing on their phones and down the row I can see some who are asleep—when Brenda strides in and flicks on the lights. Apparently we've now been taught the essentials to successfully work at The Mount. The room blinks in the glare and shudders slowly, unfurling as arms collectively reach for the ceiling. People greet each other with smiles and waves. Rows reorganise into lively groups as we file to the door.

Outside, the trestle table's now been set with rusty urns and bowls of cheap tea and instant coffee. Styrofoam cups teeter on one end where the laminate surface, like the carpet and walls, is cracked and peeling. The others mill around, and it seems everyone's found someone they know, even Steve. For a moment I miss my old hospital. Here I'm suddenly alone, apart from one other person . . . and where *is* that profile I'm looking for?

My ankles wobble in my heels, those textbooks in my bag getting heavier by the minute. I'm contemplating stirring together some instant coffee and long-life milk for something to do when there's a jab at my side.

Finally!

To my own surprise, I throw my arms around my brother, Andy. After an equally surprised pause, he returns my hug.

'Hey, kiddo,' he says with a smile and, today, I don't even mind. Andy pushes his unruly hair off his face as he's always done and punches my arm. 'You ready for your first day?'

I smile and nod. I haven't seen Andy since before Shamsi and I left for our honeymoon. He looks drawn and tired. Before I can ask if he's okay, Steve's strident voice cuts through the crowd.

'Emma! Why are you still here? You have to get to theatre.' Then he's towering above me, waving his phone. 'Jon's been operating alone all morning and he's furious at you. You didn't even send him your mobile number so he's been trying to page you—but you didn't get your pager out of the office, did you?'

I didn't even know there was a pager in our office. I thought most hospitals had moved on to contacting us on our mobile phones. Exasperated, I add this to the list of things Rod and the interminable orientation didn't tell me.

Andy and Steve look at each other warily. No time to worry about the pager, I hurriedly make an introduction. 'Um, Andy, this is Steve, who I'm working with this year. Steve, Andy's my brother and a final-year general surgery registrar.'

Andy offers him a hand and Steve sullenly shakes it.

'You'd better go, Emma. They never like to be kept waiting,' Andy says, sagely. 'I'll see you Saturday, if I don't see you before.'

For a moment a deep worry overtakes the enthusiasm I arrived with this morning. Then, I take a breath and force a smile. Andy's somehow learned what to do. I can too. Even though it's at The Mount.

Chapter Three

Daniel's slouched against a wall outside administration. He straightens when he sees me. 'Here, I found this in the office.' He presses a pager into my hands and points to the stairs. 'Shall I show you to theatre?'

I nod gratefully. While he chatters on about being an intern at The Mount last year and how he's keen to become a surgeon too, the pager screams. Of the eleven messages, six are from Jon, three are from the Emergency Department and another two I accidentally delete in my muddling.

So many questions, so few answers. A week ago, Jon was a final-year registrar here, and as of today, he's graduated and is a fully qualified surgeon and my boss. Surely one weekend hasn't robbed him of the memory of what it's like to be a registrar? This morning I felt like I was superfluous, now I suddenly feel like I'm not enough.

Am I on call today? As well as not coming to handover yesterday, Steve hasn't circulated our roster yet. As the senior registrar, it's his responsibility, and privilege, to divvy up the evenings and weekends between us. He should have done it weeks ago.

The on-call registrar takes the referrals to the Orthopaedic unit and stays until the day's work is done, however late. I've accepted that long hours will be my life for the next five years, but I didn't expect the slog to start today when Shamsi's promised to cook a celebratory dinner. Although it seems only a fool would believe a medical spouse when they say they'll be home at a certain time, for years we've been having the same conversations, making and cancelling the same plans.

I clip my pager to my skirt. Jon sounds angriest, so the Emergency Department will have to wait.

Daniel leads me down the stairs, pointing out various wards as we descend. We pass the special lifts—staff ID tag access only—that connect the critical care departments with the helipad above level nine.

The operating theatre is a place where patients are brought, not somewhere they're required to find themselves, so there's little to identify it. Only a small window for theatre reception, and non-descript locked doors leading to the change rooms. Daniel can't scan me into the female change room with his male ID tag. He shrugs while I seethe in frustration at these impediments that could have been avoided if Brenda had been more organised.

Pointing to the unattended reception, he disappears to get changed.

A small bell to call for attention is behind the locked glass and my raps go unanswered. After pacing, and knocking, and pacing some more, a nurse and a hospital technician appear, pushing a patient through a sliding door. I follow them into the theatre holding bay.

Here, patients have their names checked, their paperwork confirmed, the surgical site marked with an arrow. All the small details to make sure that once they're an anaesthetised lump of organs and blood, we'll perform the right procedure.

The holding bay at The Mount is only three beds along a narrow wall. From the other side, there's moaning and shouting, the noises of someone in pain. The racket becomes words and 'nurse it hurts, nurse it hurts' reverberates through the wall.

The three patients currently waiting for surgery in this room look worried, but the holding bay nurse hardly notices as she runs through her checklist with the latest arrival. The Mount has grown from two theatres to eleven. I'm not sure which phase of cost-limiting and poor planning placed the recovery area on the other side of a thin wall from the holding bay. Patients before surgery are not supposed to hear those who have already had surgery.

I'm still waiting for the nurse to finish her checks when the doors at the far end slide open and Jon walks in. I've met him fleetingly at conferences and hope he doesn't remember me here. He squints at the waiting patients. Should I say hello now, or after I'm changed? His eyes land on me with recognition. His frown deepens.

'Emma. You took your time getting here. What the hell have you been doing all morning?' His overgrown brows draw closer, his neck straining against the blue paper balaclava tied around it. The patients seem distracted from 'nurse it hurts' and their own terror by watching mine.

'Oh, hi, Jon—'

'Mr Trumble,' he corrects.

I open my mouth and then close it, swallowing my irritation that he's pulling rank and title after being a surgeon for—according to the clock above his head—four hours.

'Sorry, Mr Trumble. I was trying to get into the change room.'

Shit.

I should simply apologise and bring this conversation to an end, but I know I've done nothing wrong.

'No, really, what *have* you been doing?' Jon persists.

The patients and the nurse are transfixed, their heads moving back and forth as if watching a tennis match. Seems it's my shot.

'We had mandatory orientation—'

Again he cuts me off and four sets of eyes turn in response. 'Orientation isn't mandatory. *I* never went.'

By now even 'nurse it hurts' has gone quiet, and though it's possible they were given extra morphine, it feels like they've stopped to listen, like the whole hospital's stopped to listen.

'Make sure you mark the next patient, and don't be so late again,' Jon scolds before disappearing behind the sliding doors.

Angrily, I watch him go.

The holding bay nurse hands me her ID badge with a look of sympathy and points to the change room. I hesitate, and she understands and waves at the woman in the middle. 'She's yours,' she says, returning to her checklist.

Still smarting, I introduce myself to Mrs Smith who's dislocated her hip replacement.

Rummaging in my bag for a pen to draw an arrow, even though the right leg is shortened and clearly the one that needs to be put back where it should be, I ask how she did it. She taps my arm and waves me closer. I lean in and my anger at Jon, at Steve, at this whole confusing first day mess dissipates—she smells like peppermints and flowery perfume and kindness.

'You see, my dear,' she whispers conspiratorially, 'everyone thinks we're too old and ugly to have sex, except what else are you supposed to do after you retire?' She laughs at my blush. 'I forgot I wasn't allowed to sit down quite that far!'

I busy myself with her leg, avoiding eye contact, check the consent form and explain the procedure.

She gestures me closer again. 'Don't worry about that scoundrel. I'm an old nurse and they were worse in my day,' she says, patting my hands.

At last, I make it to the change room. It's after midday and there are only XXXL and XXXS scrubs left on the large shelves by the door. I realise with dismay that I remembered my textbooks but forgot my theatre shoes. Though, as a resident, I've been proud of assisting surgery in heels, I never want to ask a colleague to operate on my bunions. I set a reminder to pack my clogs tomorrow.

There are no free lockers, so I shove my crumpled clothes on top of the never-dusted shelves and dress in XXXL scrubs. The neckline sags and I need to turn up the cuffs on the pants three times. It will do. I knot a balaclava hat under my chin and slip plastic shoe covers on. The heels immediately punch a hole through them, exposing brown leather columns underneath.

Shit.

I inspect myself in a mirror. I look near enough to a real surgeon. Hopefully, no one looks at my feet.

———

The staff in theatre 9 are getting ready to bring in Mrs Smith. Every operating theatre anywhere in the world is more or less the same as every other—even at this esteemed centre of excellence. Perhaps the anaesthetic machine is shinier, perhaps the lights a bit brighter, but the floor is stained the same iodine orange and the staff bustle about in the same busy, ordered way.

Andy was assisting with a kidney transplant operation today. I wonder which theatre he's in, and whether he's sewing up the patient who now only has one kidney, or the one who now has three.

The anaesthetist is fiddling with his machine and loading syringes—some of the white stuff and some of the clear stuff, and coloured stickers to make sure the wrong drugs aren't given.

He drops them onto a green plastic tray and stands by the theatre doors, waiting for the patient. Some of the nursing staff wave as they're off to lunch. This is only a manipulation under anaesthetic, no incisions needed, so there's no lively unpacking of trays and counting of instruments. We don't even need to wash our hands.

Daniel's arrived before me. Jon hasn't acknowledged him. Instead, he leans against a wall and taps on his phone as Mrs Smith is wheeled in. I marvel, again, that yet another procedure might be done by someone who hasn't even said hello. What makes patients willing to subject themselves to such uncertainty?

The theatre technician asks if Mrs Smith can wriggle across onto the narrow theatre table, but she can't move herself with a dislocated hip so we push and pull her across roughly because we forgot to agree on 'after three' or 'on three'. The anaesthetist leans over and deftly injects some clear stuff into the drip. Mrs Smith's eyes glaze and she gives me a smile before the oxygen mask is held to her face.

As her head is tipped back and a tube's being placed in her throat, Jon puts away his phone and reanimates. His eyes land on Daniel. 'New resident?' he asks.

Daniel springs to his feet enthusiastically and puts out his hand. 'Yes, hello, Mr Trumble.'

Jon doesn't offer his hand in return. 'Okay, if you're here, you can help.' He points to Mrs Smith's leg. 'Hold it up. By the big toe.'

As Daniel hefts the leg into the air, Jon walks out of the room. Daniel looks at me curiously. I shrug. I can't help him with this, whatever 'this' is. Jon comes back a full two minutes later, when Daniel's arms are shaking and his face is glowing with sweat.

'Good job. You can stay,' Jon tells him, waving the leg back to the table.

Daniel deflates further. Jon appears calm now that his superiority has been established.

'Okay, Emma, off you go,' he waves and settles into a chair, watching with his arms crossed and a smug expression. He thinks I can't do this.

We drop the operating table height and I get Daniel to kneel on the edge of it, holding down Mrs Smith's pelvis. I might be only one hundred and sixty-five centimetres tall and fifty-five kilos, but I've learned how to use technique over force. With Mrs Smith's leg under my forearm, I bear back with my body weight and rotate precisely. The hip pops back in with a loud clunk that makes Daniel jerk and the anaesthetist shudder.

'Hmm. Not bad, Emma,' Jon concedes.

Daniel gives me a silent high five when Jon isn't looking.

The next patient has a broken wrist. The theatre technician finds me a saw and I slit their plaster cast in the small anaesthetic room attached to the operating theatre, filling the air with dust and a loud mechanical shriek. The saw cuts only the hard plaster and not the fluffy cotton underneath. Before I can tell Daniel that we'll remove the rest when she's asleep, he wrenches it apart. The patient groans in pain.

As before, the anaesthetist is on hand with his magic medicines. 'She won't remember that,' he says helpfully as amnesic drugs flow through the patient's veins and her groan is silenced.

Daniel apologises and the anaesthetist shrugs. 'It's why we exist,' he says casually. 'To save the patients from the surgeons.'

Now back in theatre, Jon lets me make the incision and start to pull the shattered bones together. He helps me fix the plate in the right position, laughing only when I stand to turn the screws. 'Only newbies who are struggling stand up,' he says, yet there's a begrudging acknowledgement that in fact I *am* doing this.

This is why they put me on the training program, I whisper in my head.

We work through the remaining cases on the operating list. I help plate a broken humerus and drive a long nail through a broken femur. Then we're out of time and being kicked out of the safe theatre and back into the yawning hospital. I'm wondering how to make it back to the ward and if I did okay today when Jon texts me from the change room to say that he'd like to do the remaining cases later tonight. What remaining cases?

Then Steve texts me to say that he's seen the patients I apparently ignored in Emergency. These must be the 'remaining cases'—more patients needing surgery who have been admitted while we were operating on and discharging others.

And then Will texts me to say the patients on the ward are fine. None of my new team must believe in doing an evening ward round to ensure there are no issues heading into the night, even though I do.

Finally, Shamsi texts me to ask when I'll be home. And before I can reply to him, my pager shrieks, confirming that I must indeed be on call, and my work for today is far from done.

And Shamsi's dinner will go cold on the table.

Chapter Four

The room is empty apart from a few cardboard boxes stacked against a wall and a ragged poster of Amy Winehouse still tacked to the closet door.

'Well, even if it all goes to shit, you've survived longer than her, babe,' Shamsi says.

'Hey! That's not nice. Poor Amy.' I nudge him under the ribs with my elbow and he laughs and wraps his arms around me, his chin resting on top of my head.

'Are you going to miss this?'

Downstairs, there's another thud and my father's deep rumble wafts towards us. He's only just managing to stay polite as the movers thump their way through his castle.

'Nah.' I shake my head. I moved out of this house where I grew up a long time ago. Since Dad retired last year, younger than most of his colleagues, Mum and Dad are moving permanently to their house on the coast. I walked down the stairs in my wedding dress a few months ago, but now the house is sold and the new owners move in next week.

Ever organised, Mum's packed my left-behind possessions into boxes and sealed them, ready for me to take home. Consolidating two houses into one has taken her months. All Dad's done is get the garden ready.

Andy and I always loved the holiday house more. It's where Dad was most relaxed and Mum hosted her best parties, where we learned to sail and surf, where we lay in hammocks and read books all summer. Still, I'm glad I'm not on call today and could come and say goodbye to this house.

I've hardly seen Andy this week, only brief glimpses as I've rushed around the hospital, everything harder and slower because the place and systems are new. I glance out the big bay window and search for their car. I'm not surprised he and Laura haven't arrived yet. A house full of movers and grumpy Dad isn't the best place for twin babies. Dad insisted that Andy's boxes could be dropped off, that Andy should study and needn't come today. Like always, he's forgotten that life is more than surgery and exams. Despite the pressures he's under, Andy wants to farewell the house too, though I expect them to come late.

'Well, shall I carry these down to the car?' Shamsi releases my waist and pushes past me into the room. 'I think they'll fit.'

'Hey, I've got a better idea,' I suggest.

Shamsi looks at me curiously.

'You know how you've always wanted to have sex in here . . .'

'Em! I said that years ago!'

'Well, today's the day. You'll never have the chance again.' I can see that Shamsi's unsure if I'm serious or not. I slide my hand under my skirt, catch my underwear with my thumb and pull it down. My eyes locked on his, I step out of one leg and then the other. He raises an eyebrow but there's a smile playing at the edges of his mouth. I flick the underwear away and turn and close the door, clicking the lock shut.

I strut up to him, press myself close and take each of his hands in mine, still marvelling at the richness of his dark skin against the translucent white of my own. 'Come on, it's been a whole week,' I murmur in his ear, feeling his stubble tickle my cheek. No matter how meticulously he shaves, his chin is rough by midday.

'Is that your fault or mine this time?' he whispers back. Outside in the driveway there's more clunking and crashing and I hear my father swear. Shamsi extracts my hands from his and holds me by the waist. Even though he's still playing coy I can feel his need in his fingers as they press into my flank.

'Oh, definitely yours, Shamsi Alam.' I start to unfasten the button on his shorts. 'You worked later than me at least two nights this week.'

'And you worked late the other three.'

'Well, we'd better make it up to each other,' I say as his shorts fall to the floor and his mouth finds mine.

Impatiently I lift my skirt as Shamsi turns me around. I lean over the pile of boxes, his hands on my hips pulling me towards him. Just as we've done so many times, yet here it feels new again, like we haven't recently spent two and a half weeks looking at faded paintings in magnificent buildings and drinking Prosecco and making love. Unlike those long languorous afternoons, this is quick and dirty, like I imagined secret sex in a childhood bedroom ought to be. And afterwards we laugh as we rearrange ourselves.

'Emma! You in there?' There's a sharp rap at the door and Laura's voice floats through. She tries the handle and it clicks against the lock.

Shamsi holds me and whispers, 'Just in the nick of time, hey?' and I laugh too loud.

'Oh my god, you two. Okay, I don't want to know.' Laura's footsteps retreat down the hall, sharp and fast.

Shamsi puts his hand over his mouth, stifling a louder laugh, while I don't even bother. Uncontrolled giggles spill out because I know Laura won't tell anyone.

———

'How's your study?'

Dad's low voice echoes up the stairs as Shamsi and I tiptoe down. From the landing I can see straight through the empty lounge room to the backyard, Dad's garden perfect as ever. The twins have been sat in the grass and my mother's blowing bubbles at them. Dad and Andy stand back holding beers. There's still some noise from Dad's study at the front of the house. It's taken an astonishing number of reinforced boxes to contain his books and the movers are still loading them.

'It's going well,' Andy says agreeably, but with the slightest edge in his voice. His exam, the biggest hurdle to finishing specialist training, is in five months, and I'm sure he doesn't want to talk about it with anyone, least of all Dad.

Although it's over a hundred years since the great minds of Boston progressed a model of medical education that allowed trainees to learn from living patients rather than books and cadavers, we're mostly still trained in the same way. Each year, registrars are given increasing responsibility until it culminates in a grand and expensive exercise known as The Exam. If the traditional methods of daily teaching by humiliation aren't enough, The Exam is humiliation writ large. The Board of Examiners, esteemed surgeons from around the country, collect examples of disease, both alive and dead, and host a weekend of brutal questioning. Over two full days, they watch us interview and examine patients, and grill us on anatomy, operative technique and what we'd do when things go wrong.

This is to make sure trainees have attained a sufficient standard before graduating to independent practice, but it seems that oratorial confidence and performance is also required. There's no room for equivocation—humility is an excellent quality in a clinician but may doom an exam candidate to failure.

Andy's been preparing for the past four years, and I'll be expected to start studying now as well. Our supervisors might not ask or care if we try to understand our patients as humans rather than diseases, or whether we were kind to them, or even if we've won a Nobel Peace Prize in our spare time—our progression is measured by the number of cases we've completed for our logbook this week, the number of topics revised that week, the number of esoteric questions we get right on ward rounds with them.

'You shouldn't have come today. You should be studying,' my father goes on, persistent.

I push open the sliding screen door and step outside into the summer warmth. Laura shakes her head and calls out a hello with false enthusiasm, like she hadn't already come upstairs to find us. Sensing something, Mum looks between us but I can see she doesn't understand.

Shamsi clears his throat in that way only I know signals his discomfort. He catches Laura's eye and busies himself by picking up Aurora, the closer baby, and giving her a cuddle, while Ava reaches up to him with a gurgle.

'Hey, no fighting,' I say to Dad, still suppressing a satisfied laugh. 'Today's a happy day, for happy memories. How about you be a father instead of a surgeon today?'

He grumbles incomprehensibly and opens another beer.

Andy puts his arm around my shoulder in solidarity. The meaning behind his gesture is clear to me, even though I'm sure it's lost on our father.

After we each agonised, deliberated and then succumbed to the study of medicine, our small rebellion was to cross the river to attend the second-best medical school and work at a hospital without the prestigious history and wall of famous doctors. According to Dad this was a mistake. These Shit Hospitals, as he calls them, lack the serious merit of Big City Hospitals. We'd end up Shit Doctors, or even worse, in general practice.

Now that we're both surgical trainees at The Mount, where *he* climbed the great ice-cream cone of medical hierarchy to be the rotund and red-faced cherry on top, we'd wondered if he'd finally be proud and stop harassing us. It seems not. At least we've only been sent to The Mount after his retirement. His torment will be limited to family get-togethers such as this and not follow us down the halls at work.

Mum, ever the artist in paint-stained jeans and her hair tied up in a scarf, puts down the bottle of soap bubbles. 'Champagne, my darling?' she asks, but before I can answer she's pouring a glass.

———

The pages of my new journal have only a few words in them when Shamsi looks up from his laptop. He's lounging on our sofa reading a thousand-page contract and boosting his billable hours for the week.

'Emma, sweetie, don't let your dad get you down,' he says. When I don't reply, he sighs, closes the computer and puts it down. 'Hey, it's barely six, we could still go to the barbecue?' We'd planned to meet friends this evening. He knows I don't want to go anymore.

The afternoon was pleasant enough. The summer sun was warm. The twins, nine months old now, happily crawled around the garden while Laura and I gossiped. She was my friend in medical school before she was Andy's wife and is training in general practice. Not his own child, Dad expresses pride in her path. This annoys me, but the alternative—him berating his daughter-in-law like he did us—would be worse.

Shamsi talked cricket with Andy, and the movers finally left. And then we took one last walk through the house together. We marvelled at our growth lines marked in the kitchen and our child-sized handprints on the walls of the upstairs hall, before we locked the front door and handed over our keys.

Even though I'd declared it a day for happy memories, Dad still intruded with a lecture about the hard work and diligence needed to be a good registrar. He interrogated me about my plans for this training year, whether I had any research projects lined up, and where I might travel at the end of five years for more training to specialise further. My answers didn't satisfy him.

In part I know he's right. Just getting onto a training program isn't enough, even though it felt like it might be when we toasted my letter of offer. These years of training are why I tried so hard to avoid medicine in the first place, and yet it found me and won't let go. But then, I never imagined my own surgical career to look like his. I'm not sure I want to be a professor or a departmental head, much less both.

So I'm writing out my own goals and the list is short: pass the training year, impress my bosses, don't kill anyone. I don't have a plan as to how to achieve these things, and there's still something missing.

Shamsi persists. 'We've hardly seen our friends since the wedding. You had to work those extra weekends and now you're on call all the time.'

'I had to make up the weekends to take leave for our honeymoon. You know that.'

Shamsi sighs. He gets up, his long legs ungainly as he lifts them off the ottoman. 'Emma, you worked so hard to get onto the training program.' He comes to sit opposite me at the dining table. 'I know your dad had a go at you today. You do understand that he's unhelpful, that it's okay to celebrate for a moment before you kill yourself again?'

I hope he has insight himself, but his earnest eyes stare innocently back at me. I lean over and take his hands in mine. 'Like you can talk, Shamsi,' I say finally. 'You're always at work, angling for that promotion to partner too.'

He smiles ruefully. 'Look, it's true,' he concedes. 'But you . . . you're on the training program now. You're guaranteed to finish and be a surgeon at the end. It's basically impossible for them to kick you off this pathway now, right?'

'They could, Shamsi. I have to pass every term. Every group of surgeons I work with has to think I'm okay. If I fail one term I'm on probation, if I fail two I'm off for good. Plenty pass but don't get jobs as surgeons at the good hospitals, and what do you do as an unemployed surgeon? And then there's The Exam. I know everyone thinks it's just an exam . . .' How do I explain how rigorous and terrifying those exams are, how studying for them destroys your life, how trainees way smarter than me have failed them more than once?

My words have come out faster and faster, higher pitched as I go on. The excitement of my first day, only six days ago, has collapsed into panic at my father's interrogation.

Shamsi tries another tack. 'Andy's okay, isn't he?'

I want to say 'no' but I say 'yes'. Andy *is* okay, in the way of all doctors studying for The Exam, whatever that looks like in their own specialty. He's exhausted and Laura's exhausted and there are months to go, but we don't apply reasonable standards to ourselves so I say, 'Yes, yes. Andy's okay,' because he's as okay as he can be, and because I don't want Shamsi to think that what *we're* about to do too is impossible.

Maybe he's right. Maybe I *am* catastrophising. Most trainees pass every term. Most trainees get through The Exam. And who ever heard of an unemployed surgeon? Maybe Dad's being as unreasonable as ever.

Shamsi sighs and stands. 'I'll go organise some dinner for us,' he says. 'And I'll tell the others that we're definitely not going over tonight.'

I nod gratefully as Shamsi tries to find inspiration in the fridge. Meanwhile, my journal's blank pages ask me why I haven't also written: *Be a good doctor.* Because isn't that what I want most? Isn't that the sole commitment we should aspire to?

Why does it feel like this will be the hardest thing to achieve?

Chapter Five

I fumble until my fingers land on the light switch. The electricity whirs through ancient copper wires and the incandescent tube sputters to life with a small buzz, filling our warm and musty office with a cold white light. I'm reminded of the backpackers' hostel in the tropics where Shamsi and I first met. I was alone among a mass of Americans waiting to check in, until, from the back of the queue, I heard, 'There's movement at the station,' in a twang that filled me with homesick joy.

Shamsi and I met the week I decided to be a surgeon. Still a medical student, I'd gone to Vietnam for the summer to experience some 'real medicine' as my father called it. 'You're not going to do, you're going to learn,' he'd told me sternly at the airport, though what I was going to learn was a little unclear to me.

Dad had linked me with surgeons he'd trained, and paid for the flight on that basis. My own pizza shop savings would pay for the backpacking holiday after. I had no interest in surgery, but tolerating it in Da Nang for four weeks, and then trekking across south-east Asia seemed a fair bargain.

What I didn't expect were the expressions of children handed a mirror after their cleft lips were repaired, or the girl who walked for the first time in twelve years after we broke and mended her crooked leg. I didn't expect the blind to leave with vision. I didn't foresee that I'd fall in love—either with surgery, or with a beautiful young man with gentle words and long eyelashes, who lived in my own city but who I'd meet on the other side of the world.

My screeching pager and growling stomach break my reminiscence and bring me back to the hard reality of a hospital on a Tuesday night. I hush the pager and survey the small room. It really is time to clean up. After two weeks, it's clear none of the boys are going to.

The desk is covered in mouldy coffee cups, patient lists from three months ago, the unopened pay slips of doctors past, and half-empty ballpoint pens, one which has leaked ink and is stuck to the grey acrylic paint. Above the desk a warped whiteboard is decorated with incomprehensible hieroglyphs, one doctor describing an unknown operation to another in squiggles and arrows. On one side, old operating lists are stuck one over another in an untidy mass of paper and cellophane tape. A computer screen flickers with a broken neck of femur. At least it's one we've already fixed.

Next to the desk is a sagging blue sofa covered in stains and heaped high with hospital-issue blankets and pillows. The bin is the only thing that's tidy—presumably emptying it is the one task required of the hospital cleaners with regard to this room.

I shove the cups to one side and punch the extension on the pager into the phone.

'Hello, Emergency?' The person answering sounds much too bright for the hour.

'Hi, it's Emma from Orthopaedics, someone paged?' I sink into the chair and lean back. My shoes come off and even the sticky carpet feels good under the balls of my feet. Andy was grumbling about being on call, but I'm happy to be here. I'm ready to take this next step in my learning.

'Not me, and there's no one else here,' says the voice from Emergency.

Ugh.

Irritated again at people who page someone to a phone number and then walk away, I hang up. I could wait until they page back, but it might be faster if I walk downstairs. As I push my chair back to stand, it hits the small bookshelf tucked under the windowsill and a book falls off the end with a thud. I fish it out from beside the bin and put it back on the shelf next to other outdated orthopaedic textbooks and copies of the *Journal of Bone and Joint Surgery (British Edition)* from 1992 to 1996. There's a small sticker stuck to the top of the bookcase. I rub off the grime and read: *Donated by the family of Dr Lyndhurst.*

Now, there's a moment from my past. I sit back down on the chair with surprise.

My father took me to Lyndhurst's funeral. He died at his desk in the private hospital next door, and the brass nameplate from the wall outside his office was prised off and affixed to the front of his coffin. I remember the speeches still. Though his children told stories about him, it was their father's absence that featured heavily. Lyndhurst's only friends were his colleagues, and their recollections were limited to how much he worked. He seemed a cautionary tale, the person I'd point to when I proclaimed I would study medicine but live differently. I'd still have long lunches with friends who weren't doctors and I'd read books and maybe even paint like Mum. Who'd want to live a life like Lyndhurst's?

The man might be many years under the ground, but some part of his professional collection has made it to this office and is curiously preserved here, a perpetual, pitiful, shrine.

I move his drab books to the bottom shelf and pull out the brand-new ones that I've been dragging around, their covers brightly coloured and glossy. I wipe dust from the shelf and arrange them there, promising myself that I can still be more than Lyndhurst, more than a body with a brass plaque.

——

I'm forced to stop at the entrance to the Emergency Department. Steve and I still don't have ID tags despite working at the hospital for weeks, because Brenda can't manage to schedule our photos at a time when we're not in theatre. We skulk in hallways, begging others to let us through doors.

The entry to Emergency is my favourite. The dingy hallway from the late 1800s opens onto a bright and sparkling modern trauma unit. Where has the money come from for the white linoleum on the floor, fresh paint on the walls and LED lights studded through the ceiling? And why isn't there more for the rest of the hospital?

The enormous glass-enclosed command bridge at the centre of the department has a raised floor so the staff can see the monitored patients in the surrounding beds, blipping ECG traces outside each cubicle as proof of life. There, I find the nurse in charge who directs me to the 'Minors and Fast Track' area.

The tall doctor from orientation is sitting at a desk furiously typing notes. Jealously, I see *he* has a brand-new ID tag pinned to the chest pocket of his fitted forest-green scrubs.

'You're the orthopaedic registrar who doesn't answer their pager,' he says as greeting.

I sigh. I'm still hearing about how I didn't answer my pager on the first day, the day I didn't know I had a pager, the day Steve hadn't told me I was on call. There seems little point in explanation. Besides, I understand the immense pressures of the Emergency Department.

'Sorry,' I offer. 'I didn't get my pager the other week and that would've made life harder for you.' This is probably the sort of apology Jon wanted on the first day, but Jon was being entitled while this emergency doctor has a genuine grievance and is trying to get by, like me.

The doctor points at a closed curtain. 'That one's for you. Guy in his seventies. Fell off a roof and broke his ankle. He's otherwise fine.' He hands me the ambulance notes and a sheet of stickers and returns to his typing, his spindly fingers moving across the keyboard like a spider.

'Er . . .' I interrupt, glancing through the notes. He turns slowly, clearly unhappy. 'Um, have you made sure he doesn't have any other injuries? Because, um, eight metres is *really* high.'

He sighs. 'Yes, of course. He's *fine*. Just a broken ankle.'

At my old hospital the patient would be admitted under general surgery for observation. As Daphne, the medical registrar, pointed out, everyone knows orthopaedic surgeons fix bones and kill people.

Seeing the patient might help with this discussion. I call out 'Hello', and whip open the green curtain. The small bay floods with light.

Tim, a retired carpenter, startles. He tells me that he was repairing his roof this afternoon when things didn't go so well. He doesn't remember why or how he fell, but he remembers the ambulance arriving.

His ankle is twisted, turned away from the rest of his leg at the wrong angle. The emergency doctor has wedged an ill-fitting plaster around it. I hide my frustration from Tim—they could have given him some sedation and pulled the ankle into a better position. The skin is swollen and purple-black, explained in part by the dangers on his drug chart. I tell Tim that I need to check something and sidle out of the cubicle.

Back at the desk, I clear my throat, hoping it will cough up some diplomacy.

The emergency doctor glances up from his computer and smiles, a terrifying expression on his long and slow-moving face. 'Finally! You've done something efficiently!'

'Well, you know what?' I lean over the bench affecting friendliness. 'Tim's not ready for us. He's on three different blood thinners, he can't remember falling, he hasn't had an ECG or an ultrasound of his abdomen or a scan of his neck. Don't you think he needs to be seen by a medical registrar and general surgery?'

'No.'

Shit.

He's towering over me. 'Orthopaedics, we don't tolerate politics here. He has a fracture, he gets admitted to your unit. He's been here over three hours and I need to get him out.'

My fury rises. Some of my colleagues play games and refuse to accept patients, but *I'm* trying to get the patient the correct care. I could go find the Admitting Officer, the senior emergency physician running the floor, to defend my honour. Instead I text Andy.

> 73 year old guy, fall from eight metres,
> broken ankle, no trauma screen. You or me?

Andy replies almost immediately:

> Me. Med reg needs to see also.

Vindicated, I scribble some notes and order the extra tests Andy will want. Switchboard tells me that Daphne is the medical registrar on call this evening so I send her a text message. The tall emergency doctor, who stalked off twenty minutes earlier, is still nowhere to be seen.

Back in the main part of Emergency, the command bridge is buzzing with unfamiliar faces. Everyone ignores me. Is this what it'll be like at every new hospital? I imagine I'm the star in a movie of my own life, the camera spinning around me as people rush by, a registrar alone in the spiralling cacophony of humanity. Oh, to be back where I knew everyone. Then my stomach growls, the fictional scene ends and my main character syndrome is replaced by the sinking reality that I'm just another cog in the wheel.

There's a tap on my shoulder. A motherly woman in neat scrubs embroidered with *Dr Julia* on the left chest is holding a bag of X-rays in one hand and a cup of tea in another.

'You look lost,' she says with a smile, and then indicates the in-charge desk. 'Sit down, new registrar, and tell me what's up.'

Uneasily, I wonder how she knew.

She thrusts the tea at me. 'Here, drink this,' she says, and then opening the drawer next to the desk, she hands me a muesli bar. 'No nuts, just in case. We don't need any extra anaphylaxis.'

I protest, unsure about such generosity. No one's ever handed me tea or food at work before.

Julia shushes me. 'You surgical lot are always starving. I can make another. Eat, drink. Then tell me who or what you were looking for.'

I tear open the wrapper and tell her about Tim in bay 31, choosing my words carefully. I don't want to criticise the other doctor, but I detail my changes to his plan.

Julia listens with a neutral expression, ignoring my loud chewing. 'Good job,' she says when I've finished. 'Brayden is one of our new registrars. He was a resident here and should know better . . .'

I slurp my tea gratefully.

'I'm the Director of Emergency. Next time, come talk to me or whoever is running the floor. Our deal with specialty registrars is that if you help us, then we help you. So thank you.'

She puts out her hand and I shake it; she laughs at my mistake and takes the empty mug, promising to straighten Tim's ankle and put on a better plaster.

Then, thoughtfully, she finds a blank ID tag in another drawer. 'Here, take this,' she offers. 'We keep a handful for locums. It won't give you access to the car park, but it'll get you through most doors in the hospital.'

I'm leaving the Emergency Department like a superhero granted a new weapon, when my phone dings. It's Daphne:

> Come up to the residents' room and tell me about this
> disaster.

———

The outward expansion of the hospital has been chaotic—a warren of corridors connecting vital services—but a hundred years of slow vertical growth now yields panoramic views to the city, the river and the distant mountains. A long sweeping balcony surrounds the residents' room, although the external doors are locked and looped with chains. The ninth floor must be, in part, why doctors keep coming to The Mount.

The residents' room is a remnant of the days when interns, residents and registrars were expected to stay overnight, or even whole weekends. No one mourns the passing of seventy-two-hour shifts, but with them went the tea ladies who'd bring up meals and the laundry ladies who'd change the bed sheets. Now, residents have shorter shifts but can't ever sleep, at best they might manage to slouch on the sofa for a short while. Now, few registrars are rostered to be on site overnight and the rest of us are only 'on call'. We provide advice over the phone, but stay or return if there's work to be done—and are always back for the daily morning ward round.

At one end of the space the old on-call bedrooms are still there, each with a bed and a small desk overlooking the city, visible through the open doors. Perhaps I won't ever have to sleep on that awful grimy sofa in our office.

The sofa up here sits between a large air hockey table and an ancient television. Someone balancing a mug of soup and an enormous laptop computer covered in statistical outputs sits in the middle, his bare feet resting on a chair.

'Nice save on the old guy!' Daphne appears suddenly from a small kitchen at the back of the room. 'ED here are great, but any department's only as strong as its weakest link, and this year that will be Brayden.'

'How did you know it was Brayden?' I ask.

The person on the sofa chuckles and shakes his head, still tapping at the computer. 'It had to be Brayden,' he says without looking up. 'He's okay. You have to know that he's low on Dreyfus' model of skill acquisition. In his blind application of rules, he fears administrators more than medical catastrophes. I heard he even went to orientation on his day off, despite working here for three years already.'

'You know, Vikram, that's because everyone saves him from clinical disaster, but no one can save us from the wrath of admin,' Daphne responds, tossing her pen at his head.

'There's a statistically significant chance of admin wrath on any given day,' Vikram pontificates, tossing it back. They laugh together, their easy camaraderie like a bubble around them.

Feeling left out, 'Daphne, that patient in ED . . .' I begin, trying not to sound aggrieved. Surely I could have told her about the patient over the phone without walking upstairs to watch these two banter.

'Hold that thought, we can talk shop in a minute,' she says, walking back into the kitchen. 'By the way, Vikram comes with the hospital, chained here by a PhD. You want a stat on anything? Ask him.'

Vikram gestures at his screen and slurps his soup. 'Yes, I *have* done a Poisson regression on how many times I've been able to answer a statistical question in the last year. Admittedly, it's not as interesting as counting how many people died from being kicked in the head by a mule.'

'Aren't flesh-eating ulcers interesting enough?' Daphne laughs again, emerging with a plate of food. 'Sit, Emma,' she instructs. There's enough hot buttered toast for all of us.

Vikram is the Infectious Diseases registrar but is only working part time on the wards this year while he finishes his PhD. Professor Brown is his supervisor. They spend their field time in plastic overalls digging in sewers, trying to find the unknown secret hiding place of *Mycobacterium ulcerans*, a bizarre flesh-eating bacteria.

Daphne tells me about her childhood friendship with a kind elderly neighbour, whose final nursing home doctor inspired her to become a geriatrician. And I don't tell them about my father, but I do tell them about the girl who walked.

By the time my pager rings with another referral from ED, I've got an ID badge and a full stomach. Most importantly, even The Mount has people in it who might be friends. And maybe, because of this, whatever else happens things will turn out okay.

Chapter Six

'You're writing notes?' Daniel asks.

We're in surgical admissions trying to locate our final patient of the morning, and I've spent too long talking to the first two.

'Yes,' I say, as if this is routine. Except four weeks into the year, Daniel knows it's not. He and Will watch me and Steve rush through our early morning assessments every day. Our hope to start ward rounds at 7 a.m. has already failed and we're now coming in at 6.30. Some days we have surgery in the morning, others we see patients in clinic, either way there are patients everywhere to see first—the patients on the ward, new patients who've arrived in Emergency overnight, new patients who've come in for elective surgery, new patients who've been referred by another unit because they've injured something or other while in hospital. And everyone needs to be seen five minutes ago.

My feeling of being superfluous on the first day was fleeting. Now we're never enough. Even at 6.30 a.m. it's a rush. Steve rampages while I follow and apologise to everyone he insults, but no one wants to arrive earlier because we're always here so late.

Today Daniel and I simply left the ward round midway because it's my first operating list with David Wright, one of the best regarded surgeons in town. He's been on holidays and I've been stuck with grumpy Jon covering those lists. I'm determined to ensure this morning goes smoothly so that I can make up for lost time.

There are three patients scheduled for surgery this morning. I take a detailed history and examine them carefully. Early to theatre, I'm relieved that the rest of the team is gathering too, but then notice something wrong. The anaesthetist is on her tablet checking emails, while a nurse and theatre technician chat about the upcoming weekend. Why aren't they hurrying? Even dropping my bag on our desk loudly doesn't provoke movement.

'Don't we need to get the patient around?' My voice is anxiously tinny, even to my own ear. The technician glances at me. The nurse doesn't even turn. The anaesthetist sends her email with a 'whoosh' that echoes around the theatre. I expect she'll spring into action but she picks up her mug of coffee.

'Rule number one. Don't bring the patient around until David has seen and marked them.'

'I've already marked the patient.'

Lowering her mug, she wipes her mouth. Her dark brown eyes crinkle, creasing the stroke of kohl underneath. 'Rule number two. The registrar should never mark the patient. Only David's allowed to do that,' she intones.

Shit.

She swivels in her chair and hands me a fistful of alcohol wipes from her drug trolley.

'Rule number three. David is almost always late. The "almost" is why you and I will always get here at 8.15, even though he'll only arrive at 8.45.' She glances at Daniel. 'And rule number four. Surgical residents ruin sterility and shouldn't be in theatre. My name is Jyothi. Come pretend you're an anaesthetic resident.'

In the holding bay, the alcohol wipe only smudges the purple ink and leaves the patient's leg red from rubbing. I hope David won't notice.

Back in theatre there's some bustle in the small set-up room. I tie on a mask and crack the door open a few centimetres. Lorraine, the lead nurse for Orthopaedics, is in a sterile gown and gloves and unpacking instruments for the first case. This is a surprise—most of her job is administrative, ordering and receiving instruments and implants. I thought she only scrubbed in for Prof Bones.

'What gives?' I ask her.

'David only works here because I agreed to scrub for him too.'

The scout nurse, who opens sterile packets for the nurse who is scrubbed in, tears open another blue paper-wrapped box and Lorraine catches it in her hands.

'Got everything we need?' I've never done an ankle replacement before so I'm relying on Lorraine.

She points to a large folder, bursting with paper. 'David has extremely precise fad cards,' she tells me. 'And, well, we also bring in anything else he might need.'

Against one wall, a mobile shelf is filled with parcels wrapped in blue sterile paper.

'You seem to have brought in the whole storeroom?' I laugh.

'Emma, do you know what "fad card" stands for?'

'Fad, like what's fashionable. What the surgeons like to use.' This is unremarkable. Nurses are forever adding and removing things from fad cards.

'No, they are a F.A.D. card. A Fucking Arsehole's Demands. And we're supposed to know, telepathically, when the Arseholes have changed their minds.'

The scout nurse giggles, almost dropping another parcel of instruments. Lorraine catches it deftly. 'Now, don't go telling people,' she says. 'We only share that with the registrars who aren't arseholes.

———

David walks in at 8.42, a bunch of folders under one arm and dragging a large bag on wheels. He nods at Jyothi, gives Lorraine a thumbs-up through the window, and turns to me with a big smile. 'You must be Emma. Pleasure! Professor Swann was very good to me many years ago.'

He's exactly the sort of person my father would have been good to, I think. My parentage can't be a secret among the surgeons at The Mount, but I swore early in my career to get ahead on my own steam and not my father's reputation. I deflect by holding out my hand. 'Pleasure to meet you, Mr Wright.' Forget about a handshake, I almost feel a curtsy is due.

He roars with laughter, his already handsome face glowing. 'Emma, only my banker calls me Mr Wright. Call me David.' He meticulously lays out the manila folders, a small speaker, a notebook and a fountain pen, the edges lined up. 'Thanks for sending me the operating list and summary of the patients,' he says with unusual warmth. That's part of my job and few other surgeons even acknowledge I've done it.

Something operatic fills the room. Jyothi's registrar asks if David would like an ankle block, a targeted injection of local anaesthetic so the patient has less pain after surgery. This used to be a blind injection but is more often now performed by the anaesthetists using ultrasound guidance.

Jyothi intervenes. 'Rule number five. We're only here to put the patient to sleep. David will put in his own ankle block if he wants one.' She drops her voice as David shuffles papers, and murmurs to me, 'Go scrub, don't prep.'

'Rule number six?'

Jyothi nods and winks.

I spend the full eight recommended minutes washing my hands, even after David gives up and goes inside, removing dirt and *Propionibacterium* from under my fingernails with a small pick and scrubbing the *Corynebacterium* from my skin with a brand-new brush. The cold water makes my arm hairs stand on end. Why doesn't this scrub sink have a warm water mixer?

Lorraine dresses me in my gown, holding it up as I find the arms. She puffs up my gloves and holds them out, snapping them over the cuff of my gown as my fingers each find the correct spot. David unties his waist strap and hands me the end. 'Dance with me?' he invites, and spins so the gown unwraps around him.

The ankle replacement is a beautiful operation, skilfully done. Andy's advice, no doubt passed on from Dad, was to admire and learn from those surgeons we might never operate as well as, and beware those we already operate better than. David's incision is short, his dissection precise, his bone cuts sharp. Even my grandmother, who won several quilting gold medals at her regional show, would approve of his sutures. I'm smitten.

In the interval between cases, after I've put a plaster on the leg and helped Jyothi transfer the patient to the bed, David calls me over to his desk. I tuck myself into the narrow space between his broad shoulders and the wall. Poor Daniel, uninterested in anaesthesia and again betrayed by my lack of introduction, gives up and disappears.

'So, Emma, I'm sure you want a research project. Can I give you one?' David asks.

I nod, my eagerness embarrassingly reflected in his designer glasses.

He hands me the folders. 'I brought these in today in case I could tempt you. I've been meaning to do something with this data, but . . .'

I'm still nodding.

'You could present it at the national conference in a couple of months and write it up for a journal as well?' he smiles indulgently at my overflowing enthusiasm. 'These are my notes from my last thirty-six ankle replacements. Now, this is the first one we've done together so you wouldn't know that my technique is a modification of what the company recommends,' he starts to explain.

I *had* noticed that he did something different. The official guide for the joint replacement is in front of me. On the page describing placement of the prosthesis I find the relevant diagram where the implant is placed in the dead centre of the bone above and below. 'You put it in a bit off centre,' I say, pointing.

David sits back and crosses his arms, a curious expression on his face. He wasn't expecting me to have noticed.

'Okay,' he says slowly. Pointing to the pictures in the book, he explains the biomechanical studies he did while he was in London after he finished his surgical training. These extra years are called a fellowship and are not mandatory but it's how experts are made—and why Dad's already started nagging me about it. David draws several diagrams of bones and angles and vectors. Producing a small packet of coloured pencils he shades in parts to demonstrate different areas of pressure within the joint.

'David, you should have been a plastic surgeon, you draw so beautifully!'

'Well, I got into both training programs. It was a hard choice. The feet of our city are lucky I chose orthopaedics.'

Most people take years of dedicated effort to get onto one surgical training program, in fact most people don't ever get accepted to any. These programs are the only way to become any sort of specialist and hospitals are run on the labour of those who hope for selection to a program of choice. At times a battle royale between junior doctors, I know how relentlessly I worked—although it's been muttered that I was only put onto a surgical training program because I was a woman, or because my father was Professor Swann. It's incomprehensible that David managed offers for two different programs.

His files handed over for me to analyse, David tells me about his wife while we wait for the next patient to go to sleep. She's an interventional radiologist, dissolving blood clots in the brain of patients having a stroke within minutes of their arrival to hospital. David's impressed by what he calls 'the technology' but doesn't think it's a great job for his wife. 'She could earn such a good income reporting scans done overseas and would still be able to drop off and pick up the kids,' he sighs.

We go through the process of washing our hands and cleaning and draping the next patient's ankle, while I tell him about Shamsi. We might have met on a holiday but Shamsi is even more career-focused than me.

David whistles in disbelief. 'You're married to a corporate lawyer? That's an exhausting combination of careers. How are you going to make it work?' he asks. An odd question, I think, from someone married to a fellow doctor.

'We're pretty good at this,' I tell David. We've spent the last few years tag-teaming when we're most busy. Shamsi had a quiet period when I was an intern in the country, he took on his biggest case in the one term I always finished at five. I've told the truth—we've been very good at supporting each other, but we've never both been as busy as we are now.

This patient has a broken ankle. At my old hospital we'd have given him a boot to wear for months. David uses a small camera and miniature instruments to remove a small bone fragment from within the joint, then finds and elevates a sunken bit of load-bearing cartilage. Offering surgery for this fracture seemed excessive when I looked at the scans last night, but now that we're inside the joint it's clear why the long-term results of doing it this way might be better.

When he's finished, he hands me the camera and lets me have a turn driving it around the joint. I've floated an arthroscope through knees before, but the knee is a big joint with lots of space and this is totally different. Tight corners and sudden turns make the straight camera stick and jam.

'Whoa, whoa,' David says, as he takes the camera from me. 'Try it this way.'

He stands closer and puts his gloved hands over mine. And then, step by step, he shows me how to manoeuvre the camera around the bends. His biceps press into my shoulder and I'm aware of the smell of his aftershave, how close his hips are to mine. This sudden closeness would be inappropriate anywhere else, but our blue paper gowns are a magical cape that transport us away from our normal boundaries. Put on a gown and you can cut into flesh, hold a beating heart or a wriggling intestine. Put on a gown and you can stick needles and deliver babies. In a gown, we stand together, smell each other's hair and inspect each other's eyelashes, together breaking so many usual rules. I wonder if, after years of wearing the gown, the edges of opposing realities start to blur. Today the case ends and we step away from each other discarding the paper gowns in the bin, as if what we've done, what we do all the time, is nothing.

The last case is a common operation I've seen many times but never performed—bunion surgery. David considers me as we scrub. He leans over and magically flicks my tap to warm water and asks if I know how to correct a bunion.

'Yes!' I answer confidently, then frantically go over the steps in my mind.

He pauses. 'I don't normally let registrars operate. How about I do one side and you do the other?' He waits for my nod. 'We'll do them at the same time. Watch me and keep up.'

This is a game I can play.

Over the next half-hour, he pushes the pace. Lorraine, understanding, hands me the right instruments at the right time. I make the same incision, pressing the blade firmly to cut the skin in one swipe, not so firmly that the tendon underneath is damaged. A few drops of blood seep from the transected veins. I reach for the cautery forceps but the pedal to activate it is under David's foot. He pauses his part of the operation to step on it for me, cheerfully accusing me of sabotage.

We retract the skin and he passes me the saw after he's done with it. Lorraine syringes sterile saline over the saw blade as we cut the bone, the fluid protecting the bone cells from the heat of friction. My plastic face shield spatters with wet bone dust, tinged pink with blood. She hands me the screws, and I fix the now straight bone together, making sure the cut ends are well compressed.

I place the last sutures in the skin only a few moments after him, flushed from the effort. And when our eyes meet, I know he's impressed.

'Nice one, Emma!' David gives me a high five and a wink.

I dress the two feet with thick cotton padding and thin stretchy crepe bandage while he drops his gown and gloves in the bin, grabs his bag, and winks again on his way out the door. Jyothi and her registrar are wheeling the patient out of theatre when Andy texts me.

Did you nail it this morning?

I sink onto a stool, tap out a '*YES*' and close my eyes in satisfaction, savouring the moment. *This* is why I'm here.

Chapter Seven

It's 5 a.m. Shamsi reaches over to stop my Wednesday morning earlier-than-usual alarm then envelops me in his arms, his broad chest rising and falling against my cheek.

'Sweetie, stay in bed,' he mutters, entwining his legs in mine. I try to conjure my enthusiasm of last week when my eyes sprung open and I leapt from bed to be on time for David's operating list. A big night out with Shamsi and a couple of nights on call at the hospital and today, I could so easily lie here with my eyes closed a bit longer. Or if Shamsi were to slide his hand further up my shirt and then slowly pull himself onto me, *that* I could rouse myself for too. Instead I have to get to Grand Round. With a sigh I disentangle myself and sit up. 'Another day,' I tell him with a kiss.

Easing myself from bed and shuddering in the early autumn chill, I stumble to the wardrobe, using my phone as a torch. The hangers are bare and I know the laundry basket in the bathroom is full. There are no ironed shirts left.

Shit.

Shamsi still has many that are neatly laundered and pressed, but the boyfriend shirt isn't the look that's expected for the weekly Grand Round. I find a crumpled dress that I haven't worn in a while and decide to iron instead of eat breakfast.

I'm fumbling my hair into a loose bun when Shamsi appears, holding a coffee and rubbing his eyes, his bare chest giving me reason to pause. We kiss, my lips lingering slightly too long for a casual morning peck, my hand a little too low on his waist. Just as he wakes enough to wrap his arms around me and let the hollow under his chin find the top of my head, I check the time. With another small kiss, I run for the door. As I back out of the driveway, he's a shadow, waving silently.

———

At least I now have an ID tag and access to the hospital car park. It's across the road, wedged between the private hospital and a tall office building. At this time of day, I can usually get a park on the second floor.

As I exit onto the street, the sun appears above the 1960s Brutalist façade, built during the stage of expansion where the original Victorian hospital was completely subsumed by modernity. The street is filthy, littered with cigarette butts and discarded bottles. I'm so early even the street cleaners haven't made it past yet.

A homeless woman sits on a flattened cardboard box near the ambulance bay. Above her, the 'P' in the glowing sign to the Emergency Department has loosened and hangs at an angle, the exterior at odds with the exceptionalism within. She glares at me as I hurry past and I avert my eyes. She's been at this spot since at least my first day, and quite probably longer. Sometimes when I pass by, I think about asking her why she lives here, but then, like today, I'm always too busy.

———

Will has the patient lists and coffee. I think, *God bless Will*, then remember I'm the one who hands him a hundred dollars every Monday morning to buy team coffee for the week.

Steve appears ten minutes later with a crinkled shirt and a scowl. Catching sight of himself in the grimy office window, he groans and digs around in his bag to retrieve a crumpled V-neck jumper, which he smooths and throws on. Suddenly, he's presentable.

He drinks his coffee in a single gulp while I give him an update. He doesn't thank me but this isn't the time to complain. As the more senior registrar he's in the firing line today. No sleep, again, won't excuse him from the onslaught. We gather our notes and wait outside the office door for the senior surgeons. Daniel slouches against the wall, eyes half closed. I restrain a parental urge to tell him to stand up straight so he makes a good impression. Will checks his blood sugar monitor and furtively eats a jelly bean. These early mornings are making his diabetes even harder to manage.

Jon arrives first, with a trimmed beard and in his five-thousand-dollar dark grey Zegna suit. He bought it during a conference in Hong Kong two weeks after he passed his exam last year. He's told me that the suit, along with his hard work and general excellence, are responsible for his appointment to The Mount.

'You forget to iron your shirt, mate?' Jon slaps Steve on the back, and they both grin like loons. The mateship of the woollen jumper is clearly a club to which I don't—can't—belong.

Paul's next, also in dark grey but with a shirt as pink as Daniel's. He's our supervisor of training, responsible for collecting all the surgeons' opinions and telling us how we're progressing—and whether or not we'll pass the term. Today he graces us with a nod before showing Jon photos of his new Maserati on his phone. Old Bill, who would have retired were it not for his costly third divorce, slowly limps down the corridor, and Albert with his wet eyes and ugly brown suit follows. Then David strides in with a broad grin and his trademark wink. Steve fits easily into their easy chitchat of cars and football, while I'm still trying to work out if I stand with my legs together or crossed over.

Sensing an audience, Jon asks me questions about bone healing. I scuff my feet and stammer through some answers until Prof 'Bones' Jones marches in, cutting short my torment and handing it back to Steve.

If normal ward rounds are for the shaming of residents and medical students, Grand Rounds are the promise that such humiliation doesn't end until you're the professor at the top of the ice-cream cone, dripping derision on those below. Senior registrars and specialist surgeons alike come to surgical Grand Rounds expecting their weekly dose of so-called humility.

We invade one room after another, tearing back curtains and towering over patients, loudly discussing their medical conditions so everyone in earshot can hear. Paul grabs someone's hand to demonstrate a particular pathology, and Steve pulls a blanket off someone else to expose a limb. On Grand Rounds, each patient is little more than a case study, a limb inconveniently attached to a sentient blob of flesh.

Cheryl, usually so kind, never says anything. Does she accept this as necessary, or has she given up trying to change how the surgeons do things after years of being head nurse? As for the patients, I'm never sure what they think about being handled so roughly, or watching their treating doctor be grilled until they fail.

Steve's only a year behind Andy, senior enough that he's expected to know quite a lot. I'm not sure if it's because he was called back to the hospital at 2 a.m. or if he hasn't studied enough, but his performance today is mediocre. Several surgeons whisper and shake their heads as he trips over the classification of various injuries and admits to not knowing the specific features of a rare bone tumour. Paul warns Steve loudly that at this rate, he's going to fail The Exam. Prof suggests that he try and guess the questions he might get asked and prepare those answers the night before. Steve, usually so haughty, slumps as the round progresses.

I've no idea how to go about guessing at possible questions, but I'll be in the hot seat of this weekly trivia game soon enough. After we shuffle into the small room at the end of the ward, where the torture continues with our weekly audit, I stand to the side and write down the questions Steve got wrong.

The room can barely hold everyone. The few seats are taken first by the most senior surgeons. There are a few medical students this morning and they retreat to the back—if they draw attention to themselves, they'll be targets too.

Cheryl's closed the door and pulled the blinds. Everyone's ready but the audit doesn't start. Prof Bones spreads his legs and puts his arms behind his head, taps his feet impatiently. Daniel pokes at the keyboard as a sense of restlessness spreads across the room. He's responsible for presenting the audit of last week's cases today.

Old Bill sits forward in his chair and looks around. 'Do we have a Chinese medical student here today to help the lads? They're good with computers.'

There's a rustling among the students as they rearrange themselves to protect those who might be most vulnerable to such a question.

Lacking a volunteer, Bill turns back to Daniel. 'Where are *you* from?'

Daniel blushes and keeps tapping at the computer. 'Australia,' he mutters.

'Oh, stop being so PC,' Bill says shortly. 'Where are your parents, your ancestors *really* from?'

Daniel might look calm but his hands shake slightly. 'I'm Aboriginal,' he says quietly. Oh that the projector would come to life.

Prof Jones leans over and taps Bill on the shoulder, shaking his head but saying nothing. The room, likewise, sits in uncomfortable silence. Bill closes his mouth momentarily then leans back in his chair, changing tack.

'In my day we got here early and set everything up so the audit was ready to go. Made sure the consultants didn't have to wait.' Bill sounds more upset than he looks. My father used to taunt us like this at home, allaying his boredom by toying with others. I will Daniel not to engage as there's no way to win.

'Bill, in your day, there were no computers,' Prof suggests.

Bill smiles and takes the cue. 'We had to walk from ward to ward finding everyone's X-rays. We even rummaged through surgeons' cars and their private offices. And then we had the X-ray boards loaded and ready to go. Young people have it so easy these days. Turn on the computer and—wham—there they are.'

David chuckles from the back. 'When you were in charge, Bill, remember we *had* computers but you didn't want us to use them?'

Bill nods and smiles, indulging in the memory. With his silent blessing David continues.

'You wanted us to use those old-fashioned projectors for the audit. The hospital didn't have any, though, because we'd moved to PowerPoint years earlier.'

David turns his attention to Daniel. 'So, I used to drive across to the rehab campus at 5 a.m., and borrow theirs, and photocopy the slides onto those plastic sheets . . . What were they called?'

Daniel shakes his head.

'Transparencies! Ha!' David is triumphant. Bill chortles and Paul slaps David on the back.

'Bill, do the registrars still print out your emails for you?' David asks.

'My daughter moved overseas last year so I worked out the email,' Bill replies. 'Turns out it wasn't too hard.'

Thankfully, with a low whir, the audit illuminates the screen. Daniel, relieved, starts his presentation.

The first case is a broken ankle which has been fixed with a plate and screws. As usual Prof Bones leads the questioning. 'Who did that? That's shit,' he declares.

Jon raises his hand and sucks in a breath. 'It was a difficult fracture, Prof. The skin was terrible and I didn't want to make a bigger incision than needed and risk it falling apart. Also the patient's in her nineties and bed-bound. I thought it best to get the skin healed, even if the position isn't quite right.' As if rehearsed, the explanation comes out in a rush.

No response.

Jon seems relieved he won't be subject to any further scrutiny this morning.

I wonder, while Daniel quickly moves on, whether the decision-making paid off, as the patient was discharged back to her nursing home and hasn't been reviewed by us since.

We don't know if the skin healed and the trade-off was justified. *Nothing ruins a good operation like long-term follow-up*, I suppose, and thus we carry on.

The rest of the audit proceeds without too much interrogation. Prof Bones glances briefly at each slide between scrolling on his telephone. I've been told the trick to a good orthopaedic audit at The Mount is to ensure that the residents don't say or show anything that piques his interest too much, and if he looks up from his phone, to move on quickly.

At last the audit ends, the lights are switched on and the blinds elevated. Everyone's shuffling to the door when Prof Bones stands and clears his throat.

'I have an announcement to make,' he begins, and gestures for Jon to stand by him. 'Jon's accepted an excellent opportunity to go to the US and undertake a fellowship in trauma surgery.'

Jon beams and Prof pumps his hand.

'The offer came up at short notice. He leaves in six weeks. This means Jon won't be around to cover the many surgeons who had leave approved in the coming months.' Prof turns to me and Steve. 'It'll be up to you two to cover the shortfall but we'll support you from a distance.'

Steve and I look at each other. He shrugs and joins the rest of the group as they file out. I sink into a chair, taking a moment to hide in the now empty room. I'm a first-year trainee. I feel hardly qualified to operate alone.

I'm still digesting the news when David's head appears at the door. 'Ah, I was taking coffee orders and thought you were missing.'

My worry must be apparent on my face. Understanding, he smiles encouragingly. 'Hey, don't stress about being on your own a bit. I've watched you operate. You'll be fine!' he says.

'I don't know, David. We did that bunion operation together. I've done lots of cases with supervision, but very little on my own.'

David comes over and sits opposite me. He folds his hands one over the other, his wide gold wedding band glinting under the ceiling lights. 'Do you want to know how *I* learned to operate?' he asks. 'There was this amazing nurse here called Mary. She's retired and more's the pity. She had some cracking stories about Bill and Prof. Anyway, she didn't know how to operate but she sure as hell knew what instruments were needed when. We had a deal—she'd hand me the instruments, in order, and I'd work out what to do with them.'

'That sounds . . . inexact,' I say, then blush, wishing my mouth wouldn't say things faster than my brain can censor.

David raises an eyebrow at me, amused. 'It was. There was also an anatomy book and an operative technique book open nearby.' He stands up, and nods to the door. 'We better get to clinic, hey? Don't worry, you'll be fine.'

In the lift, he turns to me again. 'A hot tip, Emma. Showing uncertainty is a rookie mistake. Surgeons want to see confidence in a trainee. Grasp every opportunity you're given with both hands, and don't show fear.' David links his fingers behind his back and bounces up and down on his toes. 'Believe in yourself, that's the most important thing.'

I think back through the morning's Grand Round. Steve could have said his wrong answers more confidently. Jon did believe in himself but his plating of that fracture was still, as Prof put it, shit. I can't see how David's advice is useful or contributes to good patient care. But maybe it's a rookie mistake to think this way, so I simply thank him for his advice.

Chapter Eight

The outpatients clinic is at the very back of the hospital, down the end of a long hallway that winds from the lobby past the Emergency and Radiology departments. Coloured lines painted on the linoleum mark the way—red to Emergency, blue to Radiology, yellow to Outpatients—all diverging at the foot of the main staircase with the original wrought-iron balustrades.

The waiting room is full when we arrive. Patients and family fill every orange plastic chair and stand around the edges of the room. A few weary ambulance officers lean on their stretchers, unable to leave until we've arrived. Everyone watches darkly as we troop in with coffees in hand. I duck my head in shame but the bosses parade past gaily.

Why *are* the first appointments half an hour before the ward round and meeting finish? It's not lost on me that to be a good patient, one must also be patient.

Every consultation room in the clinic has two doors, one for the patients to enter and exit, and the other for us. Patients must wonder what important tasks we undertake on our side. To me it seems to be mostly bawdy jokes and shoulder slapping while the residents and registrars do most of the work.

I slink off to the four-bed room. Here we see mostly post-operative patients who need dressings or new plasters. It's the only area designed for efficiency and is not only far from the raucous mob but also next to the plaster area and Anka, the plaster nurse. She's worked in this clinic for decades and identified me as Professor Swann's daughter within seconds.

Four patients have already been brought into the room by the clinic nurses. First, though, I've got to log on to the computers—a daily battle. I set a timer and click through multiple screens to load the three different programs we use to record notes and look at X-rays and other test results. As at our audit meeting, the computer lags. Eight and a half minutes for the software to load is a new record.

My first patient is seething. 'I've paid for ten minutes of parking while you checked your social media,' she complains.

'Social media? Oh no, I was reading your notes.'

'I'm a legal secretary. My lawyers charge fifteen hundred dollars an hour. There's no way they'd lose two hundred and fifty dollars because their computer takes ten minutes to turn on.'

'That's what we have to work with.' I remove the bandage from her lower leg.

'I was listening to the radio and someone called in about computer medical records,' she continues. 'There's a hospital that needs twenty-five million dollars to upgrade its system. Did this place spend twenty-five million dollars on *that*?'

I bin her bandages and shrug. 'You know more than me.'

Thankfully, her leg is fine and she doesn't need to be seen again. Still irritated, she asks for a medical certificate. She's had to take half a day off work to come in for such a brief check.

I find the pad of blank certificates, the last paper document we're allowed to hand out. It is, therefore, one of the few things for which I need a pen. Mine was requisitioned by Albert this morning.

'Anka, do you have a pen?'

She shakes her head, hands wet with plaster as she smooths a new cast on a child's arm.

Will's on the far side of the room and clutches his pen closer, shaking his head at me too. It's a rare and desperate resident who refuses to hand a pen up the hierarchy.

I dash out of the room. There aren't any pens at the front desk, and they only have red ones in the drawers.

David sees me scrounging and comes to investigate. 'Pen? I'd offer you one but I had to steal mine from Steve,' he says, waving a near-empty and cap-less pen at me.

'Forget about your study on ankle joints, David. I'm going to do a study on where pens go in hospitals.'

'Oh, you don't need a study. You need reinforcements. When *I* was a resident, I bought boxes of pens and brought in a handful daily to give out to my registrars and consultants,' he says, scanning the crowded clinic.

Maybe that's how he got onto two training programs: bribery with pens.

Finally, beside a pile of forms marked *Falls Risk Assessment* and under a stack of brochures about pressure sores, there's a pen. Success!

David's still lurking in the hallway, not seeing patients. 'You've managed to find a pen *and* log on to the computers today?' he asks as I wave the pen above my head in victory.

'Yes!'

'You're doing better than me. The system cancelled my password because it didn't meet their strength criteria.'

'What was it?'

'Password.'

We both laugh.

Back in the room, the legal secretary is fuming. 'Another ten minutes to find a pen!' she exclaims. 'I order stationery for my practice and fifty pens cost ten dollars. That's the same as a roll of bandage, which I also order for the first-aid box.' She points to the well-stocked dressing trolley. 'We'd never let our lawyers waste ten minutes looking for a twenty-cent pen, when they could have earned two hundred and fifty dollars in that time.' She snatches the certificate from my fingers then lowers herself off the bed and into her shoes.

'This is a public hospital. No one here is earning fifteen hundred dollars an hour and *our* clients get their care for free,'

I can't help but point out. If she wanted efficiency, then she could pay extra for private insurance and go to the private hospital next door.

'How many more people could you care for if you had the simple things you need?' she asks, huffing out the door.

'She has a point, you know,' says my next patient, who's been watching from the next bed.

———

It's mid-morning when Jacqui, the young mother from the country, walks into the room. I haven't seen her since our first day last month when she was admitted for her tests.

'Hi, Jacqui!' I greet her, assuming everything was clear.

'Hi, doctor, I've forgotten your name . . .' she trails off.

I say, 'Emma,' and flip my name badge around so she can see it. I always wear it backwards so creepy patients can't know my name.

She's more drawn than when she was in hospital. 'How's the leg?' I ask.

'Sore. And . . . your colleague never called with the results. Someone told me to come in today . . . It's a long way, and on short notice . . .'

'Oh.'

I'm mortified. Steve said he'd follow up her results and report back to Prof, so I hadn't.

'Hang on,' I tell her and go to investigate. Steve's busy with another patient and Prof Bones has ducked out 'across the road'.

I look up Jacqui's results myself. Her MRI loads slowly, but once the images appear on the screen, I don't need to read the radiologist's report.

Steeling myself against the injustice, I remind myself of the words Steve couldn't find this morning, words used to describe malignant tumours. Inhomogeneous enhancement. Prominent flow voids. Wide zone of transition. Sunburst periosteal reaction. Myxoid material. Punctate calcifications. Jacqui has more than one.

There's more on her biopsy report, like: 'divergent differentiation', 'giant cells' and 'galectin-1'.

Shit.

When we started medical school we were warned that we'd learn ten thousand new words before graduation. In early university, I was more interested in reading novels, playing pool and hanging out in the university bar with nachos and beer. My medical vocabulary didn't develop as expected. In one memorable pathology quiz we had to walk around the room and describe a variety of gross specimens—gross in size and character.

'Don't try and diagnose the condition, just describe the lesions that you see,' the pathologist had instructed.

I was proud of my answers: 'cauliflowerform', 'carrara marbled', 'chartreusian'. The lecturer was not impressed. 'You're not in art class,' was the comment that accompanied the fail mark.

Once we started seeing patients in the hospitals, I was happy to abandon the bar for the wards because it felt like learning I would use. But how these words have come back to haunt me.

Now they're more than descriptions of shadows on an MRI, more than the shape of cells or the chemicals that illuminate them in purple or pink. They're words that change lives forever. I'm glad I avoided learning them for as long as possible.

The curtain flutters, Jacqui's hand rubbing her thigh. I call Prof Bones.

'Yes?' he answers on the third ring.

'Oh Prof . . .' I walk further away, trying to avoid the frustrated eyes of the other patients in the room. 'Sorry to bother you, but—'

'The summary, Emma.'

'It's Jacqui Miller—'

'Who? I don't know names. What's her problem?'

'Sorry, um, she came in for investigation of a sarcoma—'

'Well, is it a sarcoma?'

Would I call him if it wasn't?

'Yes, it's a—'

'So, why didn't you follow this up earlier?'

Am I supposed to remember everything in case Steve doesn't?

Prof's grumpy voice becomes even more gravelly. 'Get her to see the reconstructive surgeons and the radiation oncologists. Book her into the sarcoma meeting this week. She'll need surgery after she finishes her radiotherapy. Why are you calling me?'

'Oh, I thought you liked to see—'

'Well, yes, but I'm not there, am I?' He hangs up.

I wonder how to send Jacqui to see other specialists without telling her she has cancer.

Shit.

I can't.

And she's still waiting for me.

I stall by dashing to the front desk to print her pathology report. With something to read in her hands maybe she won't notice my impending clumsiness.

'I have your results!' I say cheerfully as I re-enter the room. Good grief, there's no reason to be happy. And yet if I were glum she'd know I was about to deliver terrible news.

But I *am* about to deliver terrible news.

I sit next to her and search for those 'bad news' tutorials from medical school. Surely I didn't skip all those sessions. But these days I rarely deliver bad news like this and I'm unpractised. You're-going-to-die-and-leave-your-young-children-motherless seems in its own category. As I split hairs in my own classifications of calamity, the silence stretches out.

'It's bad, isn't it?' Jacqui finally asks.

'Yeah, it's not great.'

Shit.

But the knowledge gap broken, the punchline becomes much easier.

'Jacqui, I'm sorry, it *is* a cancer.'

The words hover in the air, dreamlike. Everyone else in the room averts their eyes. I once had a pathology lecturer who called cancer the 'Spanish Dancer'. My classmates assumed he meant a beautiful woman, whirling in flamenco, but for me the nudibranch version made much more sense—speckled, slug-like and appearing in the dark of night to feast.

'Yes, I knew it must be. Thank you for being honest,' she quavers. And so the dream is broken, leaving a cold clinic with linoleum floors and a prognosis she fears but I know. We haven't even got to that.

I show her the pathology report and underline the conclusion. 'This shows that you have a sarcoma. There are many kinds so don't go and google it. Some aren't so bad,' I explain, planning to google it myself.

Jacqui nods. 'What happens now?'

I don't know in any meaningful detail. She needs more scans and then radiotherapy to shrink the mass before we can cut it out. We'll have to remove some muscle, maybe some bone. She'll see the plastic and reconstructive surgeons to talk about the reconstruction.

As I talk, Jacqui sits silent and still. I look for the shadow. It's always there after these diagnoses are given, after people learn their hopes and dreams must change. Slightly behind the front of the eyes, it's the realisation that their life will now be split as 'before' and 'after', it's the dark hood of guessing at remaining days and facing a very different tomorrow.

'Okay, how long do I need to be in town?' she asks, with urgent resignation.

'It might be a few months, Jacqui.' Next to her, my useless hands are clasped one inside the other.

'Okay. We can manage. Emma . . . it was Emma, wasn't it?'
I nod. 'Thank you for being kind. But . . . am I going to die?
Before my kids grow up?'

I don't know any more than she does. There's no crystal ball
and these are rare cancers. Prof Bones is the only person in the
city who treats them.

'I have no idea, Jacqui,' I tell her. Anything else would be a
fabrication. 'These can be aggressive tumours but we're getting
better and better at managing them. We'll know more after the
scans and after your radiotherapy is finished. If it hasn't spread
and it responds well your chances are far better.' I'm not lying but
my words are careful, deliberately chosen to convey only empty
truisms so that time won't reveal that I was wrong.

'The resident doctors will organise those tests. And would
you like to speak to the social workers about some temporary
accommodation?' At least I'm great with logistics.

Jacqui nods, no more words. I pat her arm and move on, pulling
the curtain closed around her shadowed eyes and private grief.

———

It's 12.40 p.m. and the clinic is starting to empty. The consultants
have mostly disappeared without saying goodbye. Except David,
who incomprehensibly walked past waiting patients to tell me
he was going and to ask if I'd like to join him for a sandwich.
Who would finish the clinic if I left too?

Steve, untroubled by such thoughts, snuck off a few minutes
after the surgeons, leaving me and Will and Daniel and twenty

patients still to be seen. As a nurse directs my next patient in, I text Andy who was also in clinic this morning.

> Bloody hell, why does Steve leave clinic for lunch before it's finished?

Why don't you?

> Because clinic isn't finished.

So?

> Hello. Is this Andy? Didn't you lecture me about not leaving shit for the residents?

It's old jaded practical Andy.

> This next lady's travelled three hours from the country for her complex issues and the surgeon she needs to see has gone. How can I leave too?

Do you have answers for her?

> Oh, shut up.

See. All you're going to offer is empty platitudes.

> Platitudes will make her feel better.

Lunch will make you feel better. You'll understand in four years.

It's 1.20 when I get upstairs to theatre. There's only three minutes to see the first patient and no time for lunch. With a strict knife-to-skin time of 1.30 p.m. the anaesthetists are circling, annoyed that I'm in the way.

'Why didn't you come and see the patient earlier, Emma?' Paul asks, shaking his head. 'Are you struggling with the pressure of being a trainee? You *must* manage your time better. I was going to let you have a go at this case, but if you haven't even seen the patient properly, there's no point.'

What a morning. I'm late, I'm hungry, and I'm in trouble because I tried my hardest to see a million patients including a woman my age who's got cancer and might die. I'm about to sulk, defeated when Lorraine sticks her head into theatre.

'David left you a sandwich at reception,' she whispers and we both marvel at this uncommon kindness.

Chapter Nine

Will, who's been covering the ward this evening, has drawn me out of the residents' room with the promise of a new, different, ice cream. He knows the secret fridge where the little tubs reserved for patients are kept and after six weeks of vanilla, this has excited us both. The strawberry is made from some chemical syrup rather than anything organic, but I'm happy with any edible food, even discarded, melting, medicine-flavoured food.

I'm waiting for access to theatre to do a couple of emergency cases with Jon. Sometimes if I know theatre won't be available for a while, I'll go home for dinner. More often I'm waiting on a promise of an imminent start time, only to be bumped by more urgent cases, again, and again.

I've already chatted with Shamsi on the phone and Vikram in real life, and even David called to ask about how I was going with his research project. Now I'm at the front desk of Ward 6

East with Eliza, one of my favourite nurses, who's telling me stories about the things surgeons and other trainees have said and done in years past.

Despite our shocked laughter at some of their antics, Eliza's on edge this evening. She's recently been promoted to being in charge of nursing shifts, but this alone isn't the cause of her darting eyes and distraction. An errant rotavirus-bearing cheese-cake from the night before wiped out her roster, replacing it with inexperienced locum nurses who don't know their way around the hospital or the ward.

'Which is why you should *never* eat the night-shift food.' She pretend vomits at my lurid pink confection.

Will appears with another individual carton of semi-melted ice cream, dials up another burst of insulin on his pump and settles down to order blood tests for the next morning.

I scrape the last of the ice cream into my mouth and toss the cardboard box into the bin beside him.

'We don't need all those tests, do we?' I ask, bending over his shoulder to study his computer screen.

'Yes, we do,' he says, and orders a routine set for another patient.

'Oh my god, she's going home tomorrow anyway.'

'So?'

'Do you check the results?'

'Yes. Of course,' he retorts, offended.

Hmm. 'How often are they abnormal?'

'Not often,' he replies. 'And when they are, we tell Daphne.' He waves his ID tag in front of the computer to log off, shoves the latest patient list in his back pocket and wanders off with his ice cream.

Does Daphne want these blood tests? I group message her, and Vikram, who knows everything, and Andy too.

> Hey, do we need to order blood tests for every single patient, every single day?

Daphne responds:

> Yes.

Then Andy:

> Yes. Just do it.

But then Vikram pipes up:

> Hang on, why? Every test costs the health system $68.70.

Andy responds:

> So we don't get in trouble when someone dies.
> Enough to get in trouble for around here.

This reminds me of his latest drama.

> Speaking of getting in trouble did you end up telling Prof Wilson that his bowel anastomosis fell apart, Andy?

> Yep.

> Did he tell you that you should have told
> him you were worried about the gut during
> the case?

I did tell him I was worried during the case. He told
me he knew what he was doing.

> Did the blood tests help you find the
> bowel leak?

Oh piss off Emma. Order the damn blood tests. Like I
said, enough to get in trouble for around here.

I shove my phone into my pocket with irritation. I'm certain that ordering tests to cover our backsides, or because it's something we've always done unthinkingly, isn't good medicine. What a waste of money and effort.

My feet on the peeling desk, I flip through a dog-eared trashy magazine to read about Katie Holmes and Tom Cruise getting married in—I check the cover—2006. It'll be yet another hour until we can start in theatre.

Eliza waves at me from the end of the corridor. 'Hey, Em, can you help? They didn't design the drug room for nurses who barely reach five feet,' she calls.

I toss the magazine back onto the desk, like years of hospital staff before me, shove my feet into my shoes and wander towards her.

I haven't worn heels since my first day at The Mount. Shamsi and I went out for dinner last night and I was still feeling sexy and cheerful this morning when I slipped them back on. Ah well. Surely I won't get bunions if I only wear heels every couple of months. And even if I do, I'm still feeling fondly about bunion surgery.

What Eliza wants is on the top shelf and I can't reach it either. I climb onto the bench and stand warily, well above hip fracture height, when a pale face appears at the door. A locum nurse raps so stridently on the glass that Eliza stops spotting me and opens the door.

'Um . . . Eliza . . . um . . . the patient in bed 14 . . . I don't think she's breathing.'

'You don't *think*?' Eliza bolts from the room.

I carefully lower myself from the bench—a broken ankle won't help me resuscitate whoever's in bed 14. Ah, Beverley, a lovely retiree with a smashed leg. Her bones were in a million pieces, too fragmented to secure with a plate and screws, so we used a large metal frame called an external fixateur to stabilise the entire limb. With rods screwed into the bone and an interlocking framework to hold it together, it's Meccano for surgeons.

Teetering towards her room I swear I'll never wear heels again. Overhead the loudspeaker announces a code blue in Ward 6 East. They no longer announce the room number so that family members who have gone to the café aren't alerted to their loved one dying.

Someone dashes past me with the crash cart. In the room, Will's performing chest compressions. He mustn't have left the ward before Beverley was found. On the other side of the bed a nurse tries to put an ECG on poor Beverley's dusky-coloured chest.

As the surgical registrar I'm the least useful person here. Steve wouldn't have come, or if he had, he'd likely have pronounced there was no fracture on the ECG before leaving. Unlike him I feel compelled to participate. Beverley *is* my patient.

Her geriatric ribs crack under Will's hands as Jyothi, the anaesthetist on tonight, assumes the commanding position at the head of the bed. The rest of the emergency team, doctors and nurses from ICU, edge everyone else out of the way. Drips and lines are skilfully inserted, needles discarded without injuring anyone else, even though we're packed around, and plastic tubing taped down, even as poor Beverley's body shakes from the CPR. Jyothi asks Will to pause so she can check the ECG trace. A flat line stares grimly back at us. This is the moment they would shock the patient in a movie, but that gesture is just for cinematic effect and has no power to restart a heart that has stopped.

Jyothi calls for more chest compressions and more adrenaline and I see Will cast his eyes about. CPR is hard work and he's soaked in sweat. Everyone else in the room is occupied so I tap him out of the way and kneel on the bed next to poor Beverley's frame. Her skin is dappled bluish-grey. We have no idea how long she's been like this, but she was vigorously healthy and walking her dog only two days earlier. So we try to bring her back to life.

I was taught that chest compressions should be done to the beat of the Bee Gees' 'Stayin' Alive'. Laura was taught to match the beat of 'Achy Breaky Heart'. We had lighthearted arguments for years as to whether the Bee Gees or Billy Ray Cyrus were superior—as medical students running towards resuscitations, as interns at the country hospitals we worked in together. And then, one day, Laura found a study that said medicos bopping along to music rarely did chest compressions fast or hard enough.

So today I simply go as fast as I can while Jyothi inserts a breathing tube and injects more and more drugs. Everyone's eyes are glued to the ECG screen, which only shows bumps in time with my compressions, and not because there's any spontaneous electrical activity from her still and silent heart.

My heels fall off, one at a time, and then my phone also falls out of my pocket and hits the floor. There's no time to check if it's broken. Jyothi squeezes a plastic bubble, slowly in, slowly out. We watch the monitor.

'It's been thirty minutes, Emma, and we have nothing. Do we call this?' she asks. Even though she's asking me a question, I know it's not really a question, and it's not my call to make. Jyothi's the head of this resuscitation and the final decision is hers, but the sharing eases the burden.

At once I understand with new clarity why we order so many blood tests. It's one other decision we don't have to make in a day full of weighty decisions. Let Medicare pay $68.70, the cost of a day of parking at this hospital, so that we can save our limited mental capacity for these bigger questions: *Are we going to stop resuscitating this retired accountant, this wife, this mother, this sister, this friend, this human, even though she didn't get to say goodbye?*

I nod. *Yes, Jyothi.* It's been thirty minutes of resuscitating someone who was likely dead when we arrived. *Yes, Jyothi.* Let's hope she was already gone when we broke her ribs and stuck lines in her and filled her body with drugs she could no longer use. *Yes, Jyothi. Yes. Let's let her go.*

Jyothi nods back and removes the mask from Beverley's face, I stop bouncing on her chest, Eliza puts down the syringes of drugs, and a calmness settles over the room.

'Time of death, 22.51. Thanks team.'

Jyothi closes Beverley's eyes

———

Shamsi meets me at the door when I get home the next evening. 'Babe, you must be exhausted,' he says with worry and pity in his voice. 'Do you want to talk about it?'

Shamsi hadn't woken when I got home so late last night and barely stirred when I left this morning. I'd texted him that I'd only had a couple of hours sleep, but no details why. How would I begin to explain?

The quiet at the end of an operation has nothing on the sudden silence after an unsuccessful resuscitation. The trolley's packed away, the lines we inserted paradoxically secured further so the coroner has evidence of our efforts. There's fallen debris to clear—syringe wrappers, drug vials, scraps of ECG paper, bits of blood and body. If it's a shared room, there's someone else to talk to and comfort, some innocent patient who's sat behind a thin curtain as witness to the sound and fury of a failed code blue.

I sent Will home first. He'd overstayed his shift by an hour, an hour he won't even be paid for, because Brenda from administration told us that overtime is for his own benefit and not the patient's. As a resident he's supposed to hand over to the night resident and go home regardless of what might be happening. I was grateful he stayed late. Besides, I still had that case to do in theatre, though in the end it was bumped for an urgent Caesarean section, proof that even as Death walks those halls, life finds a way, several floors down.

'Ah, someone died,' I say dismissively.

Shamsi takes my bag and steers me to the kitchen. I see he's cleaned up and there's something that smells delicious steaming on the stove.

'Sit down, tell me what happened,' he encourages.

I sit and reflect, and then the absurdity of the whole situation hits me. 'You won't believe it. This old lady is walking her dog at some charity dog-walk thing when someone runs into her with their electric wheelchair. Totally smashes her leg to pieces.'

'Woah.'

'Anyway, it's in smithereens so we bolt this frame to her leg. It sticks out about this high'—I hold my hand about fifteen centimetres apart—'all the way around her leg. Weighs a couple of kilos. And then, she dies.'

'She . . . dies?' Shamsi is incredulous. I suppose it was a rather blunt transition in my story.

'Yeah. Who knows why? Most likely a blood clot flicked off from her legs to her lungs. We worked on her for ages. No dice.'

Shamsi is ladling soup into a bowl. He brings it over and places it in front of me. 'There's garlic bread in the oven,' he says. 'Keep going.'

'Anyway, I'm about to call her family when my case in theatre gets bumped. The night resident takes pity on me and tells me to go home, says they'll call her family. That's fair, I've been there for sixteen hours at this point.'

He nods in sympathy.

'I make it to the car park when Eliza calls me, you know that nice nurse in charge who I like? She sounds like she's drowning.'

Shamsi puts the garlic bread on the table and sits down with his own soup and a doubtful expression.

'She's not, she's in the basement of the hospital, terrible reception, gurgly. She tells me to come back because this woman won't fit in the drawers in the morgue.'

'She won't . . . fit?'

'Yeah. She's quite petite but this frame on her leg is too big. Eliza can't close the morgue drawer, and if we can't close the drawer she'll decompose on a metal table overnight.'

Shamsi looks uncomfortable so I reach for humour.

'Don't worry, it's hilarious,' I assure him. 'I go back to try to get an Allen key from theatre. They can't find one, so they send me to Maintenance. I'm still in high heels, you know those tall red ones I wore to dinner?' I point to the front hall where I dumped the red heels at 2 a.m.

'I'm teetering around the basement of the hospital to meet this bearded guy, who smells of stale cigarette smoke, in this dingy room where machinery is hissing and clanking like some steampunk movie. He gives me a set of Allen keys.'

'Was that . . . safe, Em?' Shamsi seems worried.

'Totally! So back at the morgue this old lady's lying in this open drawer with steam rising out of it because she's still warm, and the air is cold, and the drawer can't be closed. She absolutely won't fit. And then her eyes spring open and she's staring at me.

'It's now gone midnight and I'm jumping at shadows, imagining that the other drawers will start to open and I'll be victim zero of the zombie apocalypse. It takes me ages to unbolt the frame and then I have to steal the pillowcase from under her head to carry the bits back up to theatre because we reuse everything that wasn't bolted into her.'

Shamsi has put his spoon down and is looking at me. I would have thought he'd be used to my gory stories by now, but he seems to be struggling with this one.

I break off a piece of garlic bread and hand half to him.

'So at last this little woman fits in her morgue drawer and I can come home for a bit of sleep. But that's not the end . . . Back at the hospital this morning there's this middle-aged woman in a suit standing in the corridor who flew in from Adelaide last night to visit her mum and is looking for her. Oh my god, you won't believe it, the night doctor forgot to call the family!' By now I'm giggling.

Shamsi dips his bread in the soup but doesn't put it in his mouth. He studies me thoughtfully. After a few moments, as I'm shovelling soup in as fast as I can, he asks, 'You know, you told that story like it was super funny, and I guess it was absurd, but wasn't it more awful than funny?'

Both of us pause, spoons in hand, a fissure between us.

Shamsi must think I'm callous. And I don't know how to explain that if I'd told it to any of my colleagues, they'd have shrieked with laughter along with me. They would've understood that this is what was required, because otherwise, we'd have to think about Beverley's soft chest and dead eyes and full life.

Chapter Ten

'So, Emma, can you explain to me what happened the other week?'

Paul's gathering up his things at the end of the operating list. I thought the afternoon had gone well. I'd read up on all the cases, in even more detail than I do for operating lists with David, and left the last few patients in clinic for Will to see on his own. This I felt especially bad about. He was looking peaky and desperate for lunch, making me wonder again if it's possible for an insulin-dependent diabetic like him to survive a career in healthcare.

I'd guessed correctly that Paul would interrogate me on a newer and more difficult approach to hip replacement surgery so I'd been able to describe the anatomy and surgical steps perfectly. As a reward he'd let me start the operation.

'Um . . . I'm sorry, Paul, I don't know what you mean,' I say.

'Jon was pretty upset. He called me to say that you had broken protocol.'

Ah. Shit. Beverley again.

I turn away and hold the patient's legs, helping the team slide him off the operating table and onto the bed. He's still asleep, the tube in his throat. At least the patient won't witness this telling off, even though the rest of the theatre will.

'Yes. I'm sorry, Paul. I know I shouldn't have taken the ex-fix off but it was the middle of the night and she wouldn't fit in the morgue drawer and—'

Paul shakes his head at me. 'You understand coronial requirements?'

Yes. Yes, I do.

That's why we taped down the lines at the end of the resuscitation. It was a death less than twenty-eight days after surgery and it's for the coroner to decide why Beverley died and if any of us are culpable. The body is the evidence and I tampered with it by removing the ex-fix. I nod at Paul mutely. Is this the thing that will mean I fail the term?

'Okay. Look. Jon spoke to the hospital lawyers and the coroner's office and explained what happened. They'll make a note of it in the report but because the fixation itself isn't directly related to her cause of death it won't be an issue. This time.'

'I'm sorry, Paul.'

His jovial manner from earlier in the list is suddenly gone and I'm confused. How was he cracking jokes only ten minutes ago knowing he was going to have this conversation with me?

'Emma, if you're ever confused about what to do, call the supervising consultant, okay? You can't just make stuff up.' And with that, Paul's gone.

From the other side of the theatre, Jyothi gives me a sympathetic look as she waits for the patient to wake up enough to remove his breathing tube, though I'm not sure why. Is it because I got told off in public? Or maybe she can read my mind—that I *had* considered ringing Jon but was worried that at midnight he'd shout at me for waking him over something so stupid. Whatever I'd done I'd be in trouble.

The patient coughs and Jyothi pulls out the tube. She's already sent her registrar off so I grab my bag and help her wheel the bed out of theatre. The surgical side has barely spoken to her the whole operating list and I apologise and thank her for being part of the team today.

She laughs lightly. 'Emma you *are* sweet. But you know that surgeons are the heroes and anaesthetists are used to being invisible.'

'Why? We couldn't do what we do without you. You keep patients comfortable—and alive!' I counter.

We're almost at recovery.

'Let me tell you a story, Emma,' Jyothi says as we round the corner. 'A couple of years ago one of the anaesthetists here died suddenly.' She sees the expression on my face and waves her hand. 'No, it's fine and that's not entirely the point of my story. Sometimes people die. The thing is, the next week one of the senior surgeons came to theatre and spoke loudly about how he'd never met her.'

I help Jyothi push the bed into a recovery bay. The patient is starting to open his eyes. She lifts the back of the bed so he's sitting up.

'You know what though, Emma? I was the last-minute fill-in that day. It had been my colleague's list, the one who passed. She'd worked with that surgeon for four hours every week for two years, and he didn't know her name or that he'd worked with her or that I was someone different in her place. So thank you for acknowledging me today.'

I have so many questions, but Jyothi's already giving the recovery nurse her handover.

'Emma!' Andy's voice calls out across the room. His patient has arrived in recovery as well. He slouches over to me, hair falling out from under his surgical cap. 'Are you done for today?' he asks.

'Yeah, you?'

'Nah. I've got a ruptured appendix to remove yet. It's first after-hours so I shouldn't have to wait too long.'

The nurse standing next to his patient beckons and we walk over together. I watch as he checks the drain tubes coming out of the abdomen and then lifts the blankets to check the tummy itself. I've never seen Andy in action at work and it comes as a surprise to see my big brother in this role, confident and competent. And yet, there's a tiredness there too. A hunch to his shoulders. A shadow under his eyes. A sag to his gait.

He reassures the nurse that everything is as expected.

'Andy, you better eat before you have to start operating again,' I tell him. Steve's on call tonight and I'm free to go home, but I've been meaning to talk to Andy properly for a while. 'The café?' I suggest.

He glances at the clock. 'Probably can't. I don't have time to get changed out of my scrubs. The in-charge nurse said she'd be able to start the evening on time.'

'We don't have to get changed, do we? All you're getting in the tea room is dry crackers.'

'We should. It's hospital rules. It's okay, Em. Dry crackers with you will be better than anything else.'

I can see Andy slump further. Oh, for goodness' sake. I grab a couple of white patient gowns from the shelf next to us and drape one over his shoulders.

'Shush, it'll be fine. Let me buy you an actual meal.' He lets me guide him to the door.

Once we're outside, clipping down the stairs in our theatre clogs, I broach the topic I really want to know about. 'How *is* the study going?'

Andy almost stops and then keeps walking. 'Em, it's non-stop. I haven't seen Ava and Aurora in weeks, and Laura's struggling.'

I don't tell him that I know this, because she's told me herself.

'You know she's going back to work in the middle of the year. I think she's enjoying being at home with the babies, but she's doing everything on her own.'

I don't tell him that I know this either.

'Nights. Weekends. I'm not there to do important things like read them books and put them to bed, or even to do dumb things like help plan their birthday party.'

I've spent hours talking to Laura. I know that Laura's back to work weeks after Andy's exam. I know that she's asked her parents who live overseas to come and stay with them for a few months, because she doesn't think she can support Andy and take care of the babies and study for her own exam later this year on her own. I know she's worried about what will happen if Andy doesn't pass—how they'll have to do this again, with her back at work too.

But I haven't had a chance to talk to Andy.

'How are you going, Andy? How are you going to manage?' I ask.

He's quiet for a moment. 'I'm fine. I'll . . . soldier on,' he finally sighs.

We're at the bottom of the stairs. The hospital lobby is full of people arriving for visiting hours and we weave our way through the crowd to the café by the front entrance. The old hospital café where Dad bought us blueberry muffins as a bribe for going along on his weekend ward rounds is long closed. The hospital saves money by outsourcing the food to a commercial operator, but the quality of the food is abysmal. No matter, as the only food vendor there's always a lengthy line.

Next to me, Andy stiffens. 'See, Em? I'm sorry, I don't have time. I should get back upstairs,' he says, checking his pager to make sure no one's tried to find him.

Suddenly, I'm filled with fury. I'm angry at Jon and Paul for having a go at me when I was trying to do the right thing. I'm angry that Andy has to be here instead of at home with his family. I'm angry that even buying a meal is so hard that I more often drop three dollars in the vending machine and buy a packet of chips or a bar of chocolate instead of waiting for oily pasta or dry sushi. Scrubs hide any number of sins, but my skirts are starting to slip from my waist. I'm angry because we're all trying so hard and working so much and yet there's no one trying to make things even a little bit easier.

'Wait,' I tell him.

Uncharacteristically resolute, I push to the front of the queue and request two pre-made sandwiches from the surprised server.

The queue mutters in protest and an elderly person taps me on the shoulder. 'We've been waiting here a while, missy,' he says.

Andy's staring off somewhere else as if he doesn't know me, the tips of his ears red with embarrassment.

I stand tall and apologise. 'Really sorry, sir, but we're surgeons and have to go back to operating in ten minutes. Either I push in or we don't eat. And you wouldn't want your loved one to be operated on by a hungry and exhausted surgeon, would you?' I tap my credit card on the reader and thank the server.

The tension in the line subsides, momentarily reassuring me that even though our bosses and administrators don't care if we eat or not, at least our prospective patients do. I scurry off with two ham and cheese sandwiches, beaming.

Andy punches me in the arm. 'Emma, you did *not* just do that.'

I thrust a sandwich at him. 'Eat. You have to take care of yourself,' I tell him as we hurry back towards theatre.

The words come out of my mouth before I've thought too hard and they're enough to make Andy pause, mid-step and mid-chew. This is what Mum would say to Dad every time she ran to grab him food before he rushed from the house or returned long after dinnertime.

Andy swallows his mouthful of sandwich. 'Food and sleep are for the weak,' he replies, exactly like Dad used to.

Chapter Eleven

By the time the last patient of the day is wheeled out, Jon's gone. He's off to the US next week and he's mentally checked out. At least this means he's finally stopped grumping to me about Beverley, Paul's telling off clearly not enough.

The anaesthetist gives me a wave as he whistles out the door. I stretch and check my pager—thank goodness, no calls. The empty theatre, usually so full of noise, is at rest. It's a rare moment to close my eyes.

There are still patients on the ward to see before I can head home, though I'll probably still be earlier than any other evening this week. Shamsi will be surprised. There's an unexpected flutter inside. It's been a while since . . .

'You leaving or not?' a theatre technician calls from the door. I set aside that stirring and pick myself up from the stool.

Sarah's the nurse running the floor tonight and she's one of my favourites. Officious but friendly, her fire-engine red hair is always curling out from under her theatre cap. This is captured perfectly in the plasticine cartoon version of herself that she wears as a name badge.

She's sitting at the central in-charge desk as I trudge past. Behind her, the large whiteboard is covered in an explosion of blue paper slips and magnets, ready for tomorrow. Most hospitals have an electronic booking system for surgical cases. Here at The Mount, we're still filling out scraps of papers with patient and operation details, and these are shuffled around the planning board with different coloured magnets to denote the urgency. Tradition, I'm told.

'Emma!' she calls me over. 'Nic was looking for you.'

Nic? The plastic and reconstructive surgery registrar?

I know Nic only passingly from our combined sarcoma meetings. When we cut out these tumours we leave a big hole. It's the plastic surgeons who come and fill that space with bone and muscle and skin, all with their own blood supply microsurgically attached. Once a fortnight the surgeons and oncologists meet to determine every patient's treatment plan.

Jacqui is currently having radiation to the newly diagnosed sarcoma in her leg. After, we'll cut out what remains of her shrunken tumour and Nic's team will replace the muscle and skin we've had to take along with it. Nic's also a final-year trainee like Andy, and though they're in different specialties, I know they're friends and spend evenings studying in the library together.

None of this explains why she's looking for me right now.

Sarah points to the only slip on the 'after hours' part of the board, held on by a red magnet. 'For this case. It's a patient with necrotising fasciitis. They're about to start in theatre 10. Sounds bad. Everyone else has postponed their cases until tomorrow.'

Damn it. I was so close to getting home. It's not often that I'm on call and there's no outstanding cases after hours. Apart from having dinner with Shamsi, I'd been planning to write my abstract for the conference, which is due at the end of this week.

Besides, it's the reconstructive surgeons who mostly deal with this rapidly progressing infection, the treatment for which is to chop off large swathes of infected skin and the tissues underneath. There's no bone involved—what could they possibly need me for?

I scuff my way to theatre 10. Through the window, I see the patient being transferred to the operating table. His right leg is swollen and dragging. A grumpy looking man who must be the plastic surgeon scrolls through CT images on the computer, his face pinched in worried wrinkles. Most operations have one, maybe two anaesthetic doctors present, but today there are at least five.

Shit. It must be bad.

As a mask is placed over the patient's face, Nic solemnly holds his hand.

I can feel the tension through the door. Putting a very sick patient to sleep is no small thing. Machines alarm as his heart rate slows and his blood pressure dips. A tall, bearded anaesthetist is aggressively directing traffic with finger-pointing urgency. Over there, more fluid goes up. And over there, another anaesthetist is putting a line into an artery. At the head end, someone is peering down his airway with a fibreoptic camera—there's only one chance to get the breathing tube in.

Nic's somehow left the theatre and creeps up beside me, making me jump. 'Oh good, Emma, we might need you,' she says.

'Why?'

'This guy's really sick. He's only forty, otherwise well, septic to his eyeballs and has gas almost to his hip. He's been sitting on this for twenty-four hours. It was only that his sister dropped in today—she took one look and called the ambulance.'

'What do you need me for?'

'He has gas almost to his hip,' she repeats.

I still don't know what she means.

Nic sighs, irritated. 'We might have to amputate his leg.'

Should I have guessed this?

'Oh.'

'My boss wanted you around as a precaution,' she says and glances around. The anaesthetists are still harried. 'Look . . . there's a good chance he's going to die. The necrotising fasciitis patients, they never understand how serious it is . . . that they might not wake up. It's why I always hold their hand as they go to sleep.'

I shuffle my feet, unsure how to offer her sympathy for a patient I didn't even meet. 'So, I should call my boss back?'

The plastic surgeon appears at the scrub sink. 'Orthopaedics? Yes, call them in. We're going to need all hands on deck,' he says over her head.

I get my phone out and reluctantly dial the number.

'What do you want?' Jon is sharp. Down the line, there's music and chatter. Glasses clink and people laugh as I explain that a man might be dying, that he needs to come back to help save him.

'What, don't they know how to amputate a leg? Any surgeon can do that.'

No one told me that so much of my job would be managing sulky surgeons who don't want to do *their* job.

'Sorry, Jon, it's the plastic surgeon's request.' I'm not going to put myself on the hook.

In the background, I hear, 'Want another beer, Jon?'

There's a long pause. 'I'll be there in twenty minutes,' Jon says. And as the line goes dead, he's telling his friend, 'Nah, mate, I'm on call and—'

I hang up and lean against the scrub sink with my eyes closed, suddenly worried. I've set aside five years to work like this; have convinced myself, and Shamsi, that it won't be like this forever, that it doesn't have to be. But what if it is? What if it's not in my hands?

———

The theatre is in chaos when Jon arrives. The reconstructive surgeon, a grumbling hunched man called Michael, is feverishly hacking bands of skin from the patient's leg. Nic, sweating, hefts up the limb so he can get underneath. A burning smell fills the room as the cautery machine buzzes on high, sending plumes of smoke into the air, and yet there's enough blood on the floor that an anaesthetic nurse is squeezing a bag of blood into the patient's veins. Big patches of muscle on the increasingly flayed limb look dark and dead. Michael pokes at it in turn, cursing when it doesn't twitch.

'How are you going over there?' the anaesthetist asks from the other side of the drapes.

'How do you think?' Michael grunts back, dropping another sheet of skin into a small green kidney dish that's far too small for it. Slippery, it falls to the ground with a wet thud. He kicks it to the scout nurse who's putting on a pair of gloves to retrieve it.

'Well, we aren't winning up here,' the anaesthetist replies. 'He's already on fifty of noradrenaline and fifty of vasopressin.'

Beside me, Jon sucks in his breath. This is a huge dose of drugs used to bolster the blood pressure of someone who's trying their hardest to die.

Michael sees us standing there. 'Orthopaedics?' he asks and we both nod.

'This guy is critical. We need to talk about a hindquarter amputation. I've gone as high as his groin and his tissues are dishwater. You can see his muscle is dead.' Michael pokes again at the dark muscle with his cautery hand-piece. When it doesn't react to his poking, he presses the button, yet even an electric current doesn't make it contract and twitch like it should.

The anaesthetists have stopped talking and are watching over the drapes. Jon is silent. Slowly the colour drains from his face and I feel a pang of sympathy. Jon, who pretends he knows so much, has probably never seen a hindquarter amputation, much less performed one. I wouldn't be able to describe it in detail but know it involves removing the whole leg and part of the pelvis. Some organs, like bowel and brain, I never wish to see again. I'm sure Jon feels the same. And yet, here we are, called up to fossick around in the patient's guts, to conduct an operation neither of us has seen, and quickly.

The anaesthetic machine alarms melodically, the patient's blood pressure dipping again. Quietly, Michael tells Jon, 'Call Albert.'

Jon startles next to me. 'Oh, no, that won't be necessary. Emma, go get scrubbed and we can begin.'

Michael considers us and picks up his scalpel. He cuts a strip of skin from the top of the patient's thigh. We can see the layer of tissue underneath, the fascia, bubbling with the gas produced by the bacteria spreading along it.

'See this? It's infected up to here. Disarticulating the hip won't be enough. With respect to you, we need someone who knows how to do a hindquarter. Call Albert, now.'

The anaesthetist has already picked up his phone.

————

Usually I hate working with Albert. His emaciated frame, his limp brown suit and bow tie, his glasses so thick they distort his watery eyes are incongruous enough for a surgeon. But then, when he speaks, his voice escapes in a tone similar to a fart that refuses to be held in—high-pitched and wheezy. Albert is technically brilliant, perhaps even more so than David, but his ponderous manner and way of speaking irritate most registrars deeply. Even five minutes in his company is too much.

This isn't the moment to be irritated by Albert. This is a time-critical emergency, and Jon is pale and worried as he looks up the steps needed to perform a hindquarter amputation on his laptop. It's a relief when Albert lopes in, glasses sliding down his nose, a squeaky, 'Aaah, hello,' squeezed from his lips.

Five surgeons are too many surgeons, yet we work together to lift the patient onto his side and organise ourselves in order of importance—Michael and Albert around the pelvis, and Jon as the first assistant. Nic and I are relegated to the head end where we try to see what we can. I still don't know the patient's name.

'More blood,' the anaesthetist calls and a nurse disappears to get it.

'Okay, we've got him as stable as possible. Go for it,' the bearded anaesthetist instructs, and Albert picks up a number 10 blade.

'Such an orthopaedic knife,' Nic whispers. She'd rarely use anything other than a number 15, smaller and svelte.

'You called us,' I whisper back, and Jon glares at me to be silent, still smarting from his demotion, necessary though it was.

Albert and Michael work in tandem. Michael draws out an incision in purple marker and Albert cuts along Michael's lines, first with the 10 blade and then with the cautery. More smoke fills the air, the buzzing burning noise wet and gurgly as the current slices through oedematous flesh. Michael helps to retract, murmuring with relief as we reach clean uninfected tissue for the first time. Along the edge of the pelvis—what laypeople call the 'hip', even though the real hip is hidden deeper, protected by the wing of the pelvis above it—Albert releases the muscles of the abdomen above and the muscles of the leg below. And then, with a broad sweep of the hand, he moves the bowels and their coverings away from the bowl of the pelvis to reveal healthy flesh. Jon gives the anaesthetist a thumbs-up. If there was dish-water and pus in the pelvis it would have been the end, and we we'd be calling his sister with grim news.

One at a time, Albert finds major structures—a large artery, a larger vein, important nerves that make the dying muscles twitch one last time as they're transected with the 10 blade. He pushes away loops of bowel and an empty bladder, drained by the catheter Nic put in at the start of the operation. The inside of the whole pelvis is visible. Taking Michael's surgical pen, Albert draws the cuts then asks for the saw. He crouches down, and the air fills with a shriek that drowns out the still-dinging alarms from the anaesthetic side of the drapes.

Nic and I step back as bone dust flies, and I almost step on the calf of a kneeling anaesthetist who's sticking another line into the patient's neck. 'Sorry!' I whisper and move. Hidden next to her hands, under the leads for the ECG, there's an ID sticker that's been stuck to the man's chest. When all the limbs are being used for lines or for surgical removal, sometimes this is the only place left for identification. I squint and read: *Robert McInerney*. It's been two hours since we started. I don't know anything about Robert, but at least now I know his name.

As Robert's diseased leg and half his pelvis are separated from his body, Albert calls over two theatre technicians to carry it away.

'Good work, Albert,' Michael says with relief.

Albert isn't listening. He's still forearm-deep in the patient, searching for things that bleed, things that leak, things that might cause problems in the night. Nic catches my eye. We have nothing to add. We've contributed nothing to the operation so far and being silent seems the best way to keep going.

There are only three anaesthetists left in the room. They're still busy but there's a sense of calm as Robert's vital signs improve. There are still electrolytes to correct and fluid balances to adjust and blood to give. Oh, so much blood to replace what's dripped on the floor or been sucked away so Albert could see what he was doing. A hindquarter amputation is bad enough, a septic patient is bad enough; together it's such a physiological insult that it's a miracle Robert's still alive.

The halls are dark by the time we've closed the skin, inserted drains, and transferred him to an ICU bed, some thirty kilograms lighter than when he arrived in Emergency earlier today. The nurse in charge mutters that tomorrow a heart operation won't go ahead because tonight, Robert's been given that ICU bed, but this is the way of things in a hospital.

A portable monitoring screen is attached to the bed, and one by one the leads are transferred to it. Syringe pumps are attached to a pole, one for painkillers and two for blood pressure support, and a bag of fluid hung from the top. An oxygen bottle is hooked up and Robert's airway is disconnected from the anaesthetic machine and to a Laerdal bag, the plastic bubble held by the bearded anaesthetist. The sides of the bed are raised with a click, and he's ready to move. Robert will be kept asleep until he's no longer septic, or until he dies.

'Aaah, Emma. Mmm, will you take him to ICU to hand over?' Albert asks.

Nic and I both nod. Our bosses may have done the operation and the ICU team will take over to keep him alive, but we'll keep an eye on the stump and act as the go-between now. The bearded anaesthetist squeezes the bag—in, out—and we step forward together. In, out, another step. Two technicians to push, two nurses either side, an anaesthetist on the airway and another watching the portable screen. Nic falls in step beside me as we inch down the corridor, the tail end of this solemn procession, past empty theatres and under dark flickering lights.

As the corridor splits, one way to ICU and the other to the change rooms, I hear Jon quietly thank Albert for coming in, even though he wasn't on call.

'Mmm. You are, aaah, never too old or senior to bring in, mmm, reinforcements,' Albert replies. I can see that Albert has chosen his words carefully so that Jon doesn't feel like he's being put down that he had to call for help. 'Your, mmm, learning doesn't end when you, aaah, finish your training,' he adds, but as they stand in the shadows, I'm not sure if Jon looks annoyed or relieved, or perhaps just very tired.

Chapter Twelve

It's after eight on a Friday night. Three months into the year and some of the comfortable predictability is becoming a grind. We took Robert back to theatre several times—washed out his pelvis and removed a bit more skin, but despite our efforts, his life support was turned off a few days ago.

I've done twenty-four hours on call three times this week, operating alone because Jon's left and the other surgeons don't come in. The fourth evening I stayed back late with Andy to help him revise, even though I should've been working on my own presentation. I didn't even have the joy of an operating list with David this week.

Now I want to go home, but I promised to meet Shamsi for dinner. He's already had to move our booking later. So, when Laura calls, I can't quite bring myself to answer. I can't keep being so many things to too many people. Besides, I'll be seeing her this weekend for the twins' first birthday party.

I let the call go through to voicemail as I trudge to my car. Then, guilt gets the better of me.

She answers even before the end of the first ring. 'I need your help, Em,' she says, panicked. 'The twins' birthday cake.'

'What about it?'

'Their party's on Sunday.'

The sun's set and the air has a real chill in it. Dry brown leaves crackle under my feet. After an unseasonably warm autumn, the weather is turning as we head towards winter. I wave at the old homeless woman who still sits outside the Emergency Department. Since Will told me that he's tried unsuccessfully for three years to get her to wave back I'm determined to best him. I haven't had more than a dark look yet.

'I need to make a cake. Don't tell me to buy a cake because they'll look at the photos in years to come and think I didn't love them.'

I laugh. 'Laura, you're studying for your exam later this year. Andy's exam is in mere months. You have baby *twins*! Go buy a cake. The girls will always know you love them.'

'Em,' Laura's voice is cold, threatening, 'you're saying the same things as Andy.'

'God, if we're both saying the same thing, it must be true, because we never agree.' I giggle.

Laura hangs up on me.

The streets are lively. Shamsi's always worked in the city and going out to dinner or drinks after work is one of his favourite things. He's the person who's always abreast of restaurant openings and special events. When I was an intern at the Shit Hospital I'd drive in after work and join him. But even though The Mount is on the edge of the city, so close I could walk, I've only managed dinner out with him once since I've been there. The last time was the night before Beverley died. This time I haven't worn high heels.

I've found a place to park when the phone rings again.

'No, stop telling me I can't or shouldn't make a cake. Tomorrow Andy's going to spend twelve hours at his desk and I'll have my hands full with the girls. Then *I* have to study and make a cake and clean the house and organise food for forty people and ten babies because *he'll* fall asleep at his desk drooling on his notes.'

At medical school Laura used to cope by making lists and methodically ticking items off as she completed them. This isn't Laura with a plan, this is Laura trying to make do on the fly. This way lies breakdown.

'Well, the babies won't eat anything,' I suggest, trying to reduce her task list.

'Em!'

The ignition off, I swap the phone to my ear, close my eyes and indulge in my exhaustion, before pushing it and my rising irritation away. I've already put off finishing my research presentation to help Andy, and now Laura wants her pound of flesh too. But then the tone in her voice gets to me. And life *is* about more than surgery, isn't it?

'What can I do?' I ask, swinging my legs out of the car and pretending to be cheerful.

Laura's immediately happier. Sausage rolls, fairy bread and a fruit platter with grapes cut in half. There goes my day in pyjamas. There's no vegetarian food on her meal plan, and suddenly I'm also making mini quiches.

'That's a lot, isn't it?' Laura asks, worried. I've reached Chinatown, where the street's hung with fairy lights and the colourful statues outside seem to grin. The real world still exists, and it's so beautiful.

'It's totally fine.'

Two teenagers walk past with pastel hair and inspirational desserts. 'Also, for the cakes, bake some cupcakes in flat bottom ice cream cones. When you ice them, they'll look like little ice creams. Simple and fun.'

'Yes!' I can almost see Laura beaming at me.

———

We get to Andy and Laura's house early on Sunday, arms full of food and two singing elephants for the girls. In the end, it's been a lovely weekend so far. After dumplings and cocktails on Friday night, we slept in, went out for brunch and then spent the afternoon making mini quiches and sausage rolls together. Our small house filled with the scent of hot pastry and unending cups of bergamot-flavoured tea. I finished the presentation this morning in a sun-drenched kitchen and sent it to David, who immediately texted me messages of praise and satisfaction. Shamsi had to work too. We sat together, smiling at each other over the tops of our laptops. It's not quite Italy, but still a glimmering moment of who we really are. After months of late nights, today I feel like we'll be okay.

Andy opens the door and silently shakes his head at me, his finger on his lips.

'What's wrong?' I whisper.

He glances behind him, circles his finger around his temple, and points at the kitchen. 'Thank god you're both here,' he says, stepping aside.

We clomp down the long dark hallway of their single-fronted terrace, the bedroom doors pulled tightly closed. Laura's probably parented, worked, made a cake and not cleaned. I step into the kitchen to find her and the twins amidst a kaleidoscopic explosion of sunlight, icing sugar and sprinkles. Ava sits in her small chair waving a soggy banana, and Aurora crawls around in her nappy, trails of white powder in her wake.

Laura, in Schnauzer-pattern pyjamas, is squeezing icing onto lopsided ice cream cone cupcakes. Oddly, a pot of discarded beetroot peels sits on the floor next to the kitchen bench. Apart from the dining table and chairs pushed to the sides, there are no signs that there will be a party here in—I glance at the clock—one hour.

'Hi?'

Laura jumps. Andy's not wrong. She does have a frantic look in her eyes.

'Woah, this place is a mess,' Shamsi exclaims. He trips over the pot of beetroot peels as he puts the boxes of food on the bench.

'Shush, that's why we're here early, babe,' I scold.

Laura is back icing cupcakes, even though she'll need a shower, the babies need a bath, and the kitchen *is* a disaster.

'So what happened?' I ask, thinking about my own lovely Saturday afternoon and pristine house.

'I got to the cakes and icing too late last night. They're tinted with beetroot so there's no artificial colours—seriously, don't say anything.'

I wouldn't dare.

'The cakes hadn't cooled enough so the icing melted and ruined them. So I baked more, but it was midnight and the girls got up and he—' She glares at Andy, who rolls his eyes. 'He was snoring so here I am, still icing these stupid cakes.'

Ava throws her banana on the floor and claps excitedly.

Laura puts the last cupcake on the baking tray, tips sprinkles over it, and raises both hands in a flourish of victory. Another slow trickle of sprinkles falls off the bench and onto the floor, to Aurora's delight. I can imagine what my father would say.

'When do the parents arrive?'

'Shit. Half an hour.' Andy starts wiping down the bench. Laura seems to be stunned.

It's time for me to take control. As the birthday family disappears down the hall for showers and clean clothes, Shamsi gets the vacuum with a sigh.

'Shh, this is what family do,' I remind him.

———

'The garden is a mess.' Dad's low voice echoes down the corridor.

Shamsi and I glance around the kitchen. He pushes a chair back into place and I straighten the tea towel on the rail. My parents have clearly arrived. The kitchen, at least, is clean.

My father's been using his time post-retirement in his country garden. Neither Andy nor I have managed to make it down since the summer but Mum's been sending photos—lilly pilly, bottlebrush and soaring stalks of kangaroo paw neatly constrained into concrete-edged garden beds, framing a horizon of vineyards and the shimmering sea. Andy's scowl as he follows Dad into the kitchen suggests his frustration that a comparison is being made to his own small inner-city front courtyard, neglected or otherwise.

'How do you have time for this? You should be studying,' my father continues, the disconnect between these two opening sentences lost on him.

Dad gives Shamsi a handshake and me a short hug. I hand him a sausage roll and a napkin as a distraction. 'I made these, Dad, and while they baked, I worked on my paper for the upcoming national conference where I'm giving a podium presentation.'

'Good girl,' he says gruffly. He slides the glass doors open to the back garden, where he starts to rearrange the table and chairs.

My mother's stopped to collect her beloved grandchildren. Slight and sprightly, she's set aside her usual paint-stained smocks for a smart jumpsuit. She's recently stopped dyeing her white hair blonde and it's almost completely grown out now, which surprises me. We laugh as she tries to give me a hug but finds her arms already full of two clean babies in matching yellow dresses.

Shamsi takes Ava from her and spins the baby in the air as Laura appears in a simple frock, also yellow, her straight black hair clipped back with barrettes and not a drop of frosting to be seen. Ava gurgles with laughter, and apart from my father who's still rearranging deck chairs, we laugh along with her.

'It's a pity your parents couldn't be here,' my mother says kindly to Laura. She puts Aurora into her highchair and starts laying sausage rolls onto a platter.

Laura shrugs. She's used to them living overseas and they'll be here in the next few weeks anyway. I wonder where they'll stay in this small two-bedroom house.

'Will this be okay for the cakes?' Laura asks instead.

'They're lovely,' my mother coos over the ice creams.

Ava waves her chubby little arms, trying to reach for a cake and Shamsi hands her a cut grape.

I should smile at my husband doting on his nieces. Despite being an only child, or perhaps because of it, Shamsi's always wanted a big family. When the twins were tiny, he'd take them for a walk every day after work, no matter how busy he was or how much they cried. He's still the one who offers babysitting before me.

But watching Shamsi engrossed in Ava's grape-filled cheeks, I find myself suddenly wishing that our love, as it is, could be enough. I wish we could freeze time to our wedding day. Before surgical training, before his campaign for a promotion, before we think about having our own children. We'd always agreed that I might do a year or two of training and then try to start a family. Suddenly I'm not so sure. Andy and Laura are *so* tired.

Mum puts a vase of flowers she's brought on the dining table and platters of food around it. Dad's re-emerged from the back-yard and helps Andy blow up balloons. Somehow, my family have bridged that gap, from easy to hard. Somehow, despite the beetroot peels and exams, despite my father and all he is and was, here we are in a home filled with cake and love.

So maybe my problem is thinking that hard work and love are incompatible. Maybe love *is* enough to make the centre hold. Maybe if we have enough of the 'easy', then coping with the 'hard' will follow.

Laura's filled her platter with cakes. As she lifts it, every-thing wobbles, and then tips. Time slows as one ice-cream cone cupcake is knocked over, and then another and another, until every cake has capsized on the tray. The ones on the end spill to the floor, leaving a trail of beetroot-pink icing down Laura's dress, before smashing onto the wooden floorboards.

Andy and I instinctively look at Dad, but before he can pronounce how we should feel, Laura's disintegrated into tears.

'They're ruined!' she sobs.

My mother rushes to her aid, a warning in her eyes for Dad. He obediently closes his mouth. Mum and I inspect the damage. This can still be saved.

I help Laura up and point her down the hall. 'Go get changed, we'll fix this,' I promise.

'How?' she hiccoughs, still crying.

'Just watch.'

'Right. I'll scrape, you ice,' I tell Mum.

Bless him, Shamsi's handed Ava to Dad and is cleaning up the mess on the floor.

By the time Laura returns, the cakes have been re-iced and placed individually on the table. The house fills with the clinking sound of champagne glasses. A single candle is lit. Ava claps and Aurora bursts into tears as the room sings 'Happy Birthday'. On the other side of the camera lens, I snap photos of my beautiful family.

'This seems much more effort than we ever went to,' Dad mutters on the way out. Mum smiles at Andy and me. Ava's asleep on Andy's shoulder.

'Oh, you two, I'm so proud of you. Don't mind him, I once dropped an entire cake train carriage onto the floor, but he missed that whole party so he wouldn't know.'

We kiss her goodbye, and she strokes Ava's black hair.

'But look at you. You aren't missing anything. And I'm so *so* glad for that.'

We watch them walk down the street, our mother springing lightly, and our father, stooped, after years of operating. Maybe there's more of boring dead Lyndhurst in Dad than I thought. I glance over at Andy with his tired eyes. Maybe, I worry, there's more of Lyndhurst creeping in to both of us too. Maybe the way he lived his life was never a choice. Maybe it's an inevitability.

Chapter Thirteen

Shamsi gives me a kiss on the forehead. 'You'd better get up or you'll miss the plane,' he whispers. '*Or* you could miss it and we can stay in bed together for a week.'

I search for my desires but they're nowhere to be found. Besides, I do have a plane to catch—and a resident to worry about. Will's on call this week, while the rest of us fly interstate for the big annual conference.

Steve's unperturbed. This happens every year. He thinks that if a resident can't cope with extra responsibility then they don't deserve to progress. Knowing how much Will wants to be a surgeon *I* want to give him a fair chance. It's hard enough for him with his underlying diabetes, which has become more unstable as the months have gone by. Paul's the only surgeon who's stayed behind, and if Will needs to unscrub to eat, I know

Paul won't be nice about it. I've promised to keep my phone close by and help with advice by text message.

It's only 5 a.m. but the conference starts this morning on the other side of the country. I've left it until the last minute to fly out to minimise Will's time on call, even though my presentation is today. Steve, who's not giving any presentation, left last night. By 6 p.m. he was sending me photos of him and the other registrars from our state at the airport bar, all with beers in hand.

Shamsi appears with a coffee as I'm wiggling into the dress I laid out a week ago, knowing that I'd go straight from being on call to a plane today. He hands me the mug and a jacket and offers to drive me to the airport. I mutter about a taxi and he laughs as I lurch down the hall, muscles protesting.

'Look at you, you can't even stand up straight,' he says, pulling on a pair of tracksuit pants. 'Besides, we can catch up in the car.'

The roads are still dark and empty, the air cold after the warm autumn. The road's clear, the usual early morning trucks and commuters are home on a Saturday. I rummage in my bag to make sure I have everything—ticket, phone, wallet. It seems I'm always forgetting something these days.

'So, what's happening at work?' Shamsi asks, conversational as he promised, but sounding to me like a parent interrogating a child at the end of a school day.

'Nothing.' I stare out the window at the alternating light and darkness flashing by.

'Really? Nothing? You're there so much? Surely *something* interesting happens every so often?'

I have plenty of stories, not all of them medical disasters. Daphne runs a cooking blog in her spare time, sharing the Vietnamese recipes her mother taught her. Vikram's a master of the Rubik's cube. He's been trying to teach me to solve some of the patterns. Steve's a total dick, but his interstate mother is dying, painfully, of pancreatic cancer. She probably won't see next year.

My mouth is too tired to talk, the energy in those cells harvested and sent to my legs, my arms, my organs. Besides, the details of my days are somehow both tedious and overwhelming the first time around.

Shamsi smiles tolerably. 'Well, our case is going well—'

I accidentally let out a groan.

'Not interested?' His eyes frown while his mouth smiles.

I curl into the passenger seat further, pull my jacket hood up over my ears, tuck my hands into the sleeves. 'I'm just tired.'

We drive over a long bridge. I search the horizon for the gold that will follow me across the continent and then realise that I'm not ready for it. I'm living most of my life under artificial lights these days.

'Sorry, Shamsi. I know you drove me this morning so we could talk because we never see each other.'

'Yes, I did. And no, we don't.'

———

My neighbour on the plane pats me awake. I startle and blink, feel my ears filling with pressure. The plane must be descending.

He hands me a tissue, which I accept without knowing what it's for.

'You're drooling. See, there.' He points at my damp face.

Aghast, I wipe my chin.

'Baby at home? My wife drooled when ours were young.' He smiles kindly

So, despite feeling mortified, I reply, 'No, I'm training to be a surgeon.'

'Ah,' he says, uncertainly. 'I hope you don't mind my saying your level of fatigue is worrying. Pilots would *never* be allowed to fly that tired.' He points at the small airline badge pinned to his collar.

'You're in charge of hundreds of lives at once,' I say.

I desperately can't be bothered talking to a stranger, but I'm grateful he didn't let me leave the plane with spit on my face.

'Aren't you responsible for lives too?'

'Not hundreds, and not hurtling through the sky in a tin box,' I retort, shoving my unused laptop and unread textbook into my bag.

'That's how the medical industry gets away with it, isn't it?'

'Gets away with what?' I'm interested and irritated at the same time.

'The errors. The complications. The deaths. Sure, two hundred people falling out of the sky in a tin box is spectacular. Bad for the bottom dollar. Headlines write themselves.' The pilot pauses, musing. 'Do you know how much they spent looking for the black box from that plane that disappeared over the Southern Ocean?'

I shake my head, no.

'Sixty billion dollars, on the disappearance of three hundred and sixty-seven people.' He packs up his own book and glasses. 'How many people do you think die in your industry every year?' he asks.

I have no idea but am pretty sure it's more than three hundred and sixty-seven.

'Sometimes, in hospital, people die,' I counter. 'We all die. Sometimes people die, even though we did everything we could. Sometimes there're things we could have done better. Sometimes we don't even know if they died because of us, or despite us.'

I wonder what the coroner found with Beverley. Unless it was our fault, we're rarely told.

The plane hits the ground with a jolt.

The pilot frowns. 'I don't fly anymore. Too old. They retired me to work in safety systems so I know that thousands of people die each year from medical error. When you look closely at the industry, it's easy to understand why, isn't it?'

I shrug. I think we do pretty okay with what we've got. Past the pilot and out the window, I glimpse the tarmac glistening in the morning sun as we taxi to the gate. The plane stops and the pilot stays seated though the whole plane rises around him. He glances at the seatbelt sign and sighs.

'I'm only a trainee surgeon. I do what I'm told and work with what I've got.'

'You remind me of my daughter. She used to say the same thing. Eventually she learned what I've said for years—planes don't crash because the plane failed, but because people did. And you've got to constantly try and improve systems so people can't fail. As a start, you've got to speak up.'

Says the guy who's always been listened to, I bet.

'What does your daughter do?' I ask instead as we inch down the aisle.

'Oh, Mia? She flew us here today.' The cockpit door has opened, and the pilot waves to the woman standing inside.

———

A dash through the airport, a silent taxi ride, a quick registration, and I walk into the hotel conference hall a few minutes before the first session starts. Should I be proud that I always fly so close to the sun and survive, or worry if I've built my wax wings strongly enough?

Everyone is milling about, a sea of blue shirts netted in by trade stands, the sample prostheses and plates flashing under the lights. Everyone who's presenting is in a suit, everyone who isn't is in jeans. There are no other dresses to be seen. I sling my conference ID around my neck and see Steve and Rod whispering conspiratorially on one side. Later. I need coffee first.

I grab a muffin and an instant coffee from a near-empty table and slink into the back of the room. I wave at Lisa, the only other trainee I know from my state. She nods back and joins Rod, who gave me such a terrible handover, and Steve. They look away and move towards the front. Oh well, I'll sit on my own.

I hide in the back for the first session and take copious notes, even though at The Mount, we don't even have the special robot for the procedure that's being discussed. An older gentleman sitting next to me leans over and tells me to stop writing because, 'It's either in the textbooks or too new and controversial for the exams.' But I haven't read all the textbooks so I keep writing.

The session ends and I emerge into the light-drenched foyer, more sun than I've seen in months. As I'm stunned and blinded there's a poke in my back. It's Steve, flanked by Rod and Lisa.

'You made it!' he announces.

Rod looks me up and down. 'And you're wearing a dress,' he chimes in.

'You look like you should be at the plastic surgery conference.' Lisa sniggers.

I'm very confused. 'I don't even know what that means,' I say.

'You've come with a wheelie suitcase, wearing a pretty dress and heels. Honestly. Orthopaedic registrars don't have wheelie suitcases and dresses.'

'Oh, leave her alone,' Steve interrupts. 'Let's get a coffee.'

'Well, did you bring your runners? We're going for a run before the session tomorrow morning,' Lisa suggests over her shoulder in a tone which seems far from an offer.

'Um, no. I thought I'd catch up on some sleep.'

'Seriously, Emma, what kind of orthopaedic registrar are you? We have cocaine for that.'

———

At lunchtime, David finds an empty room to go over my presentation one last time. He seems to expect that I'll be nervous about speaking on stage, but this isn't something I've ever found difficult. Fitting in to this crowd on the other hand . . .

'I'll introduce you to Joe Evans after,' David promises, his eyes earnest. Professor Evans is the head of the London Centre for Foot and Ankle Surgery where David went to do his extra training. Like Dad, David's convinced an overseas fellowship is essential, and to be honest, when I see what he can do with an ankle compared to the others it makes me want to be that good too.

Although there are equally eminent centres in Arkansas, Marseille and Frankfurt, London is the one city that Shamsi's law firm has a partner practice. I'm hoping that going to London won't stall his own career progression and he'll agree to come.

The catch is that London only takes one international visiting surgeon a year—and I haven't been able to bring myself to talk to Shamsi about the possibility of my applying. These registrar hours are so much worse to live than they seemed on paper. I worry that undertaking these five years is asking enough of him and our relationship. But then, is there any point in falling short at the finish line, in accepting mediocrity over excellence because we didn't have *one* more year to give?

The session starts with Professor Evans giving the keynote. Again I take notes and this time it's David who's amused. 'You know he gives that same talk at every conference?' he asks.

I pause and then keep writing. David, with his strong handsome jaw and blue eyes who walked into every centre he wanted on his international tour can't possibly understand. I feel like he could have relied on chitchat about football and cars alone, his brilliance just a bonus, whereas I have to take notes and know more than everyone to be given the same opportunities. His glass started full whereas my feminine glass started empty.

Soon my name is called and I walk to the podium, wondering if my lavender dress is adequate among the suits the other speakers have worn. There's no time to think about it now, and besides, it's too late. At least David's face is smiling encouragingly from the front row. So, ignoring Lisa's jibes, ignoring how I feel like an imposter, I take a deep breath and start.

Joe Evans nods along and even takes some notes himself, and Albert gives me a small thumbs-up when my eyes meet his in the second row. Though it's my presentation, it's David's surgical technique and I want to do his work justice. By the end, I'm sure I have. This is confirmed when he lets me answer the questions from the crowd rather than stand to take them himself.

I've barely sat down when David taps my leg and gestures to the door. Once outside, he gives me a high five. 'Great job, Emma!'

I agree to a celebratory drink, even though a shower, maybe even a quick nap before a room-service dinner would be preferable.

The bar in the hotel foyer is largely empty. David waves me into a seat. I sink into a mauve velvet armchair while he returns with a bottle of expensive French champagne and two flutes.

'You're such a natural at research. How do we make it easier for you to give more presentations like that?' he asks as he pours me a glass.

I sip and wonder what he means.

'See, I tried to do my research around my work demands and family obligations, but it wasn't without consequence. Something has to give, and for me it was important relationships. This is why I'm so keen to make sure that trainees work within their capacity and don't burn out,' he explains. This is different from the usual 'work harder' lectures from Dad. Are surgeons' attitudes finally changing?

'You seem pretty happy, David,' I observe.

'Ha! I am, mostly. Though, after years of poor work–life balance, my marriage is a disaster.'

I choke on my champagne, surprised at this personal admission. Embarrassed, I wipe the droplets from my dress.

'Oh, don't look so uncomfortable,' he laughs. 'It's important to talk about these things. My wife—I think I've said before—is very talented. But what she wants out of her career and what I need from her to support mine are rather at odds.' He leans in conspiratorially with a lopsided smile. 'Don't let that happen to your marriage, Emma.'

An hour later, when Steve, Rod and Lisa walk past, we're still lounging on the velvet sofa, empty glasses, the crumbs of a cheese board, and many laughs between us. Steve pauses outside David's view, then waves goodbye to the others and lopes over.

'David! Emma! This looks fun!' he proclaims with astounding brashness.

David settles even further into the sofa, pushes his glasses up and cocks his head at Steve. 'Hey . . .' he says, deliberately laconic, *'we're* celebrating Emma's excellent presentation. Great effort on her part, wasn't it?'

Steve can barely hide his jealousy. But I'm tipsy and don't care. Besides, our other bosses on the unit love him. Why can't he let me have this small win? I cross my legs and wave my heeled foot at him.

'Yes, it was great,' he manages, before ducking his head to David and walking off.

David gives me his characteristic wink and hauls himself out of the sofa. 'Best get going. Well done again, though it was only as brilliant as I expected from you.' Another wink and he strides off purposefully, leaving me to smile at my own cleverness.

He's only gone a few steps when I see his hotel room key card is still on the table in front of me.

'David!'

He stops and turns, his hair falling into his eyes.

'Your card . . .' I hold it out to him.

He arches his eyebrow in a way I don't understand, before coming back and taking it from me. 'I guess I'll see you tomorrow. Have a good evening, Emma,' he says, before disappearing.

I watch him go, wondering what it is about him I don't quite get. But now isn't the time to think about it. For once my time is my own. I'm going to order room service and go to sleep.

Chapter Fourteen

It's the end of the day and Sarah, wearing the nurse-in-charge hat, is sitting at the nurses' station. She tries in vain to hide her steaming cup of tea.

'Don't worry, Sarah. I won't tell anyone.' I plonk myself into the anaesthetist-in-charge chair next to her and spin around. Work is exciting again after the conference. David introduced me to Joe Evans and several others as his 'protégé', giving me hope and purpose among the drudgery.

The more I see what David can do, the more I want to be like him. The cases he takes on are cutting edge and intellectually stimulating, and he makes me feel like I'm smart enough to keep up. The opportunity to go to London and come back with special expertise like he did is starting to feel possible. But I still haven't spoken to Shamsi about it. There's still a nagging doubt that maybe it's greedy to want *even* more.

'They're so worried about rats in this place. Honestly, what rat is going to drink tea?' Sarah asks, breaking my reverie. She swivels to peer at her board, which is messier than usual.

'I've got two waiting for surgery tonight.' I try to save her the effort of deciphering the chaotic paper slips and magnets.

Sarah squints and then pulls a couple of slips off. 'These are already done, not that it helps. You won't get in before ten,' she apologises.

'It is what it is.' There's no point getting upset about things I can't change, and access to theatres after hours is at the top of that list. We try to manage the workload by doing things in Emergency, or bringing patients back the next day, but even these strategies have limits.

Brayden, the tall annoying emergency registrar, argued with me earlier about how to manage a broken wrist. He had a full waiting room, but there were no beds in the hospital and little time in theatre for me. In this case, I won, and he set it in Emergency without my even having to appeal to Julia, head of Emergency and master of muesli bars and sensibility.

'Paul is keen?' Sarah asks.

Has to pay off the Maserati. I don't let the thought escape aloud. It's both true and unfair to put it as simply as this. Although he gets paid extra after hours, there's often no other time to operate on emergency cases anyway.

At last Sarah turns her back on her board. 'It's hard on you lot,' she says, sipping her tea. 'Are you going to wait around, or go home?'

Shamsi has to work this evening. Daphne's gone home early because her mum's unwell, and Vikram can't be roused from some statistical analysis he's running for his flesh-eating bacteria PhD—Prof Brown's given him a deadline. The Exam's only a few weeks away, and Andy and Nic are in an impenetrable bubble. Andy got the full exam treatment on his Grand Round this morning, and even Steve shuddered as he described it earlier. I have no friends to talk to and nowhere better to be.

'Hanging around, may as well eat dinner,' I laugh, fishing out a packet of dry biscuits. It's the only food that's supplied in the theatre complex, and there's usually a packet or two crumbling in my scrubs pocket.

'You can't eat that here, because of the rats,' Sarah says.

I steal a blanket from the warming cupboard in recovery and head to the tea room. There's no one else there. Lounging across the whole sofa, I flick through the channels on the decrepit television. David must be bored somewhere because he's texting an anecdote about his day. The warm blanket is soothing. I don't have the energy to reply. My eyes are starting to close when Sarah calls my name sharply from the door.

'What?' I rouse myself.

'Emma, I need your help,' Sarah says, unusually anxious. 'There's a patient who's just had a Caesarean. She's bleeding.'

I'm confused. 'Well, where are the obstetricians?'

'The operating registrar isn't answering their phone, the labour ward doctor's busy, and the obstetrician is half an hour away.'

'And the midwives?'

'Emma, you and the junior anaesthetic registrar are the only doctors in this theatre complex. Even the anaesthetist has gone to help with an airway emergency in ED. Please. We've sent for midwives, but can you help?'

We sprint down the hall, my theatre clogs catching on the yellowed linoleum floor.

Shit.

What do I remember about obstetrics, or bleeding?

I see blood on the ground even before they pull back the curtains. Pooling on the bed, soaking the sheets, dripping down the side. The anaesthetic registrar looks like he's going to vomit.

Shit.

'Is the placenta out?' I ask, and the nurses look despairing. That's right, it was a Caesarean. Placenta must be out.

They're right to despair, I haven't thought about obstetrics since that term at medical school, six years ago. Bleeding, bleeding . . . first aid for bleeding is compression. I remember how to compress a uterus because it once made me cross my legs in horror.

'Have you got gloves?' I ask.

Sarah's already opening them.

They're too small for what I'm about to do but this is a crisis. I apologise to the barely conscious patient and put one hand in her vagina and the other on her abdomen, squashing her uterus as hard as I can between them. Blood drips off from my elbow onto my scrubs, then onto the floor.

'Have we got blood coming?' I ask the nameless anaesthetic registrar.

Write your name on your fucking hat, I think, fully aware I don't have my name on mine.

'Yes, and fluids are going in. Her heart rate's up, and her BP's a bit saggy. Oh, and she's had a spinal anaesthetic so she can't feel that.'

I realise with a sinking feeling that everyone thinks I'm in charge.

Shit.

What do I do next? Compression is an emergency action, undertaken by desperate people on the side of a highway or in a place without medicines or surgeons. We're in a major hospital.

Bleeding needs compression, until blood vessel spasm and contraction stop the immediate outpouring, allows the blood clotting pathway to kick in. Normally the uterus does very well with its own contractions . . . yes!

'Have we given her more syntocinon?' I ask the room.

There's no reply, from anyone.

'Hey! Anaesthetics!' I call from my awkward position bent over the bed, my arms pinned to the patient. His face appears back in my field of vision.

'I'm Tom,' he says, helpfully.

'Great. I'm Emma. Give her some syntocinon.'

'How much?'

My brain almost explodes. '*Fuck!* I don't know Tom, and I can't exactly look it up, can I?' There's a moment of guilt that

I've shouted at someone who's as out of his depth as me. But I'm not an obstetrician and I don't want to be in charge.

Tom pulls out his phone and taps at it. The anaesthetic nurse squeezes more fluid into the patient. Blood drenches my scrubs.

Some country paramedics once told me how they learned about estimating blood loss in the field. Enthusiastically, they described getting bags of expired blood product and tossing them around in a simulation room to get a sense of what a hundred millilitres looked like spattered on a wall, five hundred millilitres soaked into a carpet, a litre pooled on the bitumen. I crane my neck to assess the bed and floor but it's futile. I've never soaked a hospital bed with a pre-measured bag of blood. Our best bet is to stop the bleeding.

Another bag of fluid is hung up. My underwear is damp, and my arms are on fire. Still, I squeeze harder.

Tom draws up something and injects it into her drip, and the bleeding slows then seems to stop, although not convincingly enough for me to let go and stand up.

At last a group of midwives appear and then, the consultant anaesthetist close behind. Someone helps me from my awkward position. In the commotion that follows, I limp to the change room.

Sarah finds me there in my bloodied underwear, a pile of sodden scrubs at my feet.

'Thank you, Emma. I think you saved her life.' She hands me a chocolate frog and a two-litre bottle of saline.

'I'll take the chocolate, but what's with the saline?' I ask.

'Top secret surgical sister trick. Wash your undies out with the saline, not water. That way it doesn't leave a stain.'

'Does that mean I'm part of the surgical sister club?' I ask.

'Yep, honorary life member. You still don't ever get to touch my sterile trolley though!'

———

There's no toast in the residents' room, but Vikram's on the sofa tapping away at his computer.

'Don't you ever go home, dude?' I ask. The door slams shut. The smell of old carpet and stale coffee reassures me that I've left the clinical spaces of the hospital. No medical emergency, no resuscitation will follow me here.

'Oh, hey, Emma. This residents' room is bigger and nicer than my flat. Especially with the plants. Do you know what rent is these days?'

He's right. Someone *has* placed pot plants around the room, their shop tags still stuck in the dirt. I can't think of a reason why.

Vikram closes his laptop and studies my face. 'You look like shit, Emma. What happened?'

Gratefully, I sink into the sofa next to him and close my eyes. It's not often that other doctors have any capacity left to notice distress in others, much less sit in the rubble with them.

'An obstetric patient tried to die on me.'

'Obstetric patient? Did you wander into the wrong theatre, Emma? I mean, they both start with an "o"—'

In the silence after I finish the story, I'm worried I did the wrong thing, made the situation worse than it needed to be.

Yet Vikram smiles at me. 'You did good, Emma. You really did,' he reassures.

'What would you know about it?' I almost clap my hand over my mouth. Shamsi often tells me to simply accept compliments, but it's so hard after a lifetime of being expected to demur when praised.

'Actually, I did a couple of years of obstetrics,' Vikram says. That's right. He's mentioned that before.

Shit.

Why am I so horrible sometimes?

'Sorry.' It seems not enough. I try to move the conversation on. 'What made you switch to infectious diseases?'

'Hmm. Numbers,' he says, and opens his laptop again.

'Seriously, Vikram. What's that supposed to mean?' I probe, this time kindly.

Vikram sighs and closes his laptop. I slip off my clogs and cross my legs under me, sensing a story.

'A mum and baby died, Emma,' he says.

My regret at being nosy is short. Vikram continues without pause, the story well practised.

'It was when I was in the UK. She had a lot of complications in late pregnancy but was determined about how and when she'd deliver. Even as she descended into a fog of pre-eclampsia, she resisted any attempt to get the baby out and save her life.

She said the baby would know when it was ready. She said she'd done the research.'

Vikram turns to the window, seemingly at the city lights. I know that in his mind's eye he's back in that obstetric ward.

'Her husband was scared but had promised to support her, so he did. She wouldn't even take magnesium. She said she didn't want to poison herself and her baby with heavy metals.

'I'm a numbers man, Emma, and I had the numbers for her. I told her what her risk of seizures was. I told her how many women around the world die every year because they can't access appropriate treatment, unnecessary deaths by any reckoning and utterly avoidable in the NHS. There was no limit to what we could offer her, if she just agreed. I even told her magnesium was a light metal hoping it would sway her mind.'

I contrive an expression that I hope conveys sympathy while wondering almost dissociatively whether this story ends with uncontrolled seizures or a stroke.

'She stroked out after prolonged seizures.'

It starts to rain outside and the noise is welcome.

'I was the one to tell her husband that she'd died, and their baby too. I'll never forget his face. We both knew we could have acted against her will and saved them both.'

I give Vikram a minute to return from the secret graveyard of the doctor's soul. He shakes his head and straightens his shoulders. The shadows fade from his eyes.

'So that was when I decided that obstetrics wasn't for me. I could be kind, I could believe in women's autonomy and their right to make medical decisions and control their own destiny—and don't get me wrong, I do believe that still—but I'm a numbers man and it hurt when she and others like her wouldn't trust our numbers, or placed other values ahead of mine. I couldn't spend the next forty years in a specialty full of grey when I see things more black and white.'

'Vikram, you've got far more insight into the rights of the pregnant patient than many other doctors.'

'Perhaps. Perhaps not. And Prof Brown would kill me if she heard me describe our specialty as black and white. Don't get me started on how badly we've managed pandemic diseases like HIV/AIDS. We still struggle to ask those affected what they need from us, rather than trying to shame, stigmatise and police them into good health.'

Vikram flips up his laptop and shows me rows and rows of unintelligible code and outputs. 'Day to day, I can grow bugs in a lab and work out what will kill them. Most patients will accept antibiotics or other medications and get better. Even if there's no treatment, there are numbers. Numbers that we can use to track and predict and prevent the spread of disease across the world.'

The adrenaline of the emergency has passed. I thank Vikram for sharing and settle into the sofa.

He hands me the blanket next to him and returns to his laptop, but then a moment later, he looks up again. 'You know, Em, you did well back there tonight.'

'Really?' I ask. It was messy and imprecise and my under-wear is still a bit damp and sticky. I'm sure there was lots I could have done better.

'No, I mean it,' Vikram says earnestly. 'One of the things about training is that it brings you closer and closer to being an expert in a small field, but also it drags you further and further away from being useful in any other crisis. And I think—I hope—you'll be one of those people who doesn't retreat into your own corner for the rest of your career. We all need to think about health more broadly and step in like you did today. It's what makes you a good doctor, Emma.'

Chapter Fifteen

Andy needs a lift to the airport. He's on his way interstate to sit The Exam. Laura has a compulsory course before she goes back to work in a few weeks and Andy's more fragile than we've ever known him, so I volunteered to drive him.

For the last month Andy and Nic have been grilled late into the night by overly enthusiastic surgeons, all of whom seem to believe that the harder they interrogate, the more the exam candidates will learn. There's a myth that telling a candidate they're sure to fail is the best way to motivate them to study. Instead, they've become even more drawn, even more pale. I'm reminded, watching this process, that surgery was performed long before anaesthesia was available. Psychopathy must be fundamental to our profession.

When I arrive at Andy's on this frosty Friday morning, it's still and quiet. Laura's already gone and Laura's parents, who came from overseas to help, have taken the girls to the park. Andy finally admitted to me that he didn't want them there, but Laura had put her foot down. In her telling it was a mutual decision. It's not often that the cracks between them show.

Laura's happier, but this hasn't come without a cost—cots are wedged into Andy and Laura's small bedroom, and a new sofa bed is installed in the former nursery. No wonder Andy looks exhausted. Toys, breakfast dishes and laundry cover the benches and floor.

'Ugh, I have to pass so we can deal with this,' he says, rattled, waving his arm around him. I pack his pile of books into the open suitcase, taking care not to crush his shirts. The leaves on the bush outside scratch against the window as the wind picks up. A winter storm is coming.

'There's more to passing than housework, Andy.'

He sighs in grumpy frustration while searching for a matching tie. 'We can't live like this anymore. There're six of us in this house.'

'Laura doesn't mind,' I say, knowing full well how much Laura does mind.

Andy ignores me.

'You know how hard it was for her to take time off. She's back full time next month. If I don't pass . . .' Andy glances out the bedroom door. 'I love them, and they try so hard, but it's such a small house,' he whispers.

At that a shoebox falls off the top shelf of the wardrobe and spills on the floor, sewing supplies scattering about the room.

'Shit.' Andy crawls under the bed to retrieve a spool of thread and a bobbin. Mum taught us both how to sew but Andy excels at it. He made Laura her wedding gown, and the girls miniature dresses to come home from hospital after their time in Intensive Care. Somehow, he seems to find more time in a day than me.

'How am *I* going to do it, Andy?'

'Do what?' he asks absently, rearranging things in the wardrobe to make the shoebox fit, as if this game of Tetris will make up for the chaos everywhere else.

I wave my arm at his house, the photos of his babies on the wall, the pile of books on the bed, the plane ticket and hotel booking, the receipt for the eight-thousand-dollar exam.

'You know how much Shamsi loves the girls and how keen he is to have our own kids. And I thought I was too but . . . I barely function as it is. How would I write a paper for David with a baby? Or ask Paul for permission to go pump breastmilk halfway through an operating list? Even childcare hours are shorter than what we work.'

Andy sighs.

Today isn't the day. I push down on his suitcase as he zips it up.

'I don't know, Emma. Nic has it much harder than me, in ways I don't even understand. You should talk to her about it, one day.'

We drive to Nic's to pick her up too. Her partner also couldn't take time off, get their child minded, fly interstate to provide support for The Exam.

The wind picks up as we wait in Nic's driveway. Andy's fretting when the quiet is broken by my phone. It's Steve:

> What time's your appointment today? We need help
> in clinic.

I lied to get a day off, made up a fictitious medical appointment that no one dares ask too much about in case it concerns Lady Things.

I reply:

> Not until later this afternoon, and I have to
> do some tests this morning.

> You could have rescheduled.
> You know today was a fully booked clinic.

> My leave form went in weeks ago. I'm sorry
> they didn't reduce clinic.

> They never do. Can you come back
> for at least part of clinic?

I hand Andy my phone and he reads the conversation silently. He types, *No, fuck off*, but before I can protest, he changes it to *No sorry*, and hits send.

'Andy!'

'He takes long weekends to go interstate and you haven't had a day off this year!'

'To visit his dying mother.'

Andy's back to moping. He's right, our one-in-two roster leaves us only four days off a month, and Steve *has* added on a few Fridays. This is exactly why I took the whole day off. Even being in the same city is enough to demand I come back to work; if I'd tried to take a half day then I'd have been fielding calls all morning.

Nic appears, a clinging toddler in her arms. Her wife extricates the crying child and holds her a moment, gives her a kiss of good luck. Slumped, Nic walks to the car. I let them sit with the facts crammed in their heads, and drive.

They're barely into the terminal when Dad calls. I haven't spoken to him since the birthday party and Andy's been avoiding him as well. I know he'll keep calling now until I answer.

'Is he off?' Dad's voice fills the car. The first few drops of rain hit my windscreen.

'Yes, Dad, and don't worry, I'll get home before the storm,' I reply, trying to pre-empt his next complaint. I've picked the wrong one.

'You know he's going to fail, Emma,' he says. 'And you will too unless you change your attitude. You didn't need a day off work to drive him to the airport.'

'Dad!'

It's raining harder. The traffic is thick and harried, hard to manoeuvre through.

'I'm still four years from The Exam, Dad,' I remind him, flicking the windscreen wipers to a faster mode. I don't need him to upset me on this tricky drive or infect the rest of my day off with his stupidity.

'Do you know how many trainees I've seen?' he blusters. 'You kids are smart, but you don't act it. Especially with the advantages you've had.'

I should say 'okay' and hang up, but I'm angry. I'm angry for Andy and the work he's done, all he's given up, to be called a failure by our own father. And I'm angry for me. I haven't even started studying and he's predicting my failure already.

'Do you have anything nice to say or did you call to tell me we're both shit?'

The freeway is slick with water, the visibility dropping. The storm is no longer glorious, it's irritating, like Dad, and work, and even Andy for being so fragile today and making everything seem impossible.

'Andy's too nice, too humble. He's going to let the examiners walk all over him.' Dad ignores my taunt.

'The examiners are supposed to examine us not lead us to failure. The Exam is different now, not like when you were mean to trainees.'

'I wasn't mean, Emma. The paediatricians can be nice to each other if they want. Surgeons have to be excellent. Above reproach. Cutting into someone is a big deal, you know.'

'Yes, and that's why you also have to be kind and respectful towards patients, win their trust.' A honk of my horn warns away the taxi that's drifting into me. I should slow down, but I'm too mad.

'Kindness doesn't get you far, surgical expertise does. They might tolerate kindness in you. Not in Andy, though. He needs to be strong, tough, the best.'

Right. I've had enough of Dad's faux wisdom. We won't change each other's minds.

'So, what if Andy does fail?'

'Oh, he'll be fine, in the end,' Dad replies dismissively, infuriatingly. 'There're two sittings of The Exam every year for a reason. We expect a third of candidates will fail each time. He can sit again in three months.'

'Why are you talking like he's a candidate and not your actual son?'

'He's both, Emma. As a candidate I know he's going to fail. Because he's my son, I know it'll be miserable for him. If he'd played this right, if he'd approached this like I told him he should, then this misery could have been avoided. All he needed to do was learn to stand up to people.'

'What people, Dad? People like *you*?'

I hang up in a huff as the car aquaplanes again.

———

Despite my father, my day off is lovely. After dropping Andy and Nic at the airport, I head to the pub two blocks from our house, the one with the excellent food and sofas in front of an open fire, and find it blissfully empty. Even though it's hard to banish the feeling that I'm failing by doing something other than work or reading a textbook or writing a research paper,

161

I manage to put that feeling aside enough to read a novel with a glass of wine in my hand.

Shamsi joins me for dinner, blowing in from the storm with rain on his face and his long winter jacket swinging around him.

'I've got a secret,' he says, turning up the sleeves on his shirt. He orders the most expensive bottle of wine on the list.

'What?'

He leans forward, pulls a small box from his coat pocket. Inside, a pair of diamond hoop earrings twinkle in the fire light.

'What's this for?'

'It's a secret, Em, still embargoed, but I've got the promotion!'

We exit the pub late, happily drunk, laughing as the rain drenches us on the walk home, laughing more as our wet clothes stick as we remove them from each other. And when we're under the sheets twisted together and Shamsi whispers in my ear, 'So when do we stop doing this for fun and start doing it to make babies,' I don't have it in me to even take him seriously or worry again about what that might mean.

———

By Monday, my happiness has turned to anxiety. I'm sitting on a bed in one of the on-call bedrooms at the far end of the residents' room, waiting for Andy to let us know if he's passed. Laura's doing her orientation at the clinic this morning and we wanted to make sure someone was free. I swapped Steve a night on call for him to do my operating list this morning, and Julia in Emergency has agreed to hold any referrals unless desperately urgent.

Andy hasn't told Laura, or me, how he felt during the full two days of The Exam. He'd endured multiple sessions of being grilled by his future colleagues over a patient or specimen, and we'd texted after each station. Every time he'd replied, *Fine*. Yesterday, soon after it was over, he disappeared, my messages unanswered. Many candidates go out for a celebratory dinner but Andy's not one to celebrate pre-emptively. I worried that he sat alone in his hotel room, brooding.

In ten minutes he'll find out if he's passed or failed. The results are delivered to all the candidates across every surgical specialty at the same time. Some years ago, the announcement was even more barbaric—a congregation on the steps of the College with the Chief Examiner calling out the candidate numbers of only those who had passed. '1, 4, 5, 7, 10 . . .' and on it went until everyone gathered had either been invited inside for a whiskey with the examiners, or, their number not called, slunk away.

Today, the candidates gather in a hotel lobby where they'll simultaneously be handed a sealed envelope. They'll scramble to find a spot to open it while the full court of examiners stand against the railings one floor up, watching. I'm told there'll be tears—of happiness and desolation—so many tears it's impossible for anyone watching to tell who cries for what reason. There'll be psychologists on site even though it's unfathomable to seek care in front of your peers, mentors, colleagues, friends.

Like before, only those with a letter that says 'pass' will join the examiners upstairs for champagne.

I suggested that Andy take the envelope back to the hotel room but it's not the done thing. Besides, once it's in his hand, it'll be impossible not to tear it open.

The minutes tick by. At 11.05, my phone dings. It's Andy.

NOPE

Shit.

Shit. Shit. Shit.

Should I call? Or let Laura call first? I call anyway.

Andy doesn't answer. I try again, and again, and again. And when he does finally pick up, there's nothing but the commotion of a crowded hall down the line.

'Andy, Andy, it's okay . . .' I say, the little speeches I practised all morning gone.

'I've let them down, Emma.'

'No, Andy, no, you haven't. Lots of people get through on their second go.' I want to reassure him. Dad said he'd be okay, that he'd pass next time, but this isn't the time to bring our father into it. We've spent enough of our lives staring down his disappointment.

'I have to go,' he says, and hangs up.

Shit.

Outside an air hockey game's in full flight, the whooping at odds with my sorrow. I'm much closer to my brother than most sisters are privileged to be. Andy helped me home when I fell off my bike on a steep hill, read me stories at night when our father had yet again missed bedtime, cheered me into medical school when I thought I wasn't smart enough, married my friend. Now, I want to be there for him but I'm in another city, sitting on a sagging bed, helpless.

Shit.

Laura doesn't answer either. I try Andy again. His phone is busy or off. There's nothing to do but sit, wait, watch the traffic below, until even that's too much and I have to close my eyes.

Half an hour later, my grace period with Julia almost up, I call Andy again. Thankfully, he answers.

'What do you want?' he grumbles. Down the line, filling the air, are the muffled sounds of . . . Jimmy Barnes?

'Andy, where are you?'

'Some pub I scoped out this morning. I knew I'd failed last night,' he says, his words halting.

'Andy . . . you can't get drunk at some dodgy pub. You have to fly home.' If Andy gets home, to Laura, to the girls, things will be okay.

Jimmy sings about God and Elvis.

'I can't come home, Emma. I can't face them.'

'Are you drunk?' This isn't the kindest question but seems the only explanation.

'No. I bought a beer, but I haven't even had a sip.'

Oh, Andy. Oh, dear Andy. Sitting at the bar in some basic establishment with hospital-torn carpets and a residents' room-scuffed pool table, in his dark blue suit with a loosened tie around his neck, a full beer in front of him. Perhaps not the sorriest character the bemused bartender has seen, but surely close.

'Andy, that's too depressing. Get your stuff and come home,' I plead.

'I can't come home, Em. I can't tell Laura's folks they have to stay for another three months. I can't face Laura knowing we have to do this again. The babies . . . I can't . . .'

Shit.

'Andy, you know you'll get through, everyone does. It's a couple more months.' Goading will make him angry, make him shout that I don't know what a couple more months means for him. Anger is energy. Anger will get him home.

Hunters and Collectors take over from Jimmy. The blue summer sky seems so far away as I wait for my big brother to react.

Out of the silence, there's a low distant voice that doesn't sound like Andy.

'My flight isn't for four hours. When I booked it, I thought I'd get to stay for the drinks. How delusional, huh? Everyone said I'd fail.'

The bastards. They tell everyone that they'll fail. It doesn't mean anything.

'Andy, get a new flight home. Look. I'll buy it for you . . .'

'Emma, no, it's fine. I have to spend another ten grand on The Exam this year. I can't afford another ticket.'

'No, Andy, it's okay . . .' I've put him on speaker phone and find a flight that leaves in an hour. 'Andy, it's not an expensive flight. It's on me. The money's been spent now so don't waste it. Call a cab and get to the airport. You've got half an hour to check in. Go, okay?'

There's a long pause, and then I hear a rustle, the creak of a barstool on the wooden floor, the sound of a suitcase handle being pulled out.

'Okay, Em. Okay.'

I feel like I've fallen into an ocean of relief.

'But . . . can you tell Dad?'

Andy's in a taxi, and this is a bandaid to tear off quickly. Text message is safest.

> Can you be nice to Andy, Dad? He didn't
> pass.

Our father's reply is almost instantaneous.

> Of course he failed. I told you he would.

Chapter Sixteen

'm running across the road to the car. I'm on call this weekend and yet I've promised to try and make it to Shamsi's work party.

In the weeks since Andy failed The Exam, since the news of his own promotion, Shamsi's enthusiastic support of my medical training seems to have given way to a quiet frustration. He's suddenly started asking how we're going to get through this.

I'm also frustrated. He's known my career aspirations since the day we met and he chose to make a life with me anyway. We've been through my years of being a resident working the evenings and weekends that Will and Daniel are doing now. I've supported his interstate travel and the late nights that he's put in to progress his own career.

Now I'm too far down the path of becoming a surgeon to turn around—who'd give up on this when you're one of the very few honoured by selection?—and I feel like I'm in trouble just for going to work. And I still haven't raised the possibility of one more year of training in London.

But today, luck's on my side. Orthopaedics has no outstanding cases; there's an organ donor harvest happening in theatre, so unless a problem is life- or limb-threatening, there's no chance of getting in to do any other surgery today; and best of all, Will's the resident covering the surgical specialties this weekend. He's obliged to be on site and I can lean on him to sort out most issues. So maybe, for once, I'll make it to this party and prove I can be a good wife *and* a good registrar.

'Emma!' David's voice is deep and piercing.

I pause mid-step and search for him.

'Emma!' he repeats, from the entrance of the private hospital next door. 'I've got something for you!'

I check my phone to see how much time I have. It's always such a relief and a pleasure to see David. Great, I can spare a few minutes. 'Hi!' I call cheerfully and walk over.

'Hey, happy coincidence! Ward round over? Let's have a coffee?' he suggests. 'I've got that USB for you.'

Shit.

I glance at my phone again. I can probably manage a take-away.

Since the conference, where my paper did so well and impressed even Joe Evans, David and I have been planning to write up our findings for a journal. I've convinced him that if I gather more data from the patients' original scans, the resulting paper will be better. I assume that's what he's got for me.

Staff at The Mount often sneak to the small coffee shop inside the private hospital to get 'good' coffee, but unexpectedly, David keeps walking, past the entrance and around the corner. Obediently, I keep up.

'Where are we going?' I finally ask.

'New café, it's just a block away. They roast their beans on site. I've been meaning to take you. You've got to try it,' he says cheerfully. 'Besides, I've got to kill some time otherwise I'll have to go talk to the other soccer parents, and there's nothing worse.'

Shit. I don't have time for this.

And yet.

I follow him to the café.

Half an hour later, I'm sprinting to the car with David's USB clutched in my hand when Shamsi sends me a message:

Are you on your way or should I go without you?

Home in ten minutes.

I tap out and run faster.

————

Shamsi's waiting in the driveway holding a bag.

'You're only twenty minutes late, that's better than usual,' he says through the car window in what sounds like a congenial tone. I still search under his words for the note of unhappiness that means I'm actually in trouble. I can't sense any today.

He puts the bag in the back seat and says, 'Swap. I'll drive.'

One of Shamsi's colleagues is leaving for New York, and the law firm's holding a farewell for her this afternoon. I hadn't wanted to go but Shamsi was insistent, refusing to accept that being on call was an excuse.

'Em, I'm a new partner even though it hasn't been announced. I really want you there, if possible,' he'd asked.

I'd tried to swap weekends and when that didn't work, I'd promised to try to get away. I've been successful and yet I still feel like a failure running late in my jeans and a hoodie on my way to a fancy shindig.

I hop in the passenger seat. As he pulls back out of our driveway, I glance in the mirror with dismay. Perhaps I can put a fake polish on my personality, but I *look* tired.

'Gosh, I'm a bit haggard,' I exclaim.

Shamsi glances over. 'You look beautiful, babe,' he replies. I know he's just being nice.

'Are *all* the WAGs coming?' We've always laughed about how masculine his workplace is; full of men in powerful suits and wives in traditional roles. Shamsi probably fits in about as well as I do in surgery, but he's always been such a high achiever that the most exclusive law firm in town made him a job offer even before he'd even finished his first university clerkship with them.

Shamsi nods and I sink even further.

'Oh man. They're so glamorous,' I moan quietly. I look at my slightly pilled hoodie, perhaps too casual to have even worn to work this morning. But dress standards drop on a Saturday and, to be honest, I couldn't quite see what I was pulling out of the closet in the dark. I'd intended to get changed before the party.

'Em, none of them work like you do. It's easier to look glamorous when you aren't slaving away a hundred hours a week and have time to exercise and eat properly,' he says gently.

The traffic is at a crawl and Shamsi checks the time impatiently.

I close my eyes and wonder if he ever imagines another life. 'Do you want me to stop working?' I ask.

Shamsi doesn't answer straight away. And when he does, it's with a sigh. 'No, I don't. It's your career. It's important. I know you love it. I know you've worked hard for it. But . . . it's pretty intense. Balancing what we both need is challenging. I didn't realise what it would be like to live when we first talked about it.'

A small voice in the back of my brain is tired with the balance too. But then, Laura's so loving and supportive of Andy, even though it's almost killing her. Mum was so patient with Dad, delaying her own exhibitions when he was busy even though she was an award-winning artist herself. If she was ever resentful, she's never admitted it. Even David's understanding and helpful.

Maybe if Shamsi's so tired, he could cut back, not be promoted—maybe go work for a smaller firm himself. All he does is make companies richer whereas I'm the one to relieve pain, restore function. I don't think his gripe is fair.

'You're so unsupportive,' I tell him.

He looks across at me, wide-eyed. 'Woah. I'm totally supportive, babe. Why is acknowledging that it's a bit hard considered unsupportive?'

'I don't tell you how hard it is for me that *you* work. I don't wish that *you'd* quit.'

'Hang on. Babe. I didn't tell you it was hard for *me* that you work. I said it was hard for *both* of us that we *both* work in these high-pressure jobs, right?' Shamsi parks the car a few doors down from the restaurant. It's a busy Saturday afternoon on a popular street and people wander past in the winter sun. Outside the world's so normal. In the car the air is thick and heavy. I don't reply.

'Em, I don't know what I'm doing wrong,' he says, finally. 'It seems we can't have normal conversations anymore. It's like . . . all you talk about and care about is surgery. I knew the hours would be long, but I didn't think . . . that it would take up every bit of you, all the time.'

His words are gentle and I feel a sense of shame welling up. Perhaps I'm being unreasonable. In fact, I'm sure that I'm the one being unreasonable. I push that feeling away.

For some people, like Paul, their choices and where they've ended up seem to be about how much they earn, and for others, like Jon, how impressed other people will be. But I'm not like them.

For me and Andy and Vikram, and probably even Dad, medicine's a calling, a true love, but it never felt like my only love. I wanted to be a surgeon, but I also thought I'd eventually work part time, take our children to the park, cultivate my hobbies. I understand that Shamsi might think I'm moving the goal posts. But how could I know where the goal posts were before I even walked onto the field? I need him to understand that this, all this, is me trying, always trying. And I'm tired of feeling like that's not enough.

Shamsi reaches into the back seat and hands me the bag. 'You look hot in those jeans, babe. I brought you your make-up and a nice jumper and some heels. I hope that's okay,' he says, even more kindly again, soft enough that the tears prick at my eyes.

'Shamsi. I . . . it's just . . . I don't know how we're going to fit in babies. I want to go to London after I finish my training to do a foot and ankle fellowship, but you've been made partner . . . I've been too worried to raise another year of training as a possibility even though it would be so important, so career changing for me because you already seem so irritated and we're barely six months in. And I'm so tired, sometimes I . . . it's so hard to talk about anything serious on the good days because then we might fight and turn it into a bad day. And there are so few good days anymore.'

I wipe furiously at my face and nose, suddenly wet.

Shamsi puts his finger against my lips to hush me and then cradles my cheek in his hand. 'Em. It's okay. We can talk about that some other time. Hard doesn't mean it's impossible. Look, I have to go in. You get yourself sorted and join us when you're ready, okay?' He gives me a small kiss on the cheek and then he's out the door.

———

The law firm has booked out the whole restaurant. Through the window, I can see there're more people here than I expected. My phone dings with a message from Will and it's a relief to have to take a moment to answer before I contemplate walking in.

I've made myself presentable. Shamsi brought my favourite teal jumper that he says brings out the colour of my eyes and my best heeled boots and even a belt to glam up my jeans. I catch my reflection in the window. On any other day I'd say I looked great and that this was totally appropriate for this trendy restaurant, but inside there's a sea of designer dresses and blonde hair. I've met the WAGs before and they've always been lovely, yet, I hesitate.

And I realise it's not them, it's me. It's not even how I look; it's what I've turned into and how I feel inside. When it comes to small talk, I haven't watched the news or read the paper, I haven't been to a football game or out to a new restaurant. I haven't even watched a TV show. At home—when we talk at all—we talk about my work, and who here wants to hear about the petty politics of a small Orthopaedic unit? Our last holiday was our honeymoon and I don't think anyone's interested in what you did six months ago, are they?

But here I am and there's nowhere to flee, so I put my phone in my bag and push the door open. The cacophony is startling. I stop and then Shamsi's at my side. With his hand on my waist he steers me to the middle of the room and re-introduces me to the other partners.

And slowly, I remember what it's like to engage in normal conversations about things that aren't full of gore. Shamsi even leaves me for a while and I see him watching me from across the room with the first genuine smile in some time. And when we walk out into the gentle drizzle of a winter evening, the world feels fresh again. Fresh enough that I can see with clarity that it's not just Shamsi who's been rattled by Andy failing his exam, but also me. Because I'm not sure that I'm all that different from my brother. And if Dad thinks Andy failed because of some character flaw, not because he didn't work hard enough or study enough or care or try, then he's right. I'm in trouble too.

Chapter Seventeen

'Hey, Em, we need a surgeon to join a committee.' Daphne's short on the phone.

David and Paul are leaning against a cupboard at the back of the outpatients clinic having a chat, even though there are forty patients still to be seen. This is typical for Paul, but David's behaviour is a disappointment.

'Daphne, I'm not a surgeon, and why would I want to join a committee?' I retreat into an empty consulting room to have this conversation.

'Emma. We need a *surgical registrar* to join a *really important* committee,' she says again, slowly.

If I know Daphne, she's not going to give this up.

She says the hospital's decided to implement new initiatives to make our working conditions better. Apparently, medical workforce wellness is trendy and Prof Brown is determined to make her mark. She's in charge of a new program along with Brenda. So far, they've bought the pot plants in the residents' room.

'They know we're burnt out, and if I'm generous maybe Prof Brown isn't doing it for her academic metrics but because she truly cares about us. However, they have *no idea* what they're doing.' Daphne's indignant. I can picture her poking Prof Brown in the chest like she did Steve. 'It's got to be about real and meaningful change. Better rosters, better teaching and mentoring, better care for patients so we don't have to carry the moral injury of always being a bit crap.'

Our conversation's interrupted by the usual mid-morning announcement over the clinic PA that we're running late, usually issued once the waiting time is over ninety minutes. In the hall, Steve's joined David and Paul in whatever joke they're sharing. Scrolling through his phone and showing them pictures, he might be asking for an opinion about an X-ray, but the way they're laughing, I bet it's not. I'm not sure the moral injury of being 'a bit crap' affects all of us. *They're* able to ignore the patients in the waiting room. And then *I'm* the one who'll get in trouble for staying, and then being late to theatre this afternoon.

'Ah, are they also distributing the fruit?' I ask Daphne. A mysterious bounty has begun appearing in odd and random places—a few apples on the desk of the Orthopaedic office; some bananas in clinic; a bowl of oranges in the residents' room, with skins too thick to peel in a kitchen that hasn't had knives in twenty years.

'Yes! Admin organised it. They think *fruit* is important.'

'They should have tried wine and chocolate and paying us,' I grumble. I'm still cranky that it took me months to extract my first pay cheque after Brenda spelled my name wrong on my paperwork, not to mention the daily overtime we never get paid for.

'If you join the committee, you can advocate for wine and chocolate and pay. It's a rare opportunity, Em. They're motivated, even if it's for the wrong reasons. We can influence change. So, are you in? We meet once a fortnight and tonight's the first meeting,' Daphne suggests.

'Ugh. Who else is on the committee?'

'Aidan from ICU for anaesthetics and critical care, me for the physicians, Olga for obstetrics, and I've got Will for the interns and residents. We need someone from surgery. We need you, because you're awesome, and because you're a Swann.'

I'm offended. 'What's that supposed to mean?'

'You have no idea, do you? What it's like being a pleb like the rest of us. By the way, I saw you having a coffee with that surgeon at that new café the other weekend. Watch out. He's totally got the hots for you.'

The line goes dead as David sticks his head into the room. 'Emma, Prof had to run out, and there's a sarcoma patient he wants you to see,' David says, and then he's gone as quickly as he appeared.

I'm not sure whether to laugh or be frustrated at Daphne's suggestion. It's laughable, and yet a common accusation when a staggeringly brilliant man chooses to support a woman. Why can't Daphne, my friend, consider that I deserve mentoring because I'm actually good at my job? Besides, if he had the hots for me, he'd be seeing patients to help me out rather than politely dumping work on my head.

———

It's been four months since I last saw Jacqui Miller. That was the time I told her that she had cancer. Today, she's back in clinic for her final check-up before surgery to remove what remains of her tumour.

Uncomfortably, I realise that I haven't thought about her or her diagnosis since. She explains to me that it's fully occupied her mind. Through misty mornings on the farm battling a poor internet connection to research her diagnosis, through staying alone in a small charity-sponsored motel room for six weeks of radiation therapy, this is what she's thought about, researched, discussed.

Jacqui's read that standard treatment is amputation of the leg, and she's been worried for months that this isn't what we've suggested. She'd rather live than have a leg. I think of Robert, who died even though we removed his. I don't tell her that this isn't always a choice.

I explain that what she's read on the internet is outdated. Yes, we used to amputate the whole limb, but giving radiation first allows us to excise only the tumour and preserve her leg. Almost halfway through my year at The Mount, I now know the names of the radiation oncologist and the plastic surgeon. I know why we offer the treatment we do. I'm not always sending other patients like her off with inanities, empty reassurance.

Although I'd almost forgotten about Jacqui, now that she's here, I'm reminded of the sadness and worry I felt when I first met her. Today, strangely, I don't want to ask after her children or hear how hard the last few months have been. I glance out of the room to see Paul holding a coffee. Am I the only one working today? And Steve had the audacity to tell me off for being ten minutes late this morning.

'My husband and I have been fighting every night,' she says, as I hand her the consent form for surgery. Her pen hangs over the page.

I stifle my impatience and fake an interested smile.

'At first, when I got scared by what I read on the internet, he said to see the GP. But my cancer's so rare, my GP couldn't help much either. It would've been nice if there was someone they could call, or I could call . . .'

My phone rings all day and all night as it is. I want to tell her that I can't give out my number to everyone. I glance at the clock on the computer. We need to finish clinic on time so Paul won't growl at me for being late to theatre.

'I try to remember everything from these appointments, but my husband can't come with me because . . . the farm, the kids. It would be nice if there was another way.'

We were told in medical school that patients only take in a third of what's said in any consultation. I'm not sure how I can change that.

Jacqui looks like she's finally about to sign then puts the pen down and gets a brochure out of her bag. 'I got in touch with these people. They make leg prostheses. But they cost eighteen thousand dollars. We don't have that kind of money. If I lose my leg will the hospital pay for one? Or will I be in a wheelchair?'

I take the brochure and glance through it, a gesture rather than interest. Prostheses aren't my area. That's why we have rehabilitation physicians.

'You won't lose your leg, Jacqui. That's not the plan. And if you do, the rehabilitation department will organise a prosthesis for you.'

'Will it be this one though? The company said that this would be suitable for the farm, that I'd be able to ride a horse with it . . .'

I have no idea. Another reason to not give out my phone number is that I couldn't answer everyone's questions anyway.

'You'll be okay,' I tell her flatly, my eye half on the corridor where the stack of patient files is growing. 'Here, sign the consent form. We have a date for your surgery in the next few weeks.'

———

I'm late to the first meeting of the 'Workplace Transformation Committee' too. Daphne, master of persuasion, has assembled the group in a matter of hours.

See, you weren't the last person I called.

Daphne's text message is no consolation for getting home late.

Paul scoffed when I mentioned the committee and then left early, leaving me to sew up the last patient. So by the time I've got them off the table and sorted out the evening with nurse-in-charge Sarah, my colleagues are already in a small meeting room in the admin block.

Brenda sits sternly at the head of the table, a yellow lined notebook in front of her. Prof Brown's in a brightly coloured sloth-print dress, still trying to be one of the people, even though she's much too old to have any idea what it's like being a junior doctor and much too senior for me to trust her. I'm still dubious about the whole thing.

Aidan also looks suspicious, whereas Will seems happy to be there. Daphne's a master of inclusion, I'll give her that.

'Thank you for coming so late in the day,' Prof Brown starts.

'I assume we'll be paid for our time as this is after hours?' Daphne interrupts, her eyes wide with pretend innocence.

Prof Brown and Brenda glance at each other. I sit back and cross my arms, glad for the first time that Daphne invited me. I'm still cynical but this should be fun.

'Er, no. This will be excellent for your CVs though,' Prof Brown responds.

Olga nods enthusiastically. Aidan makes a scoffing noise.

Brenda brings up a PowerPoint presentation, and Prof Brown explains the intention of the program.

'The Mount has been one of the busiest hospitals in the city for over a hundred years, but it's clear that younger doctors no longer wish to work in the same ways, so we must change, progress, to make it more palatable.'

On the first slide, Brenda talks about healthy food and how fruit is only the first step in the program. They're planning to talk to the café about including more nutritious options and looking at ways healthy food can also be available after hours. Brenda points to the bowl of kiwifruit on the table, and when no one moves, gets up and hands one to each of us. I'm not sure what to do with it. Aidan starts to eat it like an apple, skin and all. Olga hands hers back. 'I'm allergic,' she whispers.

'Do you think we could roster mealtimes? It's very hard to manage diabetes when you can't eat regularly, or even reliably,' Will suggests.

Brenda just looks at us.

'Any questions?' Prof Brown asks enthusiastically, proudly, even though Will's question still hangs unanswered.

Daphne's phone dings with a message. She reads it and puts up her hand. 'My boyfriend's cooked me a healthy dinner and wants to know if I'll be home in time to eat it. The bananas are great but can we hire more doctors so we can get home on time to eat dinner?' she asks.

You have a boyfriend?

She sneaks me a look and shakes her head. I'm not sure if that's a denial or if she doesn't want to talk about it.

'Mmm, let's move on to safe places to rest,' Prof Brown says. Sleeping pods in the residents' room and ensuring a sofa or a bed for everyone on call after hours is written on her list.

'What about resting arrangements for the night residents?' Will asks. 'Doing seventy-seven hours in a single week, all of it overnight, is pretty exhausting, even if you get the alternate weeks off. And it's especially hard if you have a chronic illness, like I do.'

'If you're rostered to work you shouldn't be resting or sleeping, even overnight,' Brenda replies.

Prof Brown's last slide is about an education series. Every week, after hours, she's planned lectures on how to recognise our own demise, and what to do about it. Topics jump from depression to fitting in exercise, the symptoms of burnout to the principles of nutrition. 'Early intervention is so important,' she concludes.

Brenda turns the lights back on, and the two of them grin.

I think about Andy and how he's back to working, back to studying, back to trying to pass The Exam. I can't imagine how this program will help him, or any of us.

I put my hand up. 'Um, so why *are* we here? If you had everything planned, why let Daphne bring us in at the end?'

Prof Brown smiles sweetly at me. '*Nothing for you without you*, isn't that how the saying goes? Having you all here is so wonderful—it's such an important part of our consultative process.'

I text Daphne as we're gathering our things:

Did they invite us or did you push us in?

Across the room she shakes her head and taps out a short reply. A moment later my phone reads:

What do you think?

Chapter Eighteen

The day's finally come. Jacqui's operation is tomorrow. Once again she's come in alone and full of questions, this time written down so she wouldn't forget. Nic and I went to see her after she was admitted to the ward. Now, Nic's drawing on the whiteboard in the orthopaedic office, planning her part of the operation, while I consider ways to *actually* transform healthcare.

'How can we make the patient journey better?' I ask her. Ever since Jacqui told me about the things she'd found difficult in the last few months, there's been a notion in the back of my mind that maybe once you start to listen to patients' concerns there's an awful lot that needs improvement. If pot plants and fruit aren't going to help me, then whatever the equivalent we offer patients isn't going to help them either.

Nic gives me a questioning look before returning to the whiteboard. 'Jacqui should have had her surgery four weeks ago. It was hard enough finding a time for her operation, and she's a cancer patient,' she says dismissively. 'What's the deal with the bone?'

'Hmm, we're going to save it,' I reply, finding the answer in her notes from clinic, but still more focused on Jacqui's distress. In the past, I've never thought much about patients when they aren't in front of me, and now that I'm not in an overbooked clinic and running late, her story's playing on my mind.

'Seriously, Nic. We're still young and enthusiastic. How would you reimagine our health system?'

Nic stops drawing to scroll through the MRI scans on the office computer, frowning as the screen flickers. 'I swear it's growing into the bone. See? Image 76 on the coronal view.'

'No, around it. Prof Bones is going to peel it off.'

Ever since Nic passed The Exam she's become more contrary. Planning combined cases with her is increasingly annoying, but maybe it's the straightness of her spine, the strength of her voice, the light in her eyes that's getting to me. It seems unfair when Andy, now alone, is still in The Exam trenches. I must call and check on him.

'Prof . . . Bones?' she asks, her eyes widening in surprise, her painted lips pursing. Where does she find time to put on perfect make-up?

'Jones. Bones.' I pull the blanket higher around my shoulders. None of us have managed to make the old radiator in this office turn on.

Nic closes the MRI scan, puts a cap on her whiteboard marker and stands. She places the operative technique book in her bag and peers in the dark window to adjust her hair.

'Hey, do you think our bosses are sitting somewhere planning her operation together like we are?' I ask.

In the reflection, she shakes her head in disbelief. 'Em, they can't stand each other.'

———

It's a relief to see that Jyothi's our anaesthetist today. Nic and I have already marked Jacqui—arrows and words in permanent marker saying, *operative leg* and *do not use for lines*, so anaesthetics can get started nice and early. It's going to be a long operation to remove the tumour and microsurgically reconstruct the resulting cavity.

So it's a surprise when I get to the holding bay to find that Jyothi and Tom—Tom who'll never forget how much syntocinon to give a postpartum haemorrhage—are standing around.

'So, Emma, we're removing this tumour from the right leg and you've also marked the left leg, the left arm and the right arm. Where can we put our lines?' Jyothi asks.

'Only the right leg markings are mine,' I reply, as Nic appears.

Jacqui, dwarfed by the blankets and people around her, looks from one of us to another.

'You can use her neck,' Nic suggests.

Jacqui shakes her head. 'My kids will come to visit me. Nothing hanging out of my neck, please?'

'Neck is a bit harsh, Nic,' Jyothi agrees.

Nic is getting fractious. 'Well, I don't know what *they're* going to do so I can't know what *we'll* need to do. Her arms and other leg have to be clear.'

'Sorry, you don't know what you're doing?' Jacqui asks, heat rising to her face.

Now I'm annoyed. We had a plan last night. They'd take the tissue from her other thigh. She even drew it on the board. Jacqui's hand trembles in mine as I glare at Nic.

'Of course we do, Jacqui,' I reassure her. 'It's a poor turn of phrase. The plastic surgeons famously like to keep their options open.'

Nic and Jyothi move away to have a spirited discussion. Nic pulls out her phone and walks off.

Jyothi comes back with a smile. 'This is new for you, but it's routine for us. We work as a team and sometimes we negotiate. And you're part of the team too,' she tells her.

Jacqui's hand relaxes a bit. This is a phrase to store away.

Nic reappears, frowning into her phone. 'My boss says you can have the right arm,' she mutters and stalks off.

'See, we work it out.' Jyothi smiles before she and Tom wheel Jacqui, shrinking and scared, to the anaesthetic room to start sticking needles into her.

———

Prof finds me in the tea room and interrupts my self-medication with instant coffee. 'Why haven't we started?' he bellows.

'Anaesthetics are putting in their lines. We had her marked and ready to go last night,' I say, deflecting all possible blame from myself. This doesn't calm him.

'Who's the useless bloody anaesthetist?'

I like Jyothi, but it's not my job to protect her—gosh, I can't protect myself. I down the coffee and follow Prof to theatre. He cracks open the door of the anaesthetic room while I hold my breath, but then closes it, somehow restraining himself from shouting in front of the patient.

'I'll have to come back,' he says with a dirty look.

By the time Prof does come back, Lorraine has our trolley set up and ready to go. In the set-up room beyond, at least four plastic surgery nurses are preparing several additional trolleys. Packets of instruments are opened and counted, Nic waving her hands enthusiastically. It's a good performance for when her boss walks in, but I'm sure she's not actually helping.

I've already loaded Jacqui's scans on the theatre computers when Prof throws open the doors, one of them bashing into the wall.

'Ah, well done, Emma,' he says, temporarily mollified. Twice my height and width he nudges me out of the way and takes the mouse. 'We'll definitely be able to preserve the bone,' he says, flicking through the images and pointing to a couple of spots. 'See? Here, and here, the tumour is close but clear. Better for us, better for her.'

Last night, when I was only half listening, didn't Nic raise a different view? But Prof's already walked off to inspect the instrument trolleys and berate the nurses. Jyothi and Tom wheel Jacqui into the operating theatre and transfer her to the operating table.

A piece of paper escapes from under Jacqui's pillow and flutters to the ground. I go to toss it in the bin, then see it's a childish picture of a woman and a horse and flowers. *Get well mummy* is imperfectly written across the bottom.

I tuck it into my own bag to put in her room later. And instead of leaving the theatre as Tom holds an oxygen mask to Jacqui's face, I stroke her hand as she drifts off to sleep, just in case.

The tube hasn't been in her throat a second when Prof Bones appears beside me as if teleported, snarling across Jacqui's unconscious body, 'Anaesthetics, explain yourselves.' Thank goodness she's asleep.

Jyothi, who must have gassed for Prof before, doesn't even look up from her paperwork. Only an observant witness would see her fingers tighten on her pen. Tom turns away and pretends to search for something on the drug trolley.

The silence lengthens. The anaesthetic machine whirs quietly, and the *blip blip blip* as it registers Jacqui's heartbeat fills the room.

'Hey, you, anaesthetics!' Prof says, even louder.

At this, Jyothi, lifts her eyes, an expression of total calm on her face. 'Hello, I'm Jyothi, we *have* met,' she says, coolly. I cheer on the inside.

'Did you hear me? Today's delays are absolutely unacceptable.'

191

'Well, we better go outside and talk about it in a civil manner, hadn't we?' Jyothi suggests, picking up her coffee mug.

Nic's entered theatre and stops. We catch each other's eye. I once read that when predators are in an alert or aroused state, their attention's so focused that stillness appears to them as the equivalent of invisible. Nobody moves until Prof turns on his heel. Jyothi follows after a few instructions to Tom. The room breathes a sigh of relief—it isn't over, but at least 'it' will not be conducted in front of everyone.

Jyothi has clenched teeth and Prof is purple when they return. The tension's escalated to a point where silence is no longer discomfiting but welcome; at least they're not openly hostile. On the operating table, in the middle of the room, Jacqui's chest rises and falls in time with the whirring of the machine.

Fortunately, the discord hasn't stopped the two theatre teams getting ready. Soon we're scrubbed and assembled, instruments in hand, on either side of her.

We're soon upon the rubbery mass. The whirring gurgling noise of the suction fills the room as I draw away the pooling blood. Prof works his large hands around the irradiated, shrunken tumour, trying to deliver it from her thigh. As his fingers get deeper and deeper, his scowl deepens too. The plastic surgery team have been chatting away about some TV show and he silences them with a glare. His fingers are around Jacqui's femur, and the mass is clearly attached to it.

'This tumour seems to have progressed,' he mutters. Nic peeks at me, blinking as she tries to communicate something silently.

I think about Jacqui's life on the farm and two children hoping for three and suddenly understand Nic's gestures. She can't raise what she pointed out to me last night because Prof is my boss, not hers—but *I* can.

If he thinks the tumour has grown despite radiation he might consider amputating her leg. If he knows that it was attached to the bone all along he'll be upset for having missed it, but more likely to try to preserve the limb.

I take a deep breath. 'Prof, there was one image on her original scan which seemed to show that the tumour was growing into the femur?' I blurt this out quickly and inflect upwards at the end to turn it into a question. Shamsi coached me out of doing this because he said it made me sound less confident, but sometimes it's still a helpful strategy, especially around surgeons.

Prof pauses, squints at the screen across the room, and walks over to look closer. The scout nurse scrambles to work the mouse. I grab a cotton pack, the woven fabric we use to mop up blood, from Lorraine's trolley and push it into Jacqui's leg to quell the oozy bleeding, and then another to cover the wound altogether. Nic keeps operating, but her boss has stopped and watches us both, an eyebrow raised.

'Image 76, on the coronal,' I remember, hoping this is correct. Nic glances up and nods imperceptibly. Phew.

Prof watches as the nurse scrolls through the images to land on number 76. He studies it carefully, and with a nod of his head turns back to us to survey the scene—a patient asleep on the table, an operation half done, a reconstructive plan in progress, none of it quite addressing the problem at hand. His long blue gown is streaked with blood. He folds his equally bloodied hands together over his pot belly, and closes his eyes, thinking, the image of Jacqui's thigh magnified and glowing behind his head, clearly showing the tumour growing into the bone.

'Emma, you should have shown me this earlier,' he says flatly. If he's like my father, this is the slightest chiding, better than I expected.

'I haven't planned to reconstruct the bone,' the plastic surgeon tells us.

Prof closes his eyes again, and taps his foot, the rubber of the gumboot dull on the floor, and out of time with the regular blips from the anaesthetic machine. We have to remove the bone, there's no other way. But how? He snaps off his gloves and pulls his gown away, tearing the paper straps that hold it on.

'I'll be back,' he declares and walks out.

Jyothi peers over the curtain. 'Is there a problem?'

Lorraine's taken a seat by her trolley, and she answers, 'No more than usual.' Then she adds, 'At least he didn't have a knife in his hand. I've seen them fly across the room before.'

A minute or two later, Prof's back. He tosses his mobile phone near the computer.

'Right,' he says taking a deep breath. 'We'll peel the tumour off and then resect the involved segment of bone. Emma can take it across to the cancer centre for them to irradiate further. Then we can plate it back in place. The plastic surgeons can continue with their plan, and we'll have treated the cancer adequately.'

He ties his mask back on. 'Go get me the bone saw,' he adds. The scout nurse has already anticipated this.

Prof removes the last of the tumour, marking where it was attached to the bone, and then cuts out a section of Jacqui's femur. He drops it unceremoniously in a bowl. 'The whole trip should take about an hour. Take her with you,' he says, indicating Nic, before removing his gloves and leaving. The plastic surgeon nods. It seems everyone listens to Prof.

Lorraine wraps the precious piece of bone in a cotton pack and puts it into a sterile plastic bag. We cover up Jacqui's thigh with more cotton packs and drapes to cover her gaping wound while we're gone.

'I'll drive,' Nic offers as we run down the stairs.

The cancer hospital is a ten-minute journey through the university precinct and to the other side of a large park. Nic's worried about parking, but luck is with us today. She pulls into a convenient spot with a sigh of relief, and we sprint across the still dewy grass.

The radiation oncologist is waiting. She's set up the required protocols based on Jacqui's CT scan. We stand outside the room while they speed up electrons, guiding them to surf along an electronic wave in the linear accelerator, until they smash against a tungsten target, creating high energy X-rays that destroy any tumour cells still stuck on Jacqui's bone. And then the precious thing is handed back to me, back in its wadding and bag for the return journey.

I check the time. It's been fifty minutes.

The run back to the car through the park is uphill. The car is in sight when my foot catches on a tree root, and then it's as if the world is moving in slow motion. My opposite arm hits the ground first but it's not enough and the plastic bag slips from my fingers. It hits the ground and, as it does, the Ziplock opens and Jacqui's femur rolls out, escapes the cotton pack and comes to rest in the grass a couple of centimetres from my nose.

The world lurches back into full speed, and Nic is beside me, shrieking.

'Emma! Fuck! You dropped it!' I hoist myself up, my hand throbbing, and we both stare at the chunk of bone, glistening in the green.

'What do we *do*?'

'We tell no one,' says Nic, and scoops it up with her bare hands. She roughly folds the cotton pack around it and drops it back in the bag.

'What do you *mean*?'

'You heard me. Tell *no one*. Can you imagine what your Prof will do to you if you tell him that you dropped the bone in the park?'

It's true. I might as well write my own obituary. Nic's pulling my sleeve, leading me back to the car. She opens the door and pushes me in the passenger side.

'It's basically his fault for being incompetent, a bully, rushing us like this. Once you've plated it back in, I'll give it a good wash after you've left, before we do the microsurgery. With some broad antibiotic cover for a few days, she'll be fine.' Nic has the keys in the ignition.

'Think of the open fractures on the football field. They get better after you wash them, right? This is only a bit of grass. Not even mud.' Nic's persuasive. Either way she's right, there's no choice.

We're back in theatre only ten minutes later than the allocated hour, and even Prof chooses not to complain. The staff have the plating equipment ready. I carefully tip the bone out of the bag onto Lorraine's trolley as Prof selects which plate he wants to use.

As Lorraine unwraps it from the cotton pack I spy a single blade of grass still stuck to the underside. Lorraine and I lock eyes and my panic starts to rise again. She gazes at me steadily, winks, wipes the grass off the bone, and then drops the cotton pack in one deft move. 'Oops, there's a pack on the floor,' she says, and the scout nurse puts it in the bin.

In front of me, Jacqui's chest is still rising and falling in time with the anaesthetic machine, oblivious. Maybe Nic's right, maybe it *is* hard enough to achieve the bare minimum without trying to do even more.

Chapter Nineteen

'Why are you standing in the hallway?' Cheryl asks me, curious but not unkind.

Bill's operating this afternoon and normally I'd be in theatre with him, trying to avoid him patting me on the 'back'. The frequency with which he 'misses' and pats my bottom can't be an accident.

'Waiting for Paul, to do my mid-year assessment.'

She smiles sympathetically. It's clear to everyone that Paul doesn't like me. He's never available, indignant if I call for bothering him needlessly, and irritated when I don't because he thinks the only work that gets done is what he's told about.

At the last audit Prof took objection to one of my cases.

'Who did that? That looks shit,' he exclaimed to the room.

I'd been expecting this. With everyone watching I pretended to study the X-ray but didn't need to, the images already familiar after hours peering at it in theatre, and then again in my head for days after. This was yet another fracture that Paul should have come in for, but refused to, an injury pattern that even the textbooks identify as challenging.

I had to explain publicly why it wasn't perfect, and also that Paul was supervising, which felt like a betrayal even though I'd asked for help, even though the case was clearly beyond the capability of any first-year trainee. It seems some of them don't see the point of the training program as being to provide training.

Andy tells me not to worry—that people like Paul don't matter and everyone can see through them. But bosses with unrealistic expectations are making his life miserable too.

Even though Paul doesn't like me, he *is* my supervisor of training. It's his job to collate opinions from all our supervising surgeons and tell us if we're on track to keep progressing through our training. He isn't the sole judge or jury, but he might be the executioner, and I've spent months feeling like I'm marked.

Today, though, I'm quietly hopeful there will be few criticisms, and I doubt I've failed the first six months. I'm managing the workload, have completed and presented a whole research project and the other surgeons either like or tolerate me. I haven't killed anyone and I'm even getting along with my snipey, snitchy co-registrar Steve.

Cheryl wishes me good luck and retreats into her office . She doesn't seem to like Paul either, though she'd never admit such a thing to a registrar. We're only there a year, but the surgeons are forever.

I've booked the small room on the ward for our meeting. When I get there, Eliza and the other nurses are celebrating a quick baby shower on their break. Paul's always late and I don't want to interrupt the party so they're still there when he walks up the hall in a sombre grey suit.

'I told you to book the room, Emma,' he scolds as he shoos the nurses out. Eliza mouths 'sorry' as she goes, even though it was no inconvenience and not her fault. He slams the door shut, and helps himself to a pink cupcake.

I sit at the other end of the table, nervous.

'You've passed everything, Emma. Well done,' he says at last in a begrudging tone.

I nod, relieved.

'Not everyone was universal in their opinion of you. David seems to like you, though,' he scoffs. 'Your knowledge is fine for your level, and while we disagree as a group about the adequacy of your surgical skills and judgement, according to the requirements of the College of Surgeons, we have to agree that you're at an appropriate level.'

It's not my fault Prof Jones let three surgeons go on leave because Jon was going to cover them and then Jon left for the US unexpectedly. It's not my fault that I'm a first-year trainee, who still needs supervision and training when Paul doesn't ever want to come in.

'And that expression there, on your face, that's the other problem.'

Shit.

I didn't know there was an expression on my face.

'You don't ever look enthusiastic. Here I am, giving you feedback, and you don't even look interested in what I have to say.'

I glance down at the paper he's handed me, my precious documentation that I've passed, and consider this accusation. I turn up every day and do my work, well enough that almost everyone seems happy, well enough that David is introducing me to gurus from overseas. What does 'enthusiastic' mean?

Paul offers me the plate of someone else's cupcakes. I shake my head, confused. I want an explanation, not carbohydrates.

'You know what I mean, Emma,' he says, increasingly exasperated. 'You need reminding about basic things, like getting to theatre five minutes earlier and assessing patients properly before you operate on them. You shouldn't need reminding.'

If he stayed until the end of clinic, like he's paid to, then clinic would finish on time and I'd get to theatre on time. But that's not a retort to make right now.

'And you could try smiling. You often appear tired, or distracted, or uninterested. Smiling would convey that you're enthusiastic, that you want to be here.'

This time I'm the one who's begrudging as I agree to smile more.

———

There's a thin, ashen man lurking in the corridor. Worried that Bill's peeved at me for not being in theatre even though he knew I had to meet with Paul, I almost rush past without stopping.

But then I notice that the man's younger than he first seems, aged by sun and worry rather than years. His leather boots are scuffed and dusty, and his pants are barely held up by an old leather belt.

'Are you okay?' I stop and ask.

He almost jumps, before clearing his throat. 'Uh, um, yes, um no . . .' he stammers. 'I'm Dale . . . Dale Miller, Jacqui Miller's husband and . . . I don't think she's too good.'

He points into Jacqui's room, which is dark and still. It's a week after her surgery and everything has gone smoothly since. She no longer needs hourly monitoring so she's been moved from the front room near the nurse's station to the back of the ward. I follow Dale inside. Surrounded by flowers, childish drawings, including the one I rescued from theatre, and photos of her family, Jacqui's shaking uncontrollably. Her blankets are pulled up to her chin and her breathing's laboured.

Shit.

I take her hand and feel her pulse; her skin is cold and clammy, her heart racing.

'I . . . I just started shaking . . .' Jacqui gasps. I text Will and Nic—Will as a reinforcement and Nic because I know she'll be precious about her microsurgery. Dale looks like he isn't sure if he should try to help his wife, run for the door or simply fall over. I order him into a chair. I don't need two patients at the same time.

'She's okay. Maybe a slight temperature.' Is this reassurance for Dale or myself? The blue folder on the end of Jacqui's bed contains her vital observations, documented since her admission. The last time they were recorded, an hour ago, everything was okay. What's changed since then?

Thankfully, Will's brought Eliza with him, wheeling a blood pressure machine between them. She sticks a temperature probe in Jacqui's ear and holds it steady. Jacqui's teeth start to chatter so hard I worry she'll break a tooth. Will disappears back into the hall and returns with a pile of blankets.

'No pressure on her leg. Nic will kill us,' I whisper as we tuck them in around her.

The thermometer blips and Eliza holds it towards the slant of light coming in through the door. 'It's 39.1,' she announces.

Well. That settles it. Jacqui must have an infection. But where?

'Jacqui, can I look at your leg?' I ask. Her head spasms in agreement. Will helps to nudge away her blankets, pull up her hospital gown. The piece of tissue the plastic surgeons have microsurgically transplanted appears to be healthy.

The blood pressure machine exhales and beeps. 'Blood pressure is 80 on 60,' says Eliza.

I glance at her chart again. This isn't so different from her usual blood pressure, but she's young and has a huge ability to compensate. Her heart rate will go up long before her blood pressure dips.

'Heart rate is 130,' Eliza says, reading my thoughts. 'That's MET call criteria. Would you like to call a MET call?'

Some years ago, critical care doctors realised that patients rarely crash without warning; that over time, vital signs slowly change, until an acute moment many hours later when things tip over. They also noticed that clinicians didn't always notice or intervene early, when the death spiral could be prevented.

The Medical Emergency Team and MET call system was the solution. Once certain clinical criteria are reached, a MET call brings a specialist team urgently to the bedside. There's no doubt it's saved lives, but it still feels like a weakness to call for help over the loudspeakers.

'No, I'll grab Daphne,' I tell Eliza instinctively. Her blue eyes convey her disappointment in my decision—yes, I know I should call the MET—but she doesn't argue.

'Okay,' she snips, bustling back out of the room.

'Low BP, we should give her more fluids?' Will suggests. Eliza's huffed off, so he dials up an extra half litre to run in as fast as possible.

I call Daphne only to be startled by her ringing phone.

'Eliza told me. No good nurse leaves a patient who meets MET criteria alone with two orthopaedic doctors,' she snaps as she appears in the room, our usual camaraderie now stern professionalism.

Will takes a step away from the IV fluid machine like a child caught out.

'Did any of you even listen to her chest?' Daphne sighs. I don't know what happened to the top-of-the-line stethoscope I bought as a medical student. Will still carries one, but neither of us had thought to use it.

Daphne unslings *her* top-of-the-line pink stethoscope from its permanent position around her neck, unpicking it from where it catches on the large cat brooch pinned to her cardigan. Cowed, Will and I help Jacqui sit up in bed, each of us pulling her forward by a shoulder, so Daphne can listen to her chest.

'She's got crackles up to her eyeballs,' Daphne pronounces. Will surreptitiously stops the fluid that he dialled up before. Jacqui's lungs are full of it and more will drown her faster.

Daphne's intern records the findings as Jacqui continues to shake. Daphne's moved on to inspecting the leg, poking and prodding while Jacqui shudders and groans. I want to tell her to stop, because this I do know about and have already checked. She's through with letting me have an opinion, though.

'Hey, what are you doing to my flap?' Nic calls from the door. Her resident follows her in, nudging Daphne out of the way so they can both inspect the leg again, as we've already done.

Dale recoils and Jacqui closes her eyes. We're talking about Jacqui as if neither of them were present, as if she were simply a set of lungs and a leg in a bed, but there's no time for explanations and reassurance because Daphne and Nic are arguing.

'Well, you can't diurese her because you'll kill my flap.' Daphne wants to give medications to make her pee the excess fluid out of her body and, in turn, her lungs, but Nic won't let her. 'Can you give her more fluids, please? My microsurgery needs blood, and that won't happen with her blood pressure in her boots.'

'She needs antibiotics and diuresis and maybe to go to ICU.' Daphne has her hand on her hip and the voice of one claiming leadership. 'Her blood pressure's low because of infection, not because she's under-filled with fluid. In fact, she's too full of fluid because you've been trying to artificially increase her blood pressure with it for days.'

Antibiotics?

'Hang on,' I interrupt. 'She needs X-rays and a CT scan before you give her antibiotics, because if the infection's coming from her leg, we need to open her up and get a specimen first.' I try to catch Nic's eye, thinking of the mud and grass that might be turning to pus.

Daphne looks from one to the other of us with the same expression she gave Steve on the first day. 'You're both determined to kill her, aren't you?' she scolds.

Jacqui raises herself on one elbow, a massive effort in her weakened, shaking state. 'Hang on, am I going to die?'

The question hangs in the room. Even the medical intern stops typing.

Jacqui collapses back on the bed with a long, drawn out, wet cough that doesn't seem to end. As she slowly turns blue Daphne leans over her and calmly presses the emergency buzzer on the wall, sending a peal of alarm through the ward.

She crouches down, balancing on her heels, and takes Jacqui's hand, holding it and rubbing her shoulder until she stops coughing and gasps at air.

'Get out, all of you,' Daphne orders.

Nic and I collect our juniors and back out of the room as Cheryl, Eliza and the MET team tear down the hall, the crash cart close behind.

————

I've missed Bill's operating list entirely, and my afternoon theatre list alone is awful. The fracture I'm trying to fix won't come together. I can't compute the angle, the vectors, the line of pull that will overcome the distracting force of whatever muscle, ligament, scrap of sinew is pulling every fragment into the wrong position. And somewhere Jacqui might be dying and I was kicked out of her care, useless at that as well.

Yet again, Paul told me to get going and he'd come and help. I unscrub and call him halfway through the case. Now, infuriatingly, Paul's operating somewhere else. Why did he tell me he'd be available when he must have already known he wasn't? He doesn't even speak to me, rather relays some unhelpful bits of advice via a nurse.

I call David next, though he's not on call and this isn't his problem. Charming and helpful as ever, he explains in painstaking detail what I need to do, even sketching a beautiful diagram and messaging it through. It's clear he understands the problem I've described, but I can't understand his solution.

Steve leaves clinic to assist me. He examines David's picture and struggles too, yet between us we wrestle the bits of bone back into an acceptable position, making the incision longer and retracting harder than I'd like. But the plate's on and the X-ray looks okay. Pulling the skin over the plate, I sew it up, crossing my fingers that we've done enough.

By the end of the day I'm dreaming about my old university days working in a pizza shop, in among the sugary tomato sauce and plastic cheese. I'd take a capricciosa to Shamsi's dorm room after a late shift and then stay the night, squeezed together on a single bed. The night we moved in together, we balanced a supreme and a bottle of cheap wine on a cardboard box between us. I'd never agreed to a boyfriend before I met him. I didn't imagine he'd be the only one. I'm sure neither of us knew what we were in for when we sat on the deck of the backpackers hotel in Phnom Penh, staring out over the river, and he asked me what I wanted to do. And I whispered aloud for the first time, 'I think I want to be a surgeon.'

I miss this version of us. Now we see each other briefly. My meals come from a vending machine and he seems to have moved on to a diet of cheese and red wine. And occasionally, oh so occasionally, we drink too much, laugh too loud and have wild sex. It's like we have to forget who we are to remember who we were.

Worst of all, at the end of a day like today, he won't understand anyway. He doesn't know what it's like to think your favourite patient's dying. He can't understand what it's like when you've demanded an anaesthetic and cut someone open and then can't do what you've set out to do. I can't even call Andy because he's living his own version of hell. Maybe the only person who'd understand is David.

The enormous weight of this career I've chosen is oppressive.

'What are you thinking?' asks Daniel as we make our way to ICU to see Jacqui. She's in the high dependency part, not the intensive care part. This is better than I'd feared.

Daniel's intern enthusiasm of the start of the year has given way to a deep solemnity. His drive to be a surgeon runs far deeper than my own, but I can see his resolution cracking at times.

'Oh, that I should have married a surgeon.' The words escape my mouth before my tired brain has time to censor them. 'Instead of tried to be one,' I hurriedly add.

Daniel laughs, and then stops, realising it wasn't a joke.

'Just kidding!' I force a laugh too, trying to fool him into thinking it was.

As we wait for the ICU doors to slowly open, Daniel turns to me. 'You know,' he says slowly, 'I was a bit worried when I found out you'd be my registrar this year.'

'Why?'

'Because I worked on Professor Swann's unit last year, before he retired, and, well . . . I'm glad you're not like him. I'm glad you decided to be a surgeon, because it makes me feel like I could be too.'

———

The ICU is stark, white, shining. Little pods are lined one after another, each containing a larva of a human on life support. Jacqui lies in one, covered in lines again. A mask is pressed to her face, a hissing machine pushing air into the little sponges in her lungs, squeezing the fluid out. At least she's awake. The real Dale is nowhere to be seen, but someone's brought a photo of him and the girls and left it by her bed.

Aidan, the senior ICU registrar, sees us walk in and waves. He picks up a steaming mug from the desk in front of him and comes over. 'She's going to be okay,' he starts and I'm grateful for doctors who deliver the punchline before the explanation. 'There's no signs of infection in the leg. Her lungs are full of fluid and she's got a mild chest infection. I've put a line into her neck so we can measure her fluid status and stop that plastic surgery registrar from having a pink fit. She'll be back on the ward in a day or two.' He gives Jacqui a big thumbs-up and she responds with a feebler version of the same.

This, this is something I can smile about.

Chapter Twenty

I don't remember driving home last night. Steve was stuck in theatre, and even though I could have left, Julia begged me to stay until he finished operating and see the patients waiting for orthopaedics to review them in Emergency. Ambulances were queued for a block and the ED was heaving. Every patient I saw, plastered and sent home was another patient that could be unloaded into a bed rather than spend hours monitored by paramedics in the back of a truck.

So when my phone rings I sit bolt upright, surprised that I'm in bed without knowing how I got here. The clock reads 7.30.

Shamsi stirs and groans. 'It's Saturday. Why's your phone on?' he whinges before going back to sleep.

I'm about to cancel the call but it's David. Why is *he* calling? I rub sleep dust from my eyes and stagger out of bed, into the hall, then clear my throat so it sounds like I've been up for hours.

'Morning, Emma!' he greets me through his car speaker. 'Hope I didn't wake you?'

'No, David, I've been up and for a run already,' I lie, and then cringe. Why did I say that?

'Great! A fellow runner! There's a fun run coming up, we should do it together,' he suggests.

Shit.

'Anyway, not why I called! The ankle replacement company is making a video to help teach surgeons new to the implant, starring yours truly. Would you come and assist me this morning?'

I close my eyes. I'd promised to spend the day with Shamsi, and his plan to take me to a new art exhibition has already been sidelined by Laura who needs help with the twins. Still, I don't feel like I can or want to say no to David. Learning from him is the best part of my job.

'What time?' I ask and scrunch my eyes tighter. I wish I could put Shamsi into stasis for a few hours so I can leave and come back without telling him I'm going, and why.

I make a coffee and take it into the shower. Holding it out of the stream, I let the water run over me as I lean against the glass. I haven't looked at my body closely in months. My hip bones—the iliac crests, I correct myself—jut out and even my shins look bony. Only my biceps have any mass on them from months of lifting limbs into the air. Even my breasts have shrunk.

Shit.

I haven't examined them all year. My aunt, Mum's sister, died of breast cancer at thirty-eight. Even though diagnosis and treatment have improved, this is important, something I've never forgotten to do regularly. I rub my fingertips, nails chewed short, over every quadrant, surprised to find myself wondering if a lump would get me a few months off work at least. Poor dead Auntie Liz, she'd be so upset if she could hear my flippant thoughts. What's wrong with me?

The bathroom door creaks open. 'Hey, baby,' Shamsi smiles at me through the fogged glass. He slides the shower door open a crack. 'Can I get in too?'

I frown and slide the door closed again. I can't think of anything less pleasant. 'Sorry, no time.'

I turn my back and wish my guilt away. It's nothing personal, though Shamsi does remind me often that I'm hardly ever in the mood anymore. And *that's* a tiresome conversation.

'What's the hurry?' he asks, not taking the hint.

'Oh, I have to pop into work.' I wish we could talk about this outside the bathroom, when I haven't just turned him down, when I've had more time to work out how to spin this.

'Work?' Shamsi's indignant. 'It's your day off.'

'David's asked me to assist him this morning. You know the foot and ankle surgeon?'

There's a long pause.

'What, the guy who's convinced you that to be a good surgeon you have to do even more training in London?'

Ugh, this conversation again.

'You know Dad went to Paris for the same reason. And you

know how much thought I've put into it, Shamsi. London's the only city you'd be willing to come to.'

'You're trying to blame me for agreeing to do extra work on a Saturday morning?'

Hmm. Wrong strategy. 'Shamsi, I'm sorry. Everything's so competitive, even if we haven't decided anything. I can't turn down any opportunity because every no that I say is a yes that someone else says.' Surely, he can understand this. He's done this so many times too. This is how he got his promotion. Now that his career's progressing, why's he standing in the way of mine? I turn the water off and wrap a towel around myself before opening the shower door.

'It's only for the morning. We'll take the girls out for lunch before their nap.'

Shamsi looks at me warily and then nods. 'Okay. You'll be back here by midday then?'

'Yes, absolutely. Promise.' I kiss his cheek and push him out of the bathroom.

———

David's waiting at the entrance of the hospital, a pile of blue wrapped theatre trays in his hands, and a paper box from a bakery balanced on top.

'Over there,' he says and points to the medical school across the road. 'They're opening the cadaver lab for us.'

I've never been to this anatomy lab. Across the river at my medical school the lab was much newer. There were fresh cadavers for dissections and pickled bits of people in fibreglass, called 'pots', for study, but the collection was nowhere near as extensive as it's said to be here. This anatomy lab was one of the reasons my father was so disappointed that both Andy and I chose the other university.

We're waiting to cross the lights when his phone, jutting out of the back pocket of his pants, rings.

'That will be the rep. Do you mind getting it, Emma?' he asks, then laughs at my hesitation. 'It's okay, no big deal. It's not like we're having sex.'

Is he making a pass? Was Daphne right? And then I've answered his phone and his expression has gone back to serious professionalism. I'm sure I imagined it.

A cheerful voice is on the other end, and across the street, a woman pulling a large metal suitcase waves at us. Kate's the rep from the ankle replacement company. Company reps are integral to our work—they often come along to theatre when we're using new equipment. Once upon a time they also paid for fancy dinners and conferences at ski fields, until that was regulated and they had to stop. Old Bill, thrice divorced and now skint, still talks about the good old days when surgeons got free stuff.

I haven't met Kate before because David's *the* Australian expert on using this implant and he no longer needs her to come to theatre. Today, he greets her with a kiss on the cheek and introduces me effusively. Kate's brows fleetingly knit together and I wonder what's passed between them, but then we're laughing as we try to drag her suitcase up the steps of the medical school.

———

The lab's on the fourth floor. It would be impossible to find unless you knew it was there. There's no sign on the lift and the double doors that lead to it are unmarked. As with the operating theatres, this is a hidden place.

The first part of the room houses an extensive collection of pots. Among the torsos and limbs and brains floating in formalin, my eyes pick out a pot containing a uterus cut open to show a full-term fetus inside, another holding a head with a large tumour filling the eye socket, a third with a child's skull, the bone chipped away to show the adult teeth hiding in the jaw.

I'm briefly startled before an old protective curtain automatically falls and I can blank out that these were once people, real people, who lived with awful conditions and sometimes died too young.

A cupboard at the end of the hall has a small plaque saying *Phrenology Specimens* on the door. It has locks built in and a chain looped around the handles. I shudder to think what's kept in there, the chains to prevent justice, reparation, apology, and what it must have been like for Daniel, so proud of his Aboriginal ancestry, to study here every day.

Behind the next set of double doors, the air is rich with the heady sweetness of formalin. Rows of occupied blue and green body bags lie on metal gurneys with a hole at one end and a bucket underneath to drain the formalin and juices that escape with dissection.

'We've got table 32,' David says.

'Person 32.' I correct without thinking, Laura and my crusade to humanise our cadavers from medical school still instinctive.

I grab a few boxes of gloves from the front table. On the board, someone's drawn the sacral plexus, the entanglement of nerves that leave the lowest part of the spinal cord, and I pause, studying it.

'You'll need to know that for The Exam,' David calls, his voice echoing through the dim and empty room, empty even though there are thirty bodies here with us. 'It might feel years away but it sneaks up on you, Emma.'

Don't I know it. And if I fail like poor Andy, it'll sneak up a second time; though right now it seems less like it's sneaking up on him and more like it's hunting him down.

Kate finds a switch and a cold white glow lights up the space. There are no windows. The old window frames were boarded up a hundred years ago to hide this dark science from prying Christian eyes.

David grabs some gloves and enthusiastically unzips the bag containing person 32. Someone's left a portable X-ray machine and a few lead gowns next to the table. Why did David only call this morning when clearly this had been planned for some time? With more notice maybe I wouldn't be in such trouble with Shamsi. Then again maybe it's better he didn't have longer to complain.

'We'll use the right leg,' David says. Kate's opened her metal case and is pulling out a camera, microphones, a set of lights.

I check the tag on the left big toe: *Male, aged 82, acute myocardial infarction*, a life reduced to all the student of anatomy might want to know.

It takes a while for Kate and David to set up. He checks the light by taking photos with his phone while I sit on a stool, trying to use the time to relearn the anatomy of the sacral plexus.

At last we're ready to go. David unpacks the surgical instruments he's brought from theatre and reassures me that I won't have to say anything. He instructs me to hold the leg in certain ways while he makes an incision and prepares the bone for the implant. He's relaxed in front of the camera, and Kate stops him only a couple of times to rephrase or clarify certain steps. She produces a mock implant to put into the cadaver's ankle and we check it under the X-ray. Perfect, as usual.

By 10.30 we're done. What a relief, I'll be home even earlier than promised. Shamsi can't possibly be annoyed. Laura wasn't bringing the girls until eleven, so all he would've done this morning is drink coffee and check emails like he does every weekend.

As we walk back out through the specimen lab, David stops. 'Kate, why don't you go on? I might use the opportunity to grill Emma on some anatomy.'

Kate smiles thinly and waves goodbye. I freeze, stuck.

'Here, I brought croissants,' David says, opening the paper box and putting it on the wooden bench next to a grimacing head.

I help myself to a pastry and find a stool.

———

'Midday, you said,' Shamsi grumps at my arrival. The twins are in their pram, each holding a Vegemite sandwich. A box of toys is strewn over the floor and there's a puddle of spilt juice under the bench. 'We'll go out for lunch, you said.'

Shit.

David quizzed me on at least twenty pots, including parts of the anatomy I thought he might have long since forgotten, such as how the sacral plexus supplies the clitoris with sensation. Momentarily, I thought this was an odd choice but his rationale made sense. 'We put patients in traction and you need to know how to position it so you don't leave them sexually disabled,' he explained as we studied a female perineum. His family were at the beach this weekend so he was in no hurry to leave, and lunch with my husband and minding my nieces didn't seem an adequate excuse to turn down teaching.

'Sorry . . .' I sound whiny even to me. 'Shamsi, look, go for a run. Leave them with me for a bit.'

Shamsi rests both arms on the kitchen bench and frowns at me. 'Emma, I don't need a break from the kids. That's not why I'm cross. I just wanted to spend a whole day with you.'

I'm helplessly searching for the right words, the babies babbling beside me when the moment is broken by a ding from my phone.

David's sent me a photo I didn't know he took, of me writing notes in the low light of the specimen lab, a skeleton in the background and a pot of a hip joint in front of me.

Look at you.

I lose my train of thought; the apology I was going to make to Shamsi vanishing. Standing among the sticky juice and loud babies and my husband's expectations, I wonder if perhaps David's the one who understands the essence of who I really am, while Shamsi waits for my reply.

Chapter Twenty-one

It's the phone again.

'Hello, it's Emma,' I breathe, and roll back under the covers. The streetlamp casts long shadows across the room, and Shamsi stirs and rolls away from me. A man who can sleep through anything, maybe he was destined to marry a surgeon.

'Oh. Hello. Um. Sorry for waking you. How are you?' The voice on the line quavers.

Perhaps I'm dreaming and my phone never rang . . . I feel my eyes closing, but mumble, 'As good as I can be in the middle of the night.' I'm unsure if I'm cranky in my own head or out loud.

'Um. Oh. Sorry. I'm Maya. I'm, um, an intern in Emergency,' she squeaks.

Where's the intelligent part of my brain?

'Are you calling from Emergency at The Mount, or some country hospital?' I ask tersely, waking more with every word, trying to garner enough information to make sense of this call.

'Oh, at The Mount.'

The possum that's recently moved in scuttles across the roof, only increasing my annoyance. We've been meaning to call the possum catcher for weeks but there's never time. How is it possible I'm working longer and longer hours with every passing day?

In part this is because I'm trying to get David's paper done. It's been almost two months since he gave me his patients' scans and it's taken such a long time to measure up each one. I've fallen asleep at the computer so often, that maybe I should go home and get a decent sleep before trying again. Shamsi's promotion doesn't take effect until the end of the year and he's working as hard as ever too.

'Why are you calling me? What do you need?' I ask Maya-the-intern, hoping closed questions will let me get back to sleep faster.

'Oh! Yes. Um. Sorry. There's a patient with a fractured neck of femur. She needs to be admitted.' Why has Maya-the-intern woken me to tell me this? This is the sort of referral that can wait until the morning.

'Any other injuries?' A quiet anger is welling in my chest.

'No. Um. Sorry. She fell out of bed at her nursing home,' Maya explains. This is definitely not a reason to wake me.

'Maya.' She needs to know she's done the wrong thing, but I don't want to make her cry. I remember how that felt, sobbing in the toilets on the sixth night of a seven-night run as an intern in ED. 'Maya, I started being on call on Friday morning, and won't stop being on call or working until Monday evening. I need to sleep.'

Silence.

'Call me at 7.30 a.m., before the end of your shift. We're normally up and on our way in by then.' I wait for her apology, a necessary balm to allow me to go back to sleep. I'm proud I've kept my temper.

There's a long pause and then Maya-the-intern squeaks back at me. 'Oh! Um. Sorry. Thanks for the advice.'

I'm about to hang up, tuck my phone under my pillow and drift off, but Maya's still speaking.

'Except. Um. Sorry. Um. It *is* 7.30.'

Neurons start to fire, slowly, so slowly, until at last I understand what she's said. I take the phone away from my ear, hold the screen up to my face.

7.34 a.m.

Shit. I should already be awake.

Shit. I'm going to be late.

Shit. And then my mouth and brain sync.

'Shit.'

With nothing left to say I hang up.

I'm at work thirty minutes later after a spartan shower and a coffee that would raise the dead.

Maya's in the Fast Track part of Emergency gathering up her things. She looks as much like a mouse as she sounds, with small eyes and wiggling ears and a voice even squeakier in real life.

She jumps at my hello. I try to be generous in my apology and thank her for waiting until the morning to call me, and for getting me out of bed. She brightens and nods, more excited than there seems any reason to be, but then I remember how old and sage registrars once seemed to me.

'You were so nice. And you sounded so tired, I didn't want to tell you it was 7.30 a.m.,' she replies.

'I'm glad you did. Thank you for being brave enough to speak up to an irritable registrar,' I reply, hoping the positive reinforcement might help her confidence.

After quickly writing the admission paperwork for the patient with the broken hip, I grab another coffee and head to theatre. We get half a day set aside for us to mop up trauma cases on a Saturday morning, time uninterrupted by the vascular surgeons and their ruptured blood vessels, or the obstetricians with their urgent babies. It's precious time for both me and my boss—whoever that is—to get as many cases done as possible before the rest of the weekend descends into bun fights.

With a sinking heart I remember that Albert's the surgeon on call today. I'd much prefer it were David like two weekends ago, when we snuck off for lunch after knocking over the operating list as fast as we could. Over a glass of wine—which he shouldn't have insisted on, given we were both on call—he explained the manoeuvre that Steve and I hadn't understood from his diagram the day Paul wouldn't come in, and then we laughed over stories of his adventures as a registrar in a remote country hospital.

I'm happy that I slept in and managed to get here before remembering it's Albert today. Usually I complain so bitterly through my morning routine that Shamsi asks why I bother with surgery if I hate it so much.

'I don't hate surgery, I hate Albert.'

He doesn't believe me, and rattles off a long list of other people I've told him I hate—Steve, Paul, Brayden, Prof Bones, Brenda . . .

'Well, I don't hate them, but they do annoy me, and sometimes a lot.'

Shamsi doesn't understand why I'd use a word I don't mean. 'I'm a lawyer, Emma. I always talk in nuance and never in superlatives,' he warns. 'What will you do when you truly hate something? You'll have no words left.' In the change room, hunting for the correct size scrubs and pondering this question again, I realise I'm running late.

'Mmm, Emma. Nice to, mmm, see you,' Albert wheezes, the 'mmm' sounding more gaseous each time it's emitted. The first patient's already on the operating table. He waves away my apology. I should be grateful, Paul would already be cranky. I paint a smile on my face and bring up the first patient's X-rays.

'Mmm, what can you see here?' he asks, pointing at a very simple fracture. Daniel, the most junior on the unit, would be able to describe this. Nevertheless Albert's pleased with my answer. 'Aaah, very good,' he nods, his head bobbing up and down like a seagull trying to snatch chips on the beach, his beady wet eyes watching me closely.

'I, aaah, spent five years working around the, mmm, world,' he follows with no segue, leaving me confused. 'Have you, aaah, done any aid work?'

I shake my head, no.

'That is, mmm, best, I think,' he says to my surprise. Normally surgical aid trips are valorised, both trainees and surgeons coming home with photos of the dreadful pathology they heroically fixed to share over coffee. 'Aaah, best to only do it, mmm, when you can teach, not, aaah, when you're trying to learn. Your father, mmm, he was a good teacher.'

'My father?'

'Mmm. He set up many, aaah, services, no?'

I nod in agreement. Dad helped train surgeons in Vietnam, and also in Nepal, and later, the Pacific. He was usually away for two months a year.

'Those clinics, mmm, they are self-sufficient now. Aaah, what a gift,' Albert says. I wonder if he understands the sacrifices we all made for that gift, but then, I suppose those surgeons in Da Nang gave me a gift of sorts in return. Years later I understood what Dad was trying to show me with the trip was that there are different ways of doing things in medicine, but ironically it also set me on a pathway straight back to the narrow tradition-alism of The Mount.

'A good teacher but, aaah, was he a good father?' Albert wheezes.

I'm taken aback, unsure how to answer this question to his former colleague and my current boss. Dad was absent, blunt and exacting. He was infuriating but I never doubted that he loved us, or that he didn't have our best interests at heart.

How does this ledger sheet translate into a scale of goodness or badness? Maybe this is the best that can be hoped for from a doctor parent?

Albert's watery eyes are watching me. 'Mmm. You don't need to, aaah, answer that,' he says, finally realising that this was an overly intrusive question.

'What was he like when he worked here?' I ask in return.

Albert smiles thinly. 'He, aaah, did not suffer fools lightly, mmm?'

———

The operating list progresses well, and once again Albert shows what a good teacher *he* is. When the second last patient requires a spinal anaesthetic and Tom, the anaesthetic registrar, takes too long, he doesn't complain. Instead, he reassures Tom that this is a teaching hospital and that he has a right to learn. Tom's relieved, but that's because he won't have to come back later this evening and deal with the last case. I pout behind their backs.

The patient needs a metal rod inserted down the middle of their femur bone. Try as I might, I can't get the guide wire in straight. I'm still trying to figure out how the position of my hand on the drill translates to the angle the wire will go through the bone. After watching me struggle and fail for longer than anyone else would have, and with our allocated time to use the theatre running out, Albert puts his hands over mine and readjusts.

I shudder a little at his touch. It's not like working with David whose instructions fill me with electricity. The gowns are not magic enough today. Annoyingly, the wire goes in perfectly.

'What's the trick, Albert?' I ask him.

'Aaah, experience . . . and when everything lines up, I, mmm, hear a small bell.'

'A bell?'

'Mmm, no one ever understands the synesthete,' he mumbles.

We're kicked out of theatre at midday with one case left. I offer to manage it on my own as it isn't a difficult one, and usually, surgeons don't like to come in more than once, but Albert shakes his head.

'Mmm, all operations, even simple ones, are teaching cases and, aaah, it's my job to teach. Don't worry, Emma, even, mmm, normal people like you will become, mmm, excellent technicians. It's much harder to be a good doctor than a, aaah, good surgeon.' And with that he shuffles out the door.

I breathe a sigh of relief as he goes. I can't fault a single thing he's done and, yet, he's not my people. Not that I've found many within surgery who I'd consider 'my people', perhaps that list is limited just to David.

Chapter Twenty-two

Earlier, Brayden and I stood by the ambulance bay door peering at the sky to confirm it was going to be the worst night of the month. My non-medical friends don't believe me, but the full moon doesn't just prognosticate for witches, werewolves and biodynamic farmers. It also predicts for the humble registrar when their evening will go to shit.

I delivered a hot chocolate to the homeless woman tucked under the eaves, an offering to the mystical powers of gratitude to help us through the night. I realised that waving was no way to make friends, so now I take her cash and a hot drink when I can.

Everyone else has gone home, everyone except Brayden who's on a late shift. I'm still at The Mount too, waiting for an urgent transfer from the country. Strictly speaking we don't have a bed for this patient, but it sounds as if there's a bed shortage across the state. Many other hospitals have also declared ambulance bypass, an emergency status to prevent paramedics from bringing more patients to a hospital that can't take care of them safely. Bypass is a rolling crisis—always possible, but more frequent towards the end of winter as the flu season takes its toll. Paradoxically, the hospital will be fined, rather than better funded, for being too busy.

Even if The Mount has declared ambulance bypass, as a dedicated trauma hospital, sometimes we're forced to accept a patient who's been involved in a major accident. Somewhere, the nursing coordinator will find a nurse and create a bed from thin air.

At least Andy isn't on call tonight, because there wouldn't be a moment of rest for him in this heaving Emergency Department. Laura called me in frustration earlier. She's barely seen Andy in two weeks and was both cross and worried by his absence. The Exam's looming again and he's convinced that frantic revision will get him through this time. I've realised how lucky we are to have an office—most other registrars don't, so Andy's taken to studying in one of the on-call bedrooms off the residents' room. I told him he could use our office and I'd keep him company, but he prefers the silence.

To make his little room cheerier he's taken one of the peace lilies from the residents' room and slowly nursed it back to life. The others are dying through neglect and make the residents' room feel grim. I pointed this out at the last meeting of the Workplace Transformation Committee and Brenda suggested I water them, as if I'm not overworked trying to keep actual humans alive.

Tonight even Andy's gone home, but only because I made him.

I came to Emergency to see some patients and I've stayed to watch the chaos. Julia's called two code greys for aggression. She's argued for years that if The Mount provided better chairs in the waiting room and maybe some free tea and coffee, then patient combativeness might drop. Admin don't want to 'encourage' the homeless to seek refuge in the ED waiting room so, yet again, Julia's gone home with a bruise.

Now Brayden and I are in the Short Stay Unit—also full—having a chat. We're as friendly as I suspect anyone can be with Brayden. Today I helped him pop back a dislocated shoulder so Brayden's my friend. Tomorrow I'll ask him to keep a patient down here for longer than he wants and I'll become his enemy. As long as he's never stressed about meeting the arbitrary benchmarks set by the hospital, and you don't hold consistent behaviour as a prerequisite to being amicable, getting along with Brayden is pretty straightforward.

The Short Stay Unit is the overflow bin of the hospital. This part of Emergency is indistinguishable from the rest in colour, lighting and layout, but is administratively demarcated as a fine-free zone. Once parked here, patients are considered 'admitted' to the hospital and the clock stops on their admission-time targets. It's Brayden's spiritual refuge.

'So, who *are* the people in here?' I'm spinning around in my chair, bored. Brayden's engrossed in his Sudoku.

He points to the whiteboard above the desk. 'Bed 1 is here because of an allergic reaction to hair dye.'

A person of indeterminate age with a purple swollen head is indeed in bed 1, snoring away despite the bright glare of lights.

Brayden follows my gaze. 'She needs some steroids. She can go home tomorrow.'

'Was she trying to dye her hair purple?'

'No, brown. Why would you think purple?'

I smile on the inside.

'Bed 2 has an infection of her foot. Stepped on a thumbtack. Here for antibiotics. Beds 3 to 8 have pneumonia because of the flu. And there're no beds.'

'All of them?'

Brayden registers that I lost interest after the purple pumpkin and returns to his Sudoku.

I spin some more. 'Aren't you supposed to be working?' I needle at him.

He frowns. 'Aren't *you*?'

'No. Waiting for a transfer.'

'Well, I worked my guts out getting everyone in Short Stay stable so it's fine.'

I've crossed the line. Working in Emergency is relentless, and this is likely the only twenty-minute break he's had this month.

'Want a Coke?' I ask as a peace offering. It's a core part of what I call the three C diet—Coke, chips and chocolate—and if I'm to be here for a couple more hours, I need caffeinated sustenance.

'Actually, a Coke would be nice,' Brayden agrees.

———

I wander through the noise and commotion, the blipping of heartbeats and flickering incandescent lights, the crowd around the command bridge, and hit the button to open the doors back into the dinginess of the main hospital. They slide with a hiss as Nic rounds the corner at pace and nearly knocks me to the ground.

'Woah,' I catch her and myself, steadying us both by the shoulders.

She says hello distractedly, and then rushes for the door with a wave. Were her eyes wet?

'Hey, Nic, hey, are you okay?' I jog to catch up. 'Hey, stop.'

She does, but only briefly. 'Um, yes, fine . . .' she replies, and starts walking, her eyes averted. 'Sorry!' she tosses over her shoulder.

'Nic!'

She stops again.

'I'm gonna grab a Coke. You want one?' I offer.

The doors open again, flooding the dark corridor with the overwhelming light and sound from Emergency.

A burly security guard barrels past. 'Good one, doc!' he calls out and bounds up the nearby stairs two at a time.

Nic watches him with a shudder.

I grab her by the elbow. 'Come on, vending machine.'

The closest machine is in the main hospital foyer. 'What are *you* doing here so late?' I ask, as she falls into step beside me.

'Waiting on a transfer, mostly,' she says.

Ah. We must be waiting for the same patient. Sometimes, if the extent of the injury is unclear, multiple units get put on standby. All I know so far is that the patient has a major limb trauma.

At the machine Nic pulls out her credit card first. 'How many am I getting?' she asks. The first bottle falls to the bottom with a hollow thump. I offer to pay but she's an automaton, tapping her card and numbers as Coke bottles fall one after another.

She opens hers, sinks onto the bench next to the machine, and leans against the wall. Taking a deep swig she closes her eyes. On the noticeboard above her head are flyers for the International Nurses Day afternoon tea, ads for share houses and second-hand cars, and the lecture schedule for the 'Workplace Transformation' program. I see with irritation that my name is on it, along with the other committee members, as if I've somehow contributed to this program, as if I even condone it. I'd better tell Daphne. She'll be furious.

Nic cuts a lonely figure in the shadows. Eventually she opens her eyes. 'Thanks for the suggestion,' she sighs.

'Hey, what happened back there? You look really upset.'

'Oh, I got conned by the emergency doctor,' Nic replies angrily.

That's a new one. I nod, encouraging her to go on, ignoring the pin on the noticeboard that's digging into the back of my scalp.

'We have a patient named Ella. She self-harms,' Nic starts. 'She's come in nine times this year having cut herself. She's only nine-teen and homeless. It's so sad.' Nic takes another slug of Coke and rests her head against a flyer advertising Spanish language classes.

'Her fingers don't move terribly well anymore. She's had her tendons and arteries repaired that many times everything's encased in scar tissue.'

'Why does she do it?' We barely covered mental health in medical school.

'Dunno. The psychs reckon it isn't suicidal behaviour so won't admit her. She doesn't seem to get much support outside of hospital either. So we sew her up and send her away and she's back a couple of weeks later.'

Nic stares up at the ceiling where a single light flickers, irregularly regular or maybe it's regularly irregular. Another term I failed to learn.

'Hospital admin have decided she doesn't deserve an anaesthetic to be sutured up anymore,' she continues, her voice halting.

'Doesn't . . . deserve an anaesthetic?'

Nic nods. 'Yeah, it's not like we're fixing anything, we're only closing the skin over this mass of scar. So someone, somewhere, decided we could patch her up in Emergency rather than admit her and take her to theatre. Waste of healthcare dollars or some such rubbish.'

I turn sideways on the bench to look her in the eyes. She can't possibly be telling me that someone's decided to pinch pennies on the care of a fragile nineteen-year-old woman? Nic registers the shock on my face and shakes her head, more blonde hair escaping out of her bun.

'No, no, it's mostly okay. I've done it before with Julia. She gives her plenty of sedative drugs so Ella has no idea what's going on, and then some local anaesthetic and sutures and she's ready to go. It's fine. No different from you pulling a broken bone straight and plastering it. But it wasn't Julia tonight, it was Peter, Peter Fordham, the arsehole . . .'

She hunches forward, her arms on her knees, burying her face in her hands, the forgotten Coke bottle beside her.

'He said he'd sedate her so we got everything ready. He draws up some drugs and calls a bunch of security guards in. He tells me that it's not a long cut and not to use the local anaesthetic first, that if I staple the wound quickly it won't hurt her.

'I shouldn't have listened to him, Emma, but the local *does* sting and maybe he's right, I can do it quickly while he's got her bombed. So I put the first staple in . . . and she howled in pain.'

'Sounds like he's bad at sedation. Did he give her more?'

At this, Nic starts to cry. Softly, unintentionally, the tears spill over, catching her by surprise. We scramble for something to wipe them away. Nic, in her scrubs, doesn't even have a sleeve and resorts to the back of her hand. The tears smear across her face, colouring her cheek with a streak of black mascara.

'No, Emma, that's the thing.' Her voice drops to a hiccoughed whisper. 'I stopped and told him that she needed more drugs, that I needed a second for some local anaesthetic because this wasn't working, and he starts yelling to keep going. The guards are holding her down and they join in. There are six people in the room, all men, all yelling at me to keep going. And they're pinning her down while she's wriggling and crying and I'm confused. Maybe if I do what they say they'll release her and stop yelling at me . . . so I . . . I keep going.'

I'm speechless, horrified.

'I put twenty-five staples in her arm, Emma, and she wailed with each one.'

The tears fall easily from her eyes now. She catches them and wipes them away on her scrubs pants, little paint strokes of Nars Oslo over her knee. Feathers of MAC Ruby Woo bleed from her lips.

'He told me after that it was deliberate, Em. To dissuade her from doing it again. And you heard the guard, whooping and carrying on, full of praise for me, for what I did.'

I give Nic a hug. I want to be angry at her, but what would I have done? I'm hardly beyond reproach. Every time someone asks if I've done a procedure before I say 'yes', even when the answer is 'no'. So often I promise it won't hurt even though I know it will. Can I be so sure that I've never crossed the line between 'necessary' and 'torture' to judge Nic now?

———

At 1.12 a.m., the patient from the country arrives with only a three-centimetre bridge of skin holding his leg to the rest of him. He'll be better off with an amputation than a withered reattached leg that doesn't work. Nic accepts his care and trudges off to theatre to get things going.

I'm leaving the Emergency Department past bay 10 when I'm stopped by the small waif of a girl occupying it. Her left forearm is padded thick with dressings and she has bruises to her upper arm. I pause, caught off guard, and she turns her big eyes to me, pleading for something.

'Are you okay?' I ask.

She looks away before answering. 'They took my last bra, nurse,' she replies, and for once I don't correct my title.

'What do you mean?'

'I only have one bra, miss, and they cut it off. To have a look at all of me, they said. I begged them not to cut it because I haven't got money for another. How can I leave hospital without a bra?' she asks, crossing her arms over her chest.

The bat phone is ringing, the insistent sound jangling across the department as I escape out the ambulance doors into the winter night. Somewhere, another team of paramedics has scooped and run and someone else will be brought in clinging to life. Even though we're full, we'll take care of them too.

Pausing in the yellow light, I text Nic.

> Take her a bra.

What?

> Ella, your patient. They cut off her bra and she needs one. It won't make up for what's happened but take her a bra and at least she'll be discharged with dignity.

Thank you, Em.

Under the eaves, the ancient woman raises her hand in a wave.

Chapter Twenty-three

'This is bullshit,' Daphne snorts as we wait for the lift after the latest meeting of the Workplace Transformation Committee.

'I think they're excellent interventions,' Olga replies loudly, as Prof Brown and Brenda walk past.

Daphne glares at her. 'Olga, you're only here for a year. You don't have to be so obsequious.'

'I'm not! At least they're offering us healthy food when I'm stuck here in the middle of the night, hours which *you* never have to do anymore.'

'Oh, don't let them fool you into thinking that bananas and oranges are enough!'

It's a relief when the lift arrives. It's too small for everyone. I grab Daphne's arm and hold her back, letting the others get in. The committee's unpleasant enough without us turning on each other.

'Sellout,' Daphne says to me after the doors close again.

I try not to show my frustration. Daphne is such an idealist. Maybe fruit isn't enough, but even with her best efforts, all we've achieved as a committee is getting our names on things we never approved of.

'I'm ordering pizza for dinner,' I say, changing the topic. 'Shamsi's away for work this weekend so I'm going to drink wine in the shower and eat pizza in bed.'

Daphne laughs, her mood as quickly changeable to good as bad. 'Wine in the shower?' she asks.

'Who has time to draw a bath?' I don't confess that every evening I'm not on call I go straight to the bathroom with a glass of wine and hide under the warm water, emerging to face Shamsi and the world only after making myself a bit numb.

The lift doors close, and as we lurch towards the ground, Daphne stares at a flyer for the Workplace Transformation lecture series that's been pinned to the lift wall. She points to one, *Finding a place of peace*, to be given next week by a nephrologist. 'You doing anything tomorrow?' she asks.

I shake my head no, curious, the link to the lecture unclear.

'Come pick me up. Sometime around ten? My car's getting serviced this weekend, so you'll have to drive,' she tells me, not a request.

'Where are we going? I was planning to . . .' Who am I kidding? I had no plans, apart from to check in on Andy.

'You'll see,' Daphne says mysteriously, and texts me her address. The lift doors open on the ground floor. 'At 10 a.m., be there or be square.' She pokes me in the shoulder and marches off.

————

The next morning, I park in front of a small block of identical units on a quiet suburban street, unsure what force Daphne has used to pull me from bed, make me shower, dress and leave the house. Perhaps it's curiosity, perhaps it's because there was kindness in her demand, kindness which I hear so rarely anymore.

Daphne appears at the door wearing jeans and a raincoat, so different from her usual clothes. I glance at my own spring outfit of blue dress and red leather Mary Janes with worry. What's she got planned?

She throws a bag into the boot of my car and settles into the passenger seat, unplugs my phone and plugs her own in.

'You're dressed fine,' she says, reading my thoughts, before adding, 'I control the music.'

'Daphne!' My protest falls on deaf ears.

'Pop music, female artists, songs in major keys only,' she replies, and opens my sunroof, turns up the volume and smiles. There's no point arguing.

Flicking between her music and a map, Daphne guides me onto the freeway. The city roads give way to the outer suburbs and then we're in the country, past roadside stands of regional fruit, a brewery, wide open pastures. The hills are dotted with vineyards and then we're heading into the mountains, the tree ferns, flowering gums, myrtle and tall mountain ash encroaching on the road. We slip over the river, here small and babbling, and suddenly, a swarm of motorcycles roars around. Daphne opens her window and pumps her fist as the low thrum accelerates past.

She directs me off the main road, onto dirt and gravel.

'Where are we going?' I ask, but after an hour in the country-side she knows my blood is up for this drive.

'There's hardly anyone who lives along here, you can gun it,' she says.

Without quite understanding why, I do. We race like a rally car, over bends and around inclines and depressions, the blue mountains flickering in and out of view between the gum trees. The dust's been stirred by another car before us and the sparkles of filtered light reflect off the hanging particles, a shimmering veil that never ends.

'We might die today,' I laugh. Gum trees are unyielding, not like the flimsy wood of other continents which splinter and give way. Here, cars, and bodies, wrap themselves around the road-edge trees, no crumple zone ever enough. Here, people pass too infrequently for help to be reliable.

We're soon out of the forest again, screaming along rural roads and pastures dotted with lambs until the walls and buildings of another township are upon us.

'Pull in here,' she points at a former petrol station now converted to a bakery. 'C'mon!'

We join a line with a dozen cyclists in jewel-coloured lycra. Pies and coffee are handed over and then we're back in the car, heading into the mountains again. On the other side of a small single lane bridge she directs me to stop the car.

'Where are we?' I ask, studying the National Park sign.

'Ignore the sign, come with me,' she says and leads me across a field, where families picnic under a giant oak, and into a copse of trees that almost block out the sun. They've been planted like a chessboard, like the columns of an ancient temple. Between the trees there are flashes of children running, bursts of children whooping, like a stop motion film played too slow. The regularity of the trees has been interrupted, charmingly, by giant nests made of fallen sticks and branches, where a few more children hatch imaginary dragons' eggs in the dim light.

'These are Californian redwoods,' Daphne explains, a rapturous expression on her face. 'Someone planted them for logging but long before they were mature enough to cut down, they were forgotten.'

We walk into the middle of the forest where she pulls a picnic rug out of her bag and lays it on the ground. There's so little light that there are no low plants, no grass, but the forest floor is soft with soil and brushy leaves. Hundreds of trees fan out in every direction, lining up in straight aisles or as perfect triangles, depending on where you look. Never have I known nature to so perfectly obey the intent of the designer.

'Ready or not, here I come!' rings out across the still air, the trees a barrier to wind and light and sound.

'These don't seem big enough for redwoods?'

Daphne smiles and unpacks our lunch. 'Em, they're only a hundred years old. We won't live to see them fully grown. Isn't that crazy?'

She opens the bakery box and places it between us, then plucks a bottle of wine from her bag.

'Why, Daphne? Why all this?' I ask as she pours me a glass.

I can feel her watching me, but she doesn't reply straight away, and when she does, she's quiet, so quiet that in the city, in the hospital, she might not be heard. It's only here where the surrounding noise floats away on the breeze that these words could exist.

'Because you aren't okay, Em. Because I can see you're starting to struggle. And listening to a lecture about finding a place of peace is useless. You have to *actually* find one.'

I'm offended. I take a bite of my pie, sauce dribbling on my chin which annoys me more. 'What makes you say that? I'm fine,' I tell her.

Daphne shakes her head. 'I've been around a while. I can see the cracks. The tiredness in your eyes. How short you are on the phone.' She pauses, leaving me an empty space to fill with my own words.

I refuse. Training is what it is, and what would she know anyway. Physician trainees don't work as hard as surgical trainees.

'Em, it's okay,' she continues. 'Lots of us struggle. I've struggled. We just don't talk about it. We aren't supposed to talk about it.'

'There are lots who don't struggle,' I sulk, thinking about Paul, about David.

Daphne rubs the pastry from her fingers, tries to shoo the crumbs from her jeans. 'You can't listen to *them* for advice,' she says. 'They're the survivors, the ones who made it. Because they've made it, they think anyone can make it, simply by doing the things they did. They'll tell us it's easy and they'll tell us we're failing, all in the same breath.'

I nod, though I don't entirely agree. David conceded that he'd borne some costs, that he was trying to change things and make it better for us. Now, on reflection, I'm not sure what he's actually *done* but I push this sudden uncertainty away. Daphne's still talking.

'Also, you aren't them. You might not want to do it how they did, or even be able to. You might have a chronic illness, have people to care for, be more empathetic and therefore more prone to moral injury and burnout. And even people who've faced these challenges, their solutions might not work for you. Lectures aren't the solution. They might give you the words to understand, but that's only the very *very* start.'

'Fine. How did *you* do it?'

'Badly,' she says with a smile. 'I came so close to leaving.'

'What stopped you?'

'Here,' she says and closes her eyes with a smile. 'You know why I love this place? If you think about it, it's fake, artificial, rigid. And yet, look at those trees! And this forest, it's dark, almost oppressive, but there's *always* a clear way out, a way to run, a straight path to the light. When it gets too much, I imagine that I'm here.'

Now she's making no sense. I must look as confused as I feel.

'I don't think we have the capacity to process everything all the time,' she explains a little impatiently. 'The work we do pushes us on, relentlessly. You only have space to think about what happened three days ago in the middle of something else that's happening right now. For me, I needed to find a place I could come, either in real life or in my mind. Somewhere I could think clearly and honestly, to regroup before I face it all again. It might work for you, it might not. I thought I'd bring you here in case it helps. Maybe it will be as useless as Prof Brown's lectures. If nothing else, a day in the real forest is better than a room with dead pot plants.' She picks up her wine glass, stands and walks off with a nod.

Here. What am I supposed to do with that? I lie down on the rug and try to visualise my problems, but the trees are too oppressive, whether they're trees or representations of my issues. I don't think I can stare at them directly. I close my eyes.

I'm on a river and around me, people are pulling my little boat in different directions. There's Shamsi with children and David being brilliant, there's Dad in Da Nang and Mum blissfully painting and the Shit Hospitals and The Mount and London.

Then in my meditative dream I see an island and know it has a secret port where the waters are still. And if I dock, there's a hidden door which leads me down a flight of rocky stairs to a cave overlooking a calm sea and a pink sky in a magical otherworld. And in that cave, there's a fire and a bed and I can sleep because no one can get to me.

And maybe I should be staring things down. Maybe the cave is one of indecision and avoidance and won't solve any problems, but for now it feels safe. Like the lectures, perhaps this is the first step.

Chapter Twenty-four

Steve's away for two weeks. As usual, and despite the committee's best efforts to advocate for better staffing, there's no locum to replace him. I'm working two weeks straight on call, as well as covering all the clinics and operating lists. The plan to reduce the number of patients booked hasn't translated into practice.

The exhaustion of being on call night after night is balanced by the relief of not having to see Steve. We've settled into a slightly acrimonious but otherwise professional relationship, our dislike for each other offset by the realisation that if we don't at least appear to work as a registrar team then we'll both be punished for it.

Andy's exam is now only a few weeks away. I'd promised to help him revise but I've had to cancel again, and again.

Daniel spent the day working on this week's audit. It's late Tuesday night and I'm with him in the office checking it. Normally, Steve takes care of this.

'So, we have that lady who got an infection, and . . .' I turn a few more pages and show Daniel another sticker. 'This guy, whose surgical wound fell apart and he needed to be sent to the plastic surgery team. Oh, and this lady with post-operative pneumonia, and . . .' I turn to the last page. 'This guy. We readmitted him under the haematologists for a blood clot last night.'

Daniel's sceptical. Apparently, Steve doesn't make him put in these 'minor complications'. I'd noticed that they weren't presented, but had assumed they were recorded somewhere.

'Audits are important, Daniel!' I scold him.

He's not convinced but makes extra slides anyway.

I survive the Grand Round despite being in the hot seat. Prof Bones's questions are reasonable, and David eggs me on with discreet shakes of his head and thumbs-up signs while Paul sneers.

When we get to the meeting room and the lights are turned down, Prof is less impressed.

'Why are there so many complications, Emma?' he asks, as the audit drags on. 'That blood clot? Did that patient get blood thinners appropriately? It's the first one we've had this year.' It's not, I know of at least two others. Blood clots in legs are part and parcel of long bone fractures in a major trauma unit.

Daniel, bless him, has already pulled up the drug chart from the patient's admission, showing that the correct blood thinners were ordered, administered, and provided at discharge. Prof squints at the screen and is forced to acknowledge that there's nothing to blame us for. He grumbles through the rest of the audit, and all the way out of the room.

I'm lingering behind and tallying up my scorecard when David reappears.

'There *were* more complications than usual, Emma,' David says.

'Not true. We've had stacks of minor infections and blood clots and wound breakdowns—they just haven't been presented,' I argue, feeling like I can justify myself to him at least.

He smiles like he's taking pity on me and checks how far off the other surgeons are before dropping his voice low. 'Emma, let me give you some advice. The purpose of the audit is to record *major* complications. The smaller stuff? Bring them back to your registrar clinic on a Friday when none of us are around and manage them quietly.'

I turn this over. I like David, I *really* like David, but it sounds like he's telling me to leave most of the complications off the audit of complications.

He watches me carefully and sighs at my silence. Putting his hands on both of my shoulders, he crouches down slightly so we're eye level, as if I were an angry lover or an errant child.

'Em, I'm going to be blunt because I have your best interests at heart. The audit you present reflects your performance as a registrar, and there's no point killing yourself over it. We know that we provide world-class care here. The audit has to reflect the results we already know we have. Those minor things . . . The rest of us got through surgical training without putting them up and the patients were fine. There's no learning to be had from that stuff. When you're in charge of the audit, do what everyone does and give us one that doesn't make Bones look up from his phone.' He gives my shoulders another squeeze and keeps watching me until I nod my head.

'Good girl, chin up. Well done today.'

———

I'm hiding in a closed room in clinic. The colorectal clinic is next door and someone's called a 'code brown' for some faeces-related disaster. I'm in no hurry to venture outside. Besides, with Steve away, I'll have to leave before all the patients are seen, no matter how hard I work. What's another five minutes if Will and Daniel will have to finish on their own anyway. Maybe this is why the surgeons just piss off. It's like we're trying to empty an ocean with a teaspoon and they're resigned to self-preservation in the face of inevitable failure.

There are few places to hide in a hospital and too much time in a toilet inevitably brings questions about the state of one's bowels. No one saw the last patient leave so I'm enjoying my stolen moments staring at a wall. My quiet is interrupted by a knock, followed immediately by Prof Bones barging in.

'Hi, Prof. I'm finishing up my notes. What can I help you with?' I ask airily, typing away at the computer as if this is what I was doing all along.

'Hmph. Hurry up. Will needs one of us to see that woman with the femur sarcoma.' He walks out, leaving the door open. The code brown scent wafts in.

I log out of the computer and venture into the hallway, assuming that when he says 'one of us' he means me.

Anka, the plaster nurse, points me to one of the other rooms.

Jacqui's sitting in bed, a wheelchair beside her. She beams when I walk in and raises her skirt to show me a well-healed scar on her thigh. Her kids are well, but she can't get around the farm in the wheelchair. She spends her days in quiet frustration, watching from the verandah that surrounds the old house on a hill, waiting until she can be out on her horse again. Her mother-in-law is back helping with farm duties.

'We *are* farmers in this sunburnt country,' she says as if that is explanation enough, and in fact it is. Dad left my grandparents' sheep farm for boarding school and never returned to the back-breaking work his brother took on, but I spent enough time with my cousins to understand a little of what she means.

Jacqui's had a new X-ray. I enlarge it so it fills the computer screen and search for the little trabeculae of bone, filaments sprouting and bridging across the gaps. After a long silence, I'm satisfied.

'Jacqui! By some miracle, the bone is healing!' It'll still be some time before she can bear weight on her leg, but now we've crossed this first hurdle, maybe she can get up on crutches at least.

'Miracle?' Jacqui doesn't share my enthusiasm.

'Oh, well, we irradiated you, and then irradiated the bone separately. We gave those cells a real run for their money. It's great to see that they've survived,' I explain, sure that we warned her of the risks.

'I didn't know that the bone might not heal,' Jacqui says with a frown, fixated on the possible complication that didn't happen and missing my excitement.

She's even less enthusiastic about crutches. Strange. At least *I'll* go home satisfied.

'Let's see you in another few months with a CT scan, and then we might get you walking on it.' Jacqui nods, taking the appointment slip. She's halfway out the door when she stops, and looks back, unable to swivel the wheelchair in the narrow doorway.

'Oh, one last question. I have this funny lump in my groin. That's nothing to worry about, is it?'

I freeze, glad not to be facing her directly. Pushing the heavy feeling away, I try to colour my next words with nonchalance. I ask her to come back in and close the door, let her lift her skirt, shift her underwear to one side to reveal a mass which I don't need to palpate, but do anyway, as a show of an uncertainty I don't feel.

'Well, who knows what it is?' I declare, as if we're talking about a chocolate in a box of samplers, a mystery present at the ward Kris Kringle. 'Given you live so far away, why don't we get a quick CT before you head home?'

Jacqui, however, is keen to get going.

I control my panic and press her gently. *This* is important, even if she can't be told why, not yet. 'Jacqui, you're here now and we like to tick boxes, okay?' My words are smooth, slick.

At last she agrees, but only if it won't take too long. Most of our patients expect to get a CT or an MRI scan immediately and are often disappointed that it might take days or weeks. They don't understand that an urgent scan is not the preferential treatment anybody wants.

I leave her in the room, and grab a referral slip for the CT on my way to finding Will. Thrusting the paper at him, scrawled with my notes, I ask him to run it around to radiology. He shakes his head at me. He has to order it on the computer, and they'll triage it in their own time.

'No!' I protest loudly. Even if my tone and begging doesn't convince him, the words on the paper do. He folds it in half and disappears down the hall.

No longer noticing the code brown smell, I find a phone and ask for the radiologist taking referrals today.

A gruff voice answers, without introduction or pleasantry. I've come to learn that it means the person is already beyond capacity and knows they're about to be asked to do something more. Given everyone in the health system is always overworked, this is the way most people answer the phone—the way I swore I never would. I hope those calling me understand that it's not personal.

I explain to the radiologist that there's a young patient from forever away with an aggressive cancer that has surely spread, at least to her lymph nodes and perhaps much further. I spit out the tragedy in one breath, and on the other end there's clicking on a keyboard and a shuffling of papers.

'Okay, send it on a paper slip because the e-referral won't come through fast enough,' he says and hangs up. I'm glad I sent Will. Behind me, through an open door, the waiting room is still half full, but I sit until my heart hurts a bit less.

———

Please call radiology 4242 is the message on my pager, and even though I'm in the lobby of the hospital, on my way to theatre, I call back immediately. The same gruff voice answers and identifies itself by name. Dr MacQuaid is looking for the orthopaedic registrar who referred Jacqui Miller for an urgent CT.

'Confirming the diagnosis of metastatic disease. Large node in the groin. Also, metastatic deposits in her liver and lung. I've compared it with her imaging from the start of the year, and they're all definitely new.' Dr MacQuaid is short and clinical, to the point.

I take a deep breath, in anticipation of speaking, but the breath escapes as a sigh while I search for the right expressions.

Dr MacQuaid, who I've never met or even spoken to before, unexpectedly fills my silence. 'I missed your name,' he says softly, a statement not a question, but inviting a reply.

'Um, Emma,' I tell him, wondering why this is relevant. Maybe he needs to record who he gave his verbal report to.

'Emma, I know people think radiologists aren't real doctors. Did you know that I've diagnosed more primary tumours and metastatic disease than any oncologist or surgeon?' he asks gently. 'I don't know her like you, but it says on my screen that she's only twenty-nine, and isn't currently pregnant but has two children, and lives a long way from even a rural town. And her scan shows cancer spreading through her body. I can see those growing lesions and I know, more than anyone else in this hospital, what they are. And that this cancer will kill her.'

The phone is hard against my ear. Those last words are the very ones we try hardest to avoid saying out loud. Instead, we send each other diagnoses, reports, scans—coded messages that only other clinicians can understand so that we never have to say those words.

Dr MacQuaid sighs in a sad way. 'I'm sorry you have to be the one to tell her. Rest assured, though, that you aren't the only doctor in this hospital full of sorrow.'

I feel the tears welling up, and I thank him for his caring.

'If you want to debrief afterwards, I'm here until five. Come and find me.'

It doesn't seem fair to hold this knowledge. Surely it would be right and just for patients to be the first to learn of their own impending mortality, to share that realisation with others if and when they choose, rather than have it filter to them like a rumour, passed between people who don't know them, who don't love them.

Patients and other medical staff walk past averting their gaze, and I realise I'm still standing in the lobby, my face streaked with tears. My hair hasn't been washed in a week and is falling out of a scraggly bun, my shoes are scuffed because I haven't had time to polish or repair them.

Shit.

I wipe my face, the running mascara darkening my fingers, and search for refuge. A small sign, one I've never seen before, catches my eye.

The hospital chapel is empty, the seats clean and bare. Long ago built for prayer to a Christian god, more symbolism has been added so anyone can seek comfort and silence here. The camera on my phone is close enough to a mirror. I use it to wipe the wetness from my face, still guilty that Dr MacQuaid and I are the only ones who know Jacqui's truth. My face clean, I pause. Even though the busy hospital lobby is close outside, here, among the glinting colours of the stained-glass window that tint the air pink, there is unexpected quiet. I take another minute to clear the lump from my throat and catch my breath. But medicine always find a way to intrude. My pager shatters the peace with my next task: *Patient Jacqui Miller in waiting room ward 6E please review with test results.*

————

Will goes to help Paul in theatre. I don't care if either of them is unhappy about it. Next, I call Prof Bones, a necessary conversation to understand and communicate a plan. It feels like another betrayal. He's brisk: she needs to see the general surgeons so they can remove the bulk of the tumour in her groin, and I'm to present her scans at the multidisciplinary meeting with oncology to discuss her next options. But these actions only delay the inevitable, buy her some time so her children might remember her living face. However hard we try, from this point on, we cannot stop this death.

I call switchboard, hoping Andy isn't on call for general surgery and am disappointed that he is. I didn't want to burden him with this, not so close to his next attempt at The Exam. But the tasks that land in our laps when we're on call aren't of our choosing, and always come before everything else.

Andy meets me outside the ward, hands in his pockets, satchel over his shoulder, his hair hanging in his eyes. He seems pale, but perhaps that's the effect of the white overcoat he's thrown over his scrubs. We stand in silence, before he nods in that way doctors universally nod to say, *'It's time.'*

Jacqui's by the window in the small waiting room. It's more a hallway than a room, simply a place the ward clerk can offer someone a momentary seat. It's not meant for news like this.

She waves without turning as our reflections appear in the window then spins her chair around with a smile. On seeing both of us, her words and expression falter, her eyes flicker expectantly. She must know a new face is never good.

'Jacqui, we might go to a room,' I suggest.

Her smile halts, her eyes drop, her hands go limp on the wheels of her chair. 'It's cancer again, isn't it?' she asks softly.

Even though they taught us in medical school to break bad news in a quiet room with a box of tissues and a support person handy, I've since learned that these props are rarely around when you most need them. The ward clerk's desk is vacant, the small office behind it empty. It's tiny, but it will do. Jacqui's torment does not need to be prolonged as we search for a better room, as if interior design could make a difference.

Jacqui tries but can't push her wheelchair so I push it for her, and once we've manoeuvred her in, I'm almost overcome. So Andy gets down on his knees and holds her hands, introduces himself, and speaks more gently than I've ever heard him talk before.

And this is how, in a cupboard among the fax machine and photocopier and cardboard boxes full of ink and paper, we tell Jacqui that she'll never have another baby, or see her children grow up.

Chapter Twenty-five

Cheryl, wonderful warm-hearted has-seen-everything Cheryl, finds Jacqui a bed. Her outpatient clinic appointment has turned into an admission; she won't be going back to the farm just yet. Someone will buy her a toothbrush and overpriced underwear from the hospital pharmacy and she'll cope because she has no choice.

We watch her go. Andy puts his arm around my shoulder, an intimacy I'm thankful for. An observer who didn't know we were siblings would find it odd, we don't often touch each other to offer comfort.

'It's okay, Emma. These are the shitty moments of our careers,' he says.

I'm both guilty and glad he was there to share this one.

By the time she dies, maybe a year from now, she'll be under the care of other doctors, an oncologist, a palliative care physician if she's lucky. I'll have moved to another hospital, with some other Prof Bones and some other selection of vending machines from which most of my meals come these days.

The Workforce Transformation Committee, still with our names on it, has started to install 'healthy food' machines in parts of the hospital. Soup, cheese and crackers, protein bars are on offer, slowly replacing the junk food dispensers, one by one. Daphne and I inspected one of these new machines the day it was wheeled in and filled. We never approved of such misplaced moralising, as if eating chips to ease the pain of delivering bad news or scoffing a cookie to keep going in the middle of the night were sins to be washed clean with minestrone soup.

Daphne is perfectly happy with her kummerspeck while I'm equally happy to fade away to nothing. Besides, we'd still prefer to go home at a normal hour and cook dinner with our family than exchange a chocolate bar for a protein bar. But vending machines are cheaper than adequate staffing and so here we are.

I buy a packet of potato chips, grateful that they haven't yet swapped all the vending machines.

Andy shakes his head at me.

'What?' I'm a ten-year-old child whining at my teenage brother again, and before I know it, I've stuck my tongue out at him.

He laughs, a sound that echoes around the stairwell, incongruous because Jacqui's still dying. 'Don't try to survive surgical training on that,' he warns me, pushing his stubborn hair out of his eyes. 'Those new machines are good.'

'You don't eat out of them, do you?' I ask, cramming a fistful of chips in my mouth, and crunching loudly. Andy pulls a Tupperware container out of his bag and shows me a meal clearly made by Laura's mother. It's disappointingly full of fibre and vitamins. I offer him a chip.

He laughs and takes one.

'How're things at home?' I ask, buying another packet. The weight of predicting death is greater than nineteen grams of fat and salt split between us. He'll need one of his own.

'It's hard. No privacy, no space at home. Dad's offered to help, pay for nannies so Laura's parents can go home. But she wants their support because I'm so useless. We'll get through it. Everyone does, don't they?'

I think about the forest and how much better it would be for Andy than his pot plant, but there's no hope of getting him there, not when he thinks his salvation lies in journal articles and anatomy textbooks. I hope he's right and it's not that we're both innately made to fail like Dad said.

I toss him the second packet of chips. I need to get to theatre where Paul will be raging. 'Hey, look out for yourself, okay? And thanks for explaining stuff to my patient.'

'We're a team, and now she's my patient too.' He stows the Tupperware and chips in his bag, and shoulders hunched, hands back in his pockets, we part ways.

———

Paul is, as expected, grumpy. I understand why, but *I'm* exasperated because his reasons are narcissistic and unreasonable, like Jon's expectations on my first day. At least he operates fast and leaves. No matter that he doesn't teach me anything, today I'd prefer him gone. So, at 4.45 p.m., Will and I are at the desk in an empty theatre, ensuring we've completed our tasks for the day, when both of our pagers beep at the same time.

We glance at each other warily. Simultaneous pages often mean that the hospital is calling a code of something. Code purple is a bomb threat, code yellow is an internal emergency, usually the computer network failing. Code brown is the universal indicator for deep shit of literal or metaphoric form.

'All medical staff not engaged in critical activities please attend main meeting room 2-SE in ten minutes.'

Hmm. This is curious. There's no recognised code, or precedent, for every available doctor to attend admin's lair.

My phone dings immediately with messages on the group chat. Vikram says:

> Prof Brown texted me to say I had better come, because she's running it.

Then Daphne asks:

> Running what?

Vikram replies:

> Some meeting. The blokes have been invited so at least
> they aren't gathering the women to ask you not to report
> sexual harassment like they did last year.

Daphne says:

> It'll be some stupid thing the dictators on the so-called
> committee have come up with.

Just what I didn't need, right at the end of the day. I curse
Daphne for dragging me into this, as if there was any use in
being a Swann. It seems my name's merely added authority to
their dumb ideas.

The room's half full when we arrive. Andy waves from the
third row. It's much too close to the front for my liking, but
Daphne and Vikram are there too. Will and I slide in next to
them. Nic waves from the back.

'Why are we here?' 'Does anyone know what this is about?'
'Are we going to get paid for staying after hours?'

There are almost as many people as at orientation. Prof Brown
walks in wearing a dress that Daphne would be proud of, yellow
and blue geometric patterns and a turquoise pendant.

Brenda follows, her hair bigger and her lips redder than I
remember, carrying an ancient portable CD player. She crouches
under the lectern and plugs it in.

'Welcome, welcome,' Prof Brown says as Brenda wriggles
back out, stands and inserts a CD. The front row crane their

necks to see the case. She hits play and the unexpected sound of whales fills the room. Prof Brown winces, before straightening the expression on her face. There are giggles and exclamations of surprise from the crowd.

'We're aware,' she starts, coughing slightly on the words, 'that doctor burnout is very real and must be addressed.' Behind her, a humpback lows.

She talks about the Workforce Transformation Committee— the excellent lecture series, the pot plants in the residents' room, the rotting apples in my office. I catch Andy's eye and decide not to put my hand up to tell her that, apart from Andy's peace lily, the plants are now dead.

'In addition to these other measures we've decided to introduce fifteen minutes of mindfulness and meditation every fortnight. The day and time will change but to keep it spontaneous you'll receive a summons by pager as you did today.'

Oh yay. Surprise meditation. Exactly what we need. I'm not surprised they didn't share this with the committee first.

The CD has moved on to the gurgling sound of a stream alternating with a different whale. While I'm all for nature sounds, I'm not sure why they put a cetacean in a creek.

A hand is raised hesitantly in the front row. A whale hoots like a drowning owl.

'Yes?' asks Prof Brown, wincing at the whale whistles along with the rest of us.

'Should we leave our pagers at the door? So we can't be disturbed while we meditate?' the kidney registrar asks.

Prof Brown and Brenda look at each other. They hadn't considered this. Brenda answers, 'No. You need to keep your pagers because this isn't supposed to interrupt your clinical work.'

'Okay, let's start so we can get you home,' Prof Brown says, swinging her perfect bob. She takes a piece of paper from Brenda and clears her throat.

'Everyone, close your eyes.'

'Wooo ooo,' call the whales.

'I want you to become one with your breath,' she starts, and coughs again. Vikram makes a noise that starts as a snort then becomes a clearing of the throat. Towards the back, a pager goes off, followed by scuffling as someone moves out of the row to answer it.

'Be comfortable, feel at one with the Earth around you.'

The hard seat is uncomfortable, and the whales distracting. I'm not sure I want to be at one with this plastic chair.

'Breathe in, breathe out, feel nothing but your connection to Mother Earth, and to your own life-giving breath.'

'This isn't bloody mindfulness,' whispers Vikram.

'Wooo ooo,' call the whales.

Another pager goes off, and there's more shuffling.

'Shhh!' Brenda hisses over the top.

'Pay attention to your mind. Don't let it wander away from your breathing.'

Surely the purpose of having a brainstem is that I don't have to think about breathing? This one thing, at least, my brain can do by itself. Andy's pager goes off. If he leaves to answer it he can extract me with a page too. I try to catch his eye, but Brenda sees me and glares.

The CD shifts to yet another species of whale mixed with waves crashing on the shore. Don't they understand the tragedy of a beached whale? That those magnificent creatures live in the silent depths of the open ocean, only coming to the shallows to accidentally—or perhaps deliberately—die?

And in this moment, I find I can meditate on sleep, absence, release. The tendrils of thought are like soft vines, wrapping their new leaves around my arms, my legs, my face, the flowers opening and emitting a sweet aroma.

I don't want to die, per se, but maybe I'd like to stop doing the things required of me to live—breathing, eating, hygiene, sleep all seem too hard. Even the cave with the pink sky isn't safe enough. If my eyes didn't have to open for a while then maybe I could rest suspended, free of professors and Paul and Brenda and Shamsi and singing marine mammals, and re-emerge in a better tomorrow, one where I'm in a forest with Daphne rather than trying to keep one peace lily and a million patients alive.

The nature sounds CD falls silent and Prof Brown snaps her fingers as if she's a hypnotist. She wraps up with instructions on how to practise this mindfulness at home.

The line to get out is longer and slower than expected, the reason clear when we get to the door. Brenda's there with a clipboard.

'Name please?'

'Oh, come on! Isn't it enough that you type it on every poster you make about transforming healthcare?'

She thrusts her pen at me and points to my name on the paper, wanting me to sign next to it.

'What? So, if one of us kills ourselves from overwork you can tell the coroner you left a bowl of oranges on the air hockey table and played us whale music and told us how to breathe?' Daphne snaps. Vikram stifles his laughter. Prof Brown can't be far away.

'It's up to you how seriously you take these sessions,' Brenda growls back, now thrusting her pen at Daphne. She signs but doesn't move.

'Brenda, it's up to you how much you take our welfare seriously.' Daphne holds her ground under Brenda's withering gaze. 'We've sat in meeting after meeting telling you what we need is better staffing, reliable parking, safe hours, appropriate teaching, better supervision and support, adequate sleep and meal breaks, and all you've offered is fruit and decorative plants and lectures and, now, whale meditation.'

A small crowd of other doctors lingers. Intern Maya from ED, Brayden, who backs away uncomfortably. The cardiology fellow chuckles and the urology registrar nudges his resident and points at Daphne.

Brenda scans the small crowd. 'You know that the conditions of your employment are approved by your union,' she retorts.

Daphne laughs mirthlessly. 'That's not even a little bit true,' she says, before taking Vikram by the arm and marching off to the lift.

———

Jacqui's asleep, her brown hair cascading over the pillow and her slight frame curled under the sheets. I watch her sleep and then leave without waking her. This once, leaving the room without saying anything seems the kindest thing to do.

Cheryl's already called Dale and told him the news instead of leaving that conversation for me, so I grab my bag from the office and head for the lifts. There's no one in Emergency for me to see. For once, I won't be home too late. The spring sun is setting, but the promise of daylight savings and longer days is not too far away.

David calls me in the car for our now regular end of the day chat. He asks if I'm still upset from this morning, and it takes me some time to think back that far. Ah, the audit meeting. Wasn't that at least several lifetimes ago? Before clinic, before Jacqui, before petulant Paul, before the whales? How can the days be so long and yet the year be racing by? It'll be Andy's exam and then summer, and then all of us trainees will be thrown into the air and rearranged as we fall at other hospitals, for another year of this.

I reassure David that I've long since forgotten about Prof Bones and the audit. But the paper's almost finished and I'd like to show it to him.

'Emma, that sounds amazing! We should go over it next week.'

Steve will be back next week, thank goodness, so I'll be able to find some time to duck into his office.

'Oh, I'm slammed next week. What if we meet up after work? Thursday?'

I think quickly. Shamsi will probably be working late anyway and Steve will be on call. If I have this paper submitted it might even be accepted by the end of the year. Then I have some research under my belt and a mentor who can vouch for me— surely then I've ticked enough boxes to keep my career options open and there'll be no need to spend my spare time on things like this for the rest of my surgical training. And then I can get back to being the kind of wife Shamsi wants me to be. Maybe, that will even clear enough space for babies.

'Sure, I can swing by then,' I agree.

I walk into the house feeling lighter. Every time I speak to David I'm hopeful again. The path always seems clearer, my motivation to walk it bolstered. Maybe Daphne was too harsh on Brenda. Maybe there's enough teaching, supervision and support if you know where to look, even if sometimes you have to tell someone they're going to die, even if sometimes it comes with whales.

Chapter Twenty-six

Shamsi's furious. 'Emma! It's the trivia grand final tonight!' he explodes while I try to get my eyeliner on straight. Nic's convinced me of the value of make-up to hide my sallow skin, my bruised eyes.

I glance at him out of the side of my eye, stretched out with one hand and half inked with the other. Why did he think I'd go to the grand final? It's been months since I last went at all.

'Emma, you promised! You said you weren't on call and now you're off to some research meeting?'

I line my other eyelid and reach for the rouge. 'Shamsi, we talked about that too, and you said it was okay. You know that these are the things I have to do to pass my term, pass my training, pass The Exam, get a job, not be a failure. You know they hold my entire future in their hands, that they could obliterate it with the stroke of a pen.'

'We talked about it in the hypothetical, when you didn't tell me it was the same night as the grand final. Surely even people with as extreme pressures and lofty goals as you can take a single night off.'

Pushing past his sarcasm, I head down the hall to the kitchen, where the smell of coffee fills the air.

Shamsi follows. Is he waiting for a reply? An apology? It was clearly a miscommunication.

'Since when do you wear all *that* to go to work?' he asks quietly. It's a taunt but restrained, so quiet I almost don't hear it, like he hasn't quite decided if he wants the argument to go this way and maybe it will pass unheard.

Except I did hear.

'What are you implying?'

The coffee steams out of the Italian stovetop we bought in Florence, not that many months ago.

'All you do is complain about Steve and your professor and *everyone* else at work. Except *David*. Why are you suddenly getting dolled up for them if you hate them? Or is it for *David*?'

I seethe at the unfairness. I'm trying to sort out my life as quickly as I can so we can go back to being the way we used to be. And if I enjoy David's company more than his sometimes, then this is why.

'All *you* do is complain about *me*, and this is especially jerkish.' Angry, I grab the percolator roughly from the stove. Coffee splashes and spills down my skirt.

Shit.

I drop the percolator in the sink and dab at the spreading stain on the pale cream fabric with a filthy tea towel. Have we washed these even once this year?

It's not coming out and I'm already late. Slipping it off, I put it under the kitchen tap, rubbing in dishwasher detergent. I feel Shamsi's eyes on my lacy backside.

'Maybe you could try doing some washing from time to time, so you don't keep running out of things to wear,' he suggests coldly.

'Sure, in what time?'

I squeeze most of the water out and throw the skirt on the back of the kitchen chair. Shamsi pointedly takes it over to the clothes airer.

'Maybe in the time you're going on a date with your boss you could wash your own clothes,' he says, still quietly angry.

'It's not a fucking date!' I yell, and then before I know what I'm doing, I've seized the empty coffee cup from the kitchen bench and hurled it at his head. He ducks and it hits the picture on the wall behind. Both the mug and the glass crack, shards tinkling to the floor. We look at each other wide-eyed.

Shit.

And now I'm so *so* late. I snatch a slightly damp pair of pants off the airer with a smidge of guilt because Shamsi must have washed them for me. Turning my back I pull them on, refusing to show him the tears on my face, then grab my bag and run out the door.

Fuck.

It isn't even 6 a.m.

———

Shamsi doesn't text me, nor I him. He was unfair in everything he said, but then I did throw a cup at his head.

'You forgot to order the equipment,' Paul growls at me.

Shit.

I did forget to order the implant for the first case. We hurriedly move the list around so that the company can courier it to us and the sterilisation department can drop everything and run it through.

'You know we'll have to pay extra,' Lorraine chides me.

As punishment, it seems, Paul asks Steve to theatre, even though it's meant to be my operating list. He's given the case and I'm demoted to second assistant, standing too far away to see. Heads together, they talk and laugh. I can't even hear them discuss the procedure. When we finish, Paul tells Steve he'll see him next week.

Have I been 'fired' from his operating list? Is he allowed to do that? Will I have to tell the surgeons I work with next year that the reason for my incompetence is because another surgeon didn't like me, not because I didn't read up on it, turn up, see the patient and make an effort? Steve's forgotten so many important tasks this year and every time I've saved him or he's been forgiven with no consequence. Not only has he not saved me, he's taken my whole list.

So it's a relief when David confirms he wants to meet up this evening. Vikram and Daphne and even Nic are great company but they aren't my own specialty. I need to find a way to belong *here*.

David texts me mid-afternoon to ask if I'd meet him at his home rather than his office. This shouldn't be a surprise. A parade of trainees trooped through our house when we were kids, then in starched white shirts and paisley ties. Mum used to try and feed them in spite of Dad's protests. I still don't understand why it mattered if she handed out sandwiches. Still, Shamsi's taunt and Daphne's warning play at the back of my mind, so I double check with Andy before texting my agreement to David. Andy's quick reply makes me even more irritated at Shamsi and Daphne. Why is it so hard for them to believe that the mutual respect David and I have for each other—respect I've worked so hard to gain—is anything more inappropriate or sinister? And even if I did want to seek something more, he's old, established and most importantly, married! Why would he risk all of that with me?

At 6.45 p.m. I'm outside a large two-storey inner-city terrace. I check the address again and admire the tiling on the verandah before I knock. The door swings open before my hand hits the wood.

'Emma!' David beams and ushers me in. The entry hall is wider than my old share-house bedroom. A multi-coloured Murano glass chandelier hangs from an original ceiling rose, casting sparkles of colour across the black and white chequered floor tiles.

He leads me down the hall to a glistening glass and steel extension tacked on to the back of a house as old as The Mount.

Here, a modern doll's house sits next to an Eames lounge chair, and a saxophone rests next to a piano littered with children's music sheets. A long dining table fills the space, its hardwood surface polished to a gleam.

'Nice house,' I say, dropping my bag on the floor and my laptop on the long kitchen island, trying not to eye off the board of cheese and crackers. He smiles in acknowledgement, as if everyone lives in a house that must be worth millions of dollars, then reaches under the bench and pulls out a bottle of bright blue liquid.

'A drink?'

I shake my head, no. I'm only here to show him the new analysis of his data.

Not knowing how to run any statistical analysis, I'd brazenly offered Vikram authorship of the paper in exchange for his help. He'd pulled a face. 'So, n equals 36 and you're clearly p hacking. No, thanks. Don't worry though, I'll find a statistically significant something so you can impress your boss and add it to the body of research that thankfully no one will ever read.' I still don't understand what Vikram meant by all that, but he's given me a USB stick with results and tables to pass off as my own.

'Oh, come on. You won't say no after you see this,' David says, dropping ice into a glass and pouring in some of the blue liquid. He adds tonic and laughs at my surprise as the drink changes to a pale purple.

'Here you go. Try that.' He hands me the glass and points to a stool under the bench.

'So, Emma, how's the year going?' he asks as I open my laptop, inspecting the depths of his drink, the colours swirling together gently, mesmerisingly.

I sigh, wondering how to explain. 'Fine, I guess.'

'Steve's a bit of a jerk, yeah?' he asks.

I don't reply. David might want to mentor me, but he's Steve's boss too. I'm not going to betray him to curry favour.

'How's Paul?' he asks next. Is this an invitation, or a trap?

David leans over the bench, his partially unbuttoned shirt yawning, and pushes the cheese board towards me. 'For goodness' sake, eat, hungry registrar,' he says, helping himself to a piece of apple. 'Paul's going through a difficult time. I'm sure you've heard he and his anaesthetist were caught together and it's a mess. If he's giving you grief it's not your fault. Ignore him.'

Well, I hadn't heard. And it doesn't explain why he's only mean to me and not Steve. And ignoring is easier said than done.

My glass is surprisingly empty and my head's already spinning. I pick up a cracker as if it will sate my stomach and find my glass full again.

'Where's your family, David?' I change the topic.

'Oh. They're down the coast this week. My wife's father had an operation so she took the kids to stay with them and help out.'

I'm trying to hide my discomfort. I've already analysed this from every angle and I have no reason to be uncomfortable. Apart from the odd bawdy joke, our relationship has always been strictly professional. If I were a man, wouldn't I have lunch with him after an operating list, come to his house to work on a project, share a drink?

'I hope this isn't weird, Emma. A patient cancelled today so I got to come home early,' he says as if he read my mind.

My stomach, tempted with a small cracker and a large slosh of gin, grumbles loudly. Why am I incapable of being suave?

'What a terrible host I am!' he exclaims in response, jumping up.

'What? Why?'

David rummages in the fridge then closes the door, shaking his head. 'I haven't offered you any proper food and it's 7 p.m.,' he says, grabbing his keys and phone from the bench.

'Oh, it's fine . . .' I start.

He shakes his head. 'I'm a starving bachelor this week and I have to eat too. Come, let's go.' He finishes his drink and gestures to the door.

Obediently, I stand and follow.

———

Spring is in the air this evening. We walk along a row of terrace houses, buds starting to form in their small front gardens. I concentrate on the footpath. Wine in the shower isn't much compared to two generous gins on an empty stomach.

We stop at a similarly quaint old house which has been converted into a small restaurant. David enters, his eyes scanning the room. 'Hi, John!' he calls to an older man in a striped apron. The former living room has been turned into an intimate dining area and every table is full or has a *Reserved* sign on it.

'David!' John comes over with a smile and pumps his hand, studying me curiously.

'Ah, John, this is Emma. One of my brightest trainees. The least I could do is buy her a meal.'

John bows and taking my hand, kisses it charmingly. 'Your usual table?'

We're led past the service area where John collects two wine glasses and table settings, and up the stairs. The front bedroom at the top has been converted to a small function room with a large rustic table and an impressive mirror above a fireplace, but this is not where we stop. John lifts the large window, and we step out onto a balcony with a single table and two chairs.

John pulls out a seat for me and sets the table, draping the crisp napkin over my lap, while David leans back and inspects the street below. 'I love it here, Emma. Reminds me of my time in London.'

A breath of cooler air tickles my legs under my pants. I've always marked spring by when the blackbirds start to sing in the evening, and suddenly they're here too, proof that the Earth has continued to tilt outside the artificial lights of the climate-controlled hospital.

'The usual for me is a medium rare steak and glass of red wine. What about you?' David asks. There's no menu so I agree to the same, though I'm not especially fond of steak and am definitely not in need of more alcohol. John disappears out the window.

'Is this a regular thing?' I ask, to make conversation. If we're to have a meal, I may as well be personable.

David puts his hands behind his head, his gaze fixed on the twinkling street below.

'Mmm, Jill and I have been coming here since we met. Not many people get to sit on the balcony.'

'It's a lovely part of town'.

'Jill wants to move further out, where the kids can have a garden with a trampoline and be closer to their school, but . . . It's so lovely here, and over there is bland suburbia, full of surgeons who didn't quite make it in the city.'

Why don't his kids go to the local school?

'What's your husband up to tonight?'

'Pub trivia final,' I say lightly, and thank the waiter for my wine.

'I used to love pub trivia! I was pretty good too,' he says.

'You should come sometime,' I say, then wince. Did I invite David to the pub? What would Shamsi say if he turned up?

Shamsi . . . I would have refused to go out for dinner with him. Maybe I do save the best of myself for work, for my patients and my friends, and hell, even for Steve and Paul and Albert and Prof. If I can put rouge on my cheeks and be pleasant on a balcony with my boss, maybe it's not unreasonable to expect that I can do the same with my husband.

Shit.

This morning *was* my fault.

Shit.

We used to do this, Shamsi and I. Dinner and wine was always in the 'easy' column of my ledger, surgical training and babies were 'so hard love might not be enough'. When did dinner and wine and friends become 'hard'? When did a meal in a restaurant with my husband become something he had to coax out of me rather than something I did because I enjoyed it?

Is it because Shamsi can't understand me, or because I'm too tired, too singularly focused to be interesting anymore?

Maybe I should reach for my bag, discard the napkin, flee through the window to my car and join him at the pub, but steaks and a bowl of garden-fresh salad are placed on the table, so I pick up my knife and fork instead of my phone.

David refills my wine glass and tells me about his last diving holiday to Ningaloo, where he floated with the whale sharks and rays in a primordial sea, and then we crawl back out the window, wave at John and wander back through the gossamer night.

———

David leaves me in the front room this time before disappearing down the hall, a slight wobble in his step, or is that in my eyes? I've tallied up my drinks this evening when he comes back with my laptop and another bottle of wine.

'Oh my god, no, I have to drive home,' I tell him.

He puts the bottle on the table, the label facing me, and says, 'Sure, suit yourself.'

It's a Grange. For a Thursday night at home? David pours himself a glass, sits beside me, and fiddles on his phone. The room fills with piano jazz.

He catches me eyeing the wine and wordlessly pours a glass. Carefully, despite being quite tipsy, I find Vikram's tables and haltingly provide the explanation he gave me.

'Emma, I had no idea you knew how to perform this sort of complex analysis,' David says when I'm done, wonder in his voice.

'I did have some help—' I start, but David's having none of it.

'Help or not, you've managed to write a brilliant paper this year and it doesn't matter how.' He pauses and looks deep into my eyes. 'Don't worry about Steve and Paul, they're too stupid to understand how exceptional you are.'

I shake my head and stand. 'It's getting late. I'd better phone my husband to tell him I'm still here.'

David stands too, waving his hand at me. 'Go ahead, I'll pop to the loo.'

Sneaking to the kitchen I tip the rest of my Grange into the sink. I've got to get home.

Shamsi answers after many rings. The background noise tells me he's still at the pub.

'What do *you* want?' he asks. His anger is deserved, I know this now.

'Shamsi, I'm sorry—' I start, and there's silence. I take a deep breath and press on. 'I . . . I'll make it up to you, but can you help?'

'What do you *want?*' he repeats in the same cold voice.

'I've had maybe a glass too much wine and I . . . I'd like to come home,' I whisper, glancing furtively down the hall.

'Good date gone sour?'

'What? No. Uh. It was just a couple of glasses but I don't drink anymore and it's gone to my head.' I don't mention the gin, or the dinner on the balcony, or that I poured one of Australia's most lauded wines down a drain.

'I can't take a taxi because my car will be stuck here and I have to work tomorrow. Can you get a taxi here and drive me home?' I sound ridiculous, even to me.

I know I need to apologise for being absent, mean, tired, miserable, distracted, overly focused, and I should've done that *before* I asked a favour. But we've loved each other for so long. I hope he'll realise that I'm afraid, of David, and myself.

'Shamsi—'

He hangs up on me.

Shit.

David appears from the hall. 'All good?' he asks.

I nod, mute.

'Hey, I plied you with too much wine. You might need to wait a bit before heading off,' he says casually. Opening the freezer, he pulls out a box of ice cream. 'Want some?' David puts it on the counter. From a cupboard, he brings out two bowls and slides them across the bench.

I sit on the stool and watch as he comes to sit next to me, starts to spoon out vanilla ice cream.

And then his hand is on my leg, his breath is hot against my cheek, and his lips find mine.

'Emma, you're the most beautiful girl I've even seen,' he whispers. I pull away, he moves closer. 'Everyone else is an idiot. You're beautiful and brilliant and will be the best surgeon in the world.'

I'd like to dismiss his words as empty flattery, but among so many people who don't understand, who only tell me my sins—there it is. My heart *is* willing to listen. So I let him kiss me, and then kiss me some more, and at some point, I'm kissing him back.

I can feel the smooth skin on the small of his back, the angle of his jaw in my hand, his slight stubble against my chin. His hands creep under my shirt and he unclips my bra, and his hand is on my breast. And I have no neurons left to make any sense of this.

He removes my shirt and is starting to undo the button on my pants, when at last something snaps in my head.

'No.'

He moves away but doesn't break the unrelenting gaze I'm now so familiar with. My brain starts to clear. Perhaps it's the ridiculousness of being topless in my married boss's kitchen or maybe my liver is doing its job. Whatever it is, I grab a tea towel and hold it in front of my chest. David steps back. God, if he would only look away.

'You wanna go?' he asks.

I nod, yes.

'Okay,' he says, and thankfully leaves the room.

I search under the bench for my bra—what the hell—and get dressed, straighten my hair.

David is waiting in the front room, the Grange back in his hand.

I collect my laptop and bag, completely ignoring him as he watches me equally silently. In fact I almost leave without saying anything, but in the foyer, I remember my manners. 'Thanks for dinner, David,' I mumble, my hand on the front doorknob.

He's followed me to the door and steps forward to brush the hair from my cheek. 'Drive safe, Emma,' he whispers into my ear. 'And I meant everything. You're incredible. Don't let anyone beat you down.'

My knees weaken and the room spins with the broken shards of colour from the chandelier, but in a burst of effort, I yank open the door.

———

I sit in the car for half an hour, the window open. The blackbirds have stopped, the magical streets are silent. The fog lifts enough that I feel safe to start the car and drive home, but as I pull onto a main road, the world is still spinning and my exhaustion hits me hard. I have to keep going. I have to get home. I'm about to call Shamsi so he can keep me awake like he instructed at the start of the year. 'Call me anytime, even in the middle of the night. I'd rather be woken than lose you,' he'd said. But his support was apparently conditional on my not being lost in the first place.

I make a call anyway.

'Good evening. The Mount. This is Leanne,' answers the switchboard operator.

'Leanne, it's Emma from Orthopaedics.'

'Emma,' she says, a smile in her voice. 'You aren't on call tonight?'

'No, I popped back in to check on a patient,' I lie. 'I'm so tired though, could I chat with you for ten minutes while I drive home? So I don't fall asleep.'

Leanne's finishing her recap of the latest episode of a dating reality show I've never watched when I pull into our driveway. I turn off the ignition then hesitate, wondering if I smell like David.

I don't have to worry though, because Shamsi's asleep on the sofa. I creep past him, past the broken picture and the clean floor, and sink into bed. I know I should think about what happened but I can't, not yet, not tonight. So I force myself to close my eyes and the rest of the night is full of dreams of David and Shamsi and singing whales and failed suburban surgeons, but even in my dreams I'm unclear as to what exactly makes a surgeon a failure or, conversely, a success.

Chapter Twenty-seven

I have a hangover and an existential crisis, and the café isn't open yet. The residents' room is still quiet as the world spins ever so slowly towards the sun. A couple of dozy night residents loll on the sofa, only half awake, and the TV silently flickers with some infomercial. I find a mug that isn't completely filthy and run it under boiling water for good measure. There's instant coffee but no milk. Oh well. I tip in some extra granules.

What the hell happened last night? I thought David was my mentor, my friend. I thought he was there to help my career. Did he get drunk and make a silly pass or was this a long-term plan of seduction? Or does his emotion run deeper?

There's a familiar poke in my side. It's Daphne, looking dishevelled. Her polka dot dress is crinkled and she has bags under her eyes. She pushes past me and likewise starts spooning instant coffee into a mug.

'Don't mind me. Bad night. Slept here. Will be fine after coffee,' she says vaguely.

I'm suspicious. She isn't normally required to be on call overnight. Was the night registrar sick? Daphne shakes her head, drops her voice and pushes the stray hairs off her exhausted face.

'Oh Em, don't tell anyone. My mum's been unwell my whole life, and she got readmitted last night. It was hours before they could get her under control.'

I decide not to pry, besides my head's still full of David. Daphne did warn me. How did I miss the signs?

Daphne slurps her coffee and looks at me expectantly. Oh. She does want to talk about it. Fine.

'Is she okay?'

'She's had mental health issues since we arrived on a boat from Vietnam. She'd been tortured, my father had been killed. She escaped with her brother and me, the only family she had left. But her brother died soon after we arrived. So then, it was just toddler me and broken mum.'

In my ruminations about David I know I'm ignoring the elephant in the room—which is myself. I'm not sure this is a monster I can face. I'd thought my admiration and affection were all about the intellectual satisfaction of our relationship, but is there something more?

Daphne's still looking at me over the top of her mug. Shit. I need to say something.

'Aren't you a bit young to be a refugee from Vietnam?' is the first thing that comes to my mind.

She shames me with her glare. Shit. Shit.

'People left because it was unsafe for them long after the war ended, Emma,' she says, with more patience than I deserve. 'Anyway, I've been taking care of Mum for as long as I can remember. She still doesn't have great English. I've been interpreting for her at psych appointments since primary school. Honestly, our health system used to ask an eight-year-old to translate stories of torture and sexual violence rather than fund interpreters.'

Daphne keeps talking while I make another coffee. My head hurts.

In the quiet that follows, I gather I'm supposed to say something supportive. What's happened to me? It's like I've lost the ability to speak, to say even the important things that only need one word, like 'no' and 'sorry'.

'Well. Wasn't that a good chat.' Daphne gives her mug a cursory rinse and drops it loudly in the drainer with the other half-clean crockery.

'I'm sorry, Daphne, really. You've had a rough time.'

She studies me curiously, perhaps noticing for the first time that I'm as rumpled as her. 'Emma, are you okay? You're here unusually early too.'

No. No, I'm not, I want to scream. There was a brief time this year that life was okay, and now it's not okay, and I don't know how we got here.

'Yep, just a busy week and not enough sleep last night. My frontal lobe hasn't had enough coffee. I'm sorry for being a jerk,' I say instead.

Mollified, she gives me a hug. 'Better go find a shower and steam some of these creases out.'

I offer to get her scrubs, but the face she pulls is one of pure repulsion.

'I'd *die* rather than have people mistake me for a surgeon,' she says and waves goodbye. Daphne walks off purposefully, but as she's almost out the door her shoulders collapse into a hunch. For the first time, I wonder how much of her strength is an act.

For the first time, I wonder how much of mine is an act too.

The day's a blur. Shamsi doesn't answer his phone. Albert lets me be the primary operator while he supervises from the desk, but halfway through I'm struggling. He asks for a sterile gown and gloves and takes over. Though it doesn't feel like Paul's rejection, I resent his kindly gesture, further proof of my own incompetence. I used to be good at this. I got on the training program because I was better than almost anyone else. What happened?

Then, I go up to the ward to explain test results to Jacqui and Dale. Their visiting children fight over an ancient phone, their bickering boring holes into my head. Why would anyone want to have children? You're everything to them for a while and then they have to watch you die, sooner or later. Next week,

Andy will remove the mass from Jacqui's groin. She also needs another course of radiation, surgery to remove the mass from her lung, and *then* chemotherapy to top it off.

Afterwards, I sit in our office with my head in my arms, sad. I wish radiation therapy and experimental drugs would make her a superhero, like in a comic book. But maybe we tell the wrong stories. Maybe the real heroes don't have exceptional bodies and brains, maybe they're the ones like Jacqui, those who get by, survive, thrive with broken ones.

I keep checking to see if there's a message from Shamsi, or from David. Nothing.

By three o'clock, I can't take it any longer. Shamsi *will* speak to me again, if only to serve me divorce papers. I know what's happened between us, how we've drifted apart and ended up fighting, resentful. If he gave me another chance then we could mend our relationship. But I honestly don't know what happened with David. He started it but I didn't push him away. I've admired him, maybe even been seduced by his immense cleverness. I don't feel like I can start to interrogate my own complicity without knowing his intent.

I can't risk anyone overhearing this conversation. Next to Emergency, there's a small semi-dead garden, separated from the street by a low wall. I dial his number.

'Hi, Emma.' David's voice coos down the line, the affection with which he says my name sounding like an insult today. 'What's up?'

What's up? What's fucking up with you, David?

Am I going to do this? An unnecessary update about one of his patients would justify the call.

'David, we need to talk. About last night.' I manage to spit out a cliché. My heart is pounding in my chest, and the world is spinning a little. At least the watching homeless woman might come to my aid, or at least raise an alarm, if I faint.

'Last night? What do you mean, Emma?' he asks.

What?

'Oh dear, Emma, this is quite embarrassing, but I did have a lot to drink last night. I started hours before you arrived. I . . . can't quite remember what happened after dinner.'

Oof. Does the man have no shame?

'Emma, I'm sorry. I can see something's upset you. Tell you what, why don't I swing by The Mount later and we can have a chat, clear the air?'

I'm crying. I want this resolved. I think about calling Daphne for advice—she's dated many men and maybe this is what men do—but I've been with Shamsi for so long and this is all unfamiliar. Whatever 'this' is, because last night wasn't supposed to be a date, and yet he half undressed me and now I care that he didn't call.

'I've got to go. It's okay, Emma. I'll see you this evening,' he says and hangs up. I resist the urge to throw my phone at the wall and angrily wipe the tears from my face. Crying at work twice in as many weeks is not acceptable.

There's a tap on my shoulder. It's the homeless woman, she's moved from under the eaves. Her hand outstretched, she offers me a cigarette.

'Take one, for the hot chocolates,' she says, in a gravelly voice, and I do. And we sit on the low stone wall and blow smoke rings together.

———

Julia's at the desk in Emergency but I give her a wide berth. If she were to hand me a cup of tea and ask what was wrong, I'd tell her everything, and then how awful would I look? I don't need my failures laid out for everyone to see.

My stomach churns from the hangover and too much coffee, and my head's still pounding. I guess the cigarette didn't help. Maybe a Coke will.

Unexpectedly, Andy's by the Coke machine in the lobby, sitting on the bench with an unopened drink and staring into space. Is this the bench of contemplation?

I wave my hands in front of his face. 'Andy! What's up?'

He startles and then focuses. I'm pleased he looks relieved rather than annoyed to see me. 'Emma. I . . . I fucked up,' he says, and slumps back, resting his head against the noticeboard.

I'm confused. His exam is not for a couple of weeks yet.

'I'm sure you didn't,' I say, getting a Coke. Besides, there's no way he's fucked up more than me.

'No, I did.'

What the hell is wrong with everyone today? It's not a full moon. I sit and pat his knee. 'Okay, tell me, bro.' I don't have the time or capacity for this, but he's even more distressed than me.

'I killed someone, Emma.'

What?

'Andy, surely that's not true.' Surgeons *are* prone to hyperbole.

He stamps his foot impatiently, like a child, and glares at me. 'Okay. You tell me. Woman comes in. She's terrible at giving her history. Has a massive list of medical issues, some of which are not exactly, uh, widely accepted medical conditions. Full of woo. Sounds like a hypochondriac.'

Uh-oh.

'What did you miss, Andy?'

Andy sighs and closes his eyes. 'Acute mesenteric ischaemia.'

I've never heard of it.

'She came in with abdominal pain. Like a million other patients. There didn't seem to be much to find. Her tummy was unremarkable to examination, but she said she was in agony, while also complaining her daughter had taken some of her crystals away and this had flared her chronic pain. She didn't mention a recent procedure, and there was no visible scar. So I sent her home.'

'How is that your fault?'

'It was in her notes. But the operation details had been incorrectly entered under a different admission in her file . . .'

'Well, you had no chance, Andy. She didn't give you a history and the records weren't there.'

'I should've looked harder. She came in twice. The night registrar sent her home first, and I sent her home a second time. I kind of wanted my boss to come review her, but didn't push because *I'm* supposed to be in charge soon. I should've known

I wasn't up to the task. I failed The Exam for a reason, and now she's dead.' Andy slaps the bench and grits his teeth. 'Pain out of proportion to the examination findings is the classic sign, and often missed. If I'd scanned her, we could have fixed it before she came in too late, septic, with a belly full of dead guts.'

'Andy, mistakes happen.' Like last night. That was a mistake, fuelled by alcohol and loneliness and exhaustion.

'Emma, mistakes like this shouldn't happen. Even though it was a classic red herring, I thought she was making it up.'

He thought . . . I grab Andy by the shoulders and shake him. 'Don't say that to anyone! Don't say it. They'll hang you for it.'

'I'm hanged either way, Em.'

'Andy, she was a poor historian, the records weren't right, she was seen by multiple doctors, and your boss wasn't worried. This isn't on you. It's classic Swiss cheese.'

I don't add that he's up to his eyeballs in exams, hasn't slept in years, and has non-sleeping babies, and barely a home. I don't add that he's spent this year being told he needs to step up to the plate, speak up, stand up for his beliefs and not show any vulnerability. I think of the pilot on the plane to the conference and understand. Their systems fail occasionally and spectacularly, but ours fail every single day. We kill one at a time.

'Sometimes, in hospital, people die,' I remind him, trying to hide this death among the others.

Andy closes his eyes. 'Yes, but I didn't ever want it to be because of me.'

I also close my eyes. I have nothing left to give anyone, not even my brother, who hasn't noticed that I'm broken too. So, we sit, two Swanns, shattered, in the house our father helped build.

———

At 6 p.m., my work is done. Shamsi still isn't answering his phone, and David still isn't here. I want to go home, but facing Shamsi without resolving things with David seems too much to bear.

I curl up at one end of the sofa in the residents' room with Vikram perched at the other, thankfully sane unlike everyone else today. There are fresh bananas in the wellness fruit bowl, and even some leftover pizza from the wellness Friday pizza lunch the hospital has started to provide. I've never made it to the lunch, but the cold pizza is a gift for my hangover.

'What are you hanging around for?' Vikram asks, as he packs up his things.

What *am* I hanging around for? Redemption? Is there any to be had?

'Patient transfer from the country.'

Vikram tells me I work too hard, slings his bag over his shoulder, mysteriously mentions he's off to meet someone and whistles his way out the door.

The specialty surgical and medical residents are playing a very loud game of air hockey. Andy's on-call room is empty, a refuge. I tip some water into his rescued pot plant and curl up on the bed, finding some vapid new romance movie on my laptop to occupy my time.

At 8.30 p.m., David calls from the lobby, full of apologies. I nearly tell him to piss off, then agree he should come up to the residents' room. It's handover time in the hospital and no one is likely to appear.

He perches on the windowsill in Andy's room, the city glittering behind him, his shirt unbuttoned at the collar, looking calm and debonair. I pull the door closed and sit on the bed as far away as I can get.

'So, Emma. What did you want to talk about? You sounded very upset.'

My heart's racing, and I feel dizzy. Where was the medical school lecture on navigating this situation?

'Last night, David. You don't remember . . . anything?'

He shakes his head and raises his hands in a gesture of helplessness. 'I'm sorry, but I'd drunk half that bottle of gin before you arrived,' he says, as if this is explanation enough.

Who invites their registrar to a research meeting and drinks that much?

'You didn't seem drunk, not until much later,' I snap.

I almost apologise for my tone. My first instinct is to keep speaking to him as my boss, but given he's seen my breasts, he can put up with my anger too.

'Sorry. It was a hard day. Jill and I had a fight . . . It was an accident.' He waves his hand in the air, as if to clear it. 'So, tell me, what did I say that upset you so much.'

What did he *say?*

I lived it, and then relived it all day, and now he wants me to describe it because he can't remember. Fuck you, David.

Focusing on a button on his shirt, rather than on his face, I take a deep breath. 'You offered me ice cream. You told me I was an excellent registrar . . .' I pause, embarrassed that I fell for his flattery.

David nods for me to go on.

'And then you started to kiss me, and you took my shirt off.' I rush this bit, spit it out quickly and hope that my words will float away. But in this small, unventilated room, they hang like miasma between us.

'Emma.'

I don't look up. Then he's moving, a shadow in my peripheral vision. He crouches in front of me, and lifts my chin, forcing me to meet his gaze. Is he going to apologise?

'I'm so very sorry I have no recollection of that.'

Hang on. I'm confused. Why is he sorry he doesn't remember? He should be sorry it happened. Maybe not even that it happened at all—maybe if we weren't both married, if he wasn't my boss, things might be different—but surely, he's sorry it happened like *that*?

And he's kissing me again, softly, gently, and this time there's no alcohol on his breath. And I realise this is entirely him, and that I'm kissing him back too.

How are we here again? I pull my head away.

'I'm sorry, Emma,' he says, as if a kiss were no big thing. 'I should have asked. Except, you're so beautiful, and you look so sad.' He takes both my hands and holds them to his lips.

'David, this isn't cool.' Of all the words that have ever been invented, thought, expressed, this is what I hear myself say.

'Emma, my brilliant, beautiful Emma,' is his reply and we're kissing again.

I close my eyes. Didn't someone warn that if faced with these moments, we'd be better to succumb than run?

Anyway, I'm too tired to resist, to tell him to stop, to deal with the repercussions of fleeing the room, of losing my only mentor and ally. In a world of disease and death and bully bosses and psychotic mums and missing spouses, I'm too tired, too scared to say no to love and validation, whatever form they take.

And maybe it doesn't matter what his intentions are because he's made me feel clever and important and understood in a way no one else has. And even though the magic gowns are supposed to protect us from this, strip them away and we're still human underneath. People who've stood hip to hip and hand in hand doing great things for so long that maybe I can no longer tell where my love for the art finishes and my need for this man begins.

So, I let David kiss me, I let him lay me down, I let him remove my clothes, and I don't even check if he has a condom because I had contraception implanted when I was an intern with big dreams. And afterwards, I let him hold me, while I contemplate Andy's rescued plant, thriving in the dusty corner.

Chapter Twenty-eight

We always start earlier on Monday, but it wasn't enough today. After a flood of weekend admissions, we're at risk of being late for clinic. Steve taps at his watch, asking me to hurry, when I stop to answer my ringing phone.

'Do you know where Andy is?' his intern asks.

I have no idea.

Somehow, after David left the residents' room on Friday, I got dressed and drove home to a house with no lights. On the dining table there were flowers, tins of soup, a loaf of bread, fruit, muesli, chocolate, an apology.

Shit.

Shamsi's work retreat. He *had* told me it was this weekend, that he'd be gone until Monday, that there wouldn't be any phone reception and I'd have to call the firm in case of emergency.

I watched him write out the relevant phone numbers and stick them on the fridge.

Shit.

I took the food to bed and stayed there for two days, eating directly from the packaging in a nest made of blankets, breaking my silence only to call Andy on Saturday morning.

From the local library, he told me that he'd had a meeting with his head of unit. They reassured him he wasn't responsible for the patient's death. It would be presented at the audit and looked at by the coroner, but they said it was an easy miss, a rare condition, complicated by a poor historian and failed medical records.

I thought about asking him to come over so at least he had company, but instead returned to watching TV in the dark and ignoring the brief message on my phone from David:

That was fun.

Andy ruminates, but so do I. And there's still a lot to think on before I can reply to David. It was a weekend for brooding.

'Andy's never late,' his intern says now. 'There's nothing in theatre, and he hasn't texted me.'

I glance at the clock. It's 8 a.m. Andy *is* late.

I call Laura. She takes a long time to answer, and when she does one of the girls is crying in the background. She's distracted, uninterested, running late for work.

'Andy? He was gone before I woke up,' she mutters, the typical spouse of a surgeon, never surprised when their partner's absent.

And then she pauses. I hear her hand the baby to a parent. 'Why, Emma? What's up?' she asks, with a slight note of concern.

'Oh nothing, his intern's looking for him. He's probably in theatre.' I don't tell her that the intern sounded worried, or that she'd already checked theatre.

Andy still isn't answering. Julia hasn't seen him in ED this morning. The only theatre running is a neurosurgeon evacuating a brain clot. The morning operating lists won't be underway for half an hour. Vikram and Julia haven't seen him either.

Andy, where are you?

'Emma, we have to get to clinic,' scolds Steve from the end of the hall. He's finished the round on his own while I made calls.

'You go . . . I . . . have to do something first.' There's a growing unease deep in my stomach.

Steve looks to say something then stops. 'Emma, you don't look okay. You're green.'

It's true. I almost hurl into a nearby bin then choke back bilious minestrone.

'My brother, Andy, the general surgery registrar, he hasn't turned up to work.'

Dan and Steve glance at each other, their faces heavy with meaning.

'Do what you need to, Em,' Steve replies.

For the first time I hear authenticity in his voice. This is enough to unbind my legs. I turn and run.

First, I head to the car park to check if his car's there. Maybe he didn't make it to work. Maybe he's bleeding by the road.

Maybe he was scooped up and dumped in Emergency, a John Doe, his head too swollen for Julia to recognise him. He always parks in the same spot on the top level. I once asked him why, given it was exposed to the weather.

'Sometimes, at the end of the day, I sit in my car and look over at the hospital. I leave behind the baggage of the day, committing it to the building, so that I don't worry about things at home.'

'Really? Every day?'

He'd laughed in his easy way. 'Also, if you always park in the same place, you don't forget where your car is.'

Consistent, sensible, dependable Andy.

Today I curse his choice of the top level. The lifts are too slow, so I gasp up the stairs. Even from the door of the stairwell, the tail of his car is visible.

Shit.

Andy, where are you?

Vikram calls, asking if I've found the lazy bugger, a contrived phrase that poorly hides his concern. Only his car, I tell him. The silence roars.

Emergency next. Surely that's where he must be, the place is a maze, Julia didn't see him come in. I push past patients and staff in the lobby, trying Andy's phone again, casting about in case I hear his stupid, distinctive ringtone.

'Choose the worst ringtone you can, Emma, because after you're a registrar, you'll never want to hear it again,' he said to me the day I was accepted onto the training program. We were sipping champagne in Mum and Dad's garden, under the wisteria that flowers sooner and sooner each year.

I'm at the door of the ED when I hear it—switchboard Leanne's official voice booming through the hospital.

'Code blue residents' room. Code blue residents' room.'

The world disappears and all I can see is the stairwell door and the steps in front of me. I stumble and crack my shin on the edge of a step. There's blood but I keep running. The stairs pass under my feet, one at a time then two at a time, floor after floor until I burst onto the ninth floor.

A gaggle of people stand at the door of the residents' room. The code blue team hasn't arrived. They try to stop me, these babies with horror on their faces, but they're no match for me.

Inside, the door to Andy's on-call room is broken and hanging off its hinges, a medical registrar guarding it. I'm close enough to see Vikram doing chest compressions on the bed before I collapse on my knees and vomit.

A small pair of hands holds my shoulders. 'It's a surgical registrar,' Maya whispers, her eyes wet. I vomit again, my insides emptying themselves onto the filthy carpet. A crash cart whizzes past. Aidan and the ICU team have arrived. Aidan checks for a pulse, and a nurse takes over the chest compressions.

The anaesthetic team arrives next. I see them stick him with lines, fill him with drugs. Jyothi, wonderful Jyothi, takes over at the head of the bed. I've seen her do this. I know she can do this. I forget, wilfully, that Beverly didn't survive.

'Get everyone out!' Aidan shouts, and the last few residents retreat to the door.

The medical registrar tries to urge us out too. 'You have to go,' he says, his voice high and quavering.

Still on my knees, I shake my head. 'It's my brother,' I whisper, and then retch again.

Only Maya's heard, and she hugs me closer, her spindly arms shaking.

'You have to *go*!' The medical registrar is insistent.

Maya stands up to him, half his height. 'No,' she says. 'She has to stay. You sit with her. You tell her what's happening.'

She ties up her hair, and heads into the room. She's only an intern but the ICU nurse is flagging. Even interns can do chest compressions as well as anyone else. She taps him out of the way, and they let her take over.

'Let me in!' Daphne pushes through the crowd, throws her arms around me. Someone hands in some towels and they're placed over my purge.

'It's okay, Em, it's okay,' she soothes, but we both know it's not okay, that it might never be okay. The awkward medical registrar relinquishes his spot. He's better at guarding doors than comforting strangers. I look around, numb, and see a crowd of eyes watching from the entrance, mute, white, silent, hands clutching hands.

'I need to see.'

Daphne shakes her head, *no*.

'I need to see, he's my brother, I need to see.'

Daphne doesn't argue any more. She helps me up and we hobble to the broken door.

It *is* Andy, dear beautiful Andy, on the bed, that same sullied damaged bed where I lay three days earlier. Jyothi presses a mask to his face and Maya jumps on his chest, and Vikram is waiting to tag in. And on a portable screen, next to Andy's rescued plant, is the flat line of his broken heart.

Daphne wraps her arms around me and buries her head in my shoulder, but I can't look away.

'Is this wise, Emma?' Jyothi asks gently, her hand squeezing air in and out, in and out. She doesn't tell me to leave.

'I need to watch, please,' I whisper, and she nods.

So here, in this room, in this wretched hospital, I watch a team of colleagues and friends resuscitate one of our own, *my* own.

'Swap!' calls Maya, and Vikram takes over. She backs away, sweaty and spent.

And as I hear Andy's ribs crack under Vikram's hands, I notice the empty boxes of drugs stacked neatly on the table, and below them a piece of paper with Andy's handwriting. Now, I do look away. I will not see those words unless I have to.

Aidan and Jyothi confer, and Aidan makes a call. He asks if I want him to explain what's going on, but I understand what this is, all of it except the most important part. That, he can't explain either.

'Swap!' says Vikram. I step forward.

Daphne stops me. 'No, that isn't for you,' she says, clutching my arm.

Andy's grey, and Maya's sweating and Vikram's panting and Aidan's crying and Jyothi, appearing calm, is injecting drugs, drugs that may save us all, and at the faraway doors, a hundred pairs of eyes are watching, and waiting.

Julia appears with Brayden. Aidan's brought in reinforcements.

'Emma, he might not make it. We need another senior clinician to make the call if he doesn't. Jyothi shouldn't have to do it on her own,' Aidan explains, his voice cracking, shattering, tinkling over the floor.

Daphne clutches me harder as my knees buckle. How will I face Laura who loved him and made her life with him, his babies who don't really know him yet, my mother who carried him, held him, nursed him, sent him on this path with her blessings? And my father. How will I face my father, who thinks he's his legacy?

'Please try,' I whisper.

Aidan takes my hand and gives it a squeeze. 'We try for everyone, Emma, but we'll try hardest for him.'

Maya and Vikram swap, and swap again, and swap again, and the ICU nurse and anaesthetic registrar join in the rotation. More drugs are sent for and arrive. A tube is placed in his throat. The sun moves higher in the sky.

Jyothi finally speaks, quietly, softly in a room full of noise. 'Stop the compressions for a moment, please.'

The room of heads turn to the monitor. And there, just beginning, are a repeated series of regular bumps, the manifestation of spontaneous electrical activity shimmering across Andy's heart.

———

The Chief Medical Officer and Chief Executive Officer arrive. I've never seen either of them before. It seems they don't meet with their staff unless one of them tries to die.

A pod's being prepared in ICU for Andy. The ambulance service is coming to move him. A hydraulic trolley is needed, but the hospital doesn't have one, because medical crises are not supposed to happen in non-medical beds.

Daphne sits with me on the sofa outside as people rush around. Still no joy, not yet. His heart might be working but we don't know how long he was gone, how well Vikram and Maya pushed his blood around while his heart couldn't. Did his brain cells, famously greedy, get enough? We don't know if he'll wake up. At least for now, we know that more of his cells are alive than dead. Are they enough to make a human? Are they enough to make an Andy?

I'm allowed to stay, but not to help. I don't argue, even though I want to sit with him, hold his hand, examine him, read his chart, kiss his cheek—a doctor's curiosity coupled with a sister's despair. I need to know how he did it. Laura will need to know how he did it.

'The drip he put in was still working when we arrived,' I hear Aidan tell Julia. 'Maybe we should lock up the syringe pumps,' Jyothi says to the CEO. Hints, clues, to a terrible, pre-meditated plan.

My nails dig into my palm, longer than the regulation length set by infection control. A familiar guilt rises and I don't know how to deal with it. It's the guilt of knowing what's happened to someone else's loved one before they do. Laura's still seeing patients in her clinic, my father's probably digging in his garden, my mother immersed in her paints. Everyone's going on with their lives not knowing that everything's changed. Everyone except me, because this time Andy was my loved one too.

Once they've secured everything, stabilised him, made sure he'll make it to ICU, the CEO wants to call *the family*, as if we aren't individual people, as if we're not *his* people. Jyothi has a heated conversation with him, pointing at me. He asks why I was allowed to stay, his legal concerns ahead of why or how this happened. Jyothi's fists curl but she doesn't say anything.

'Emma, would you like to tell the rest of your family?' she asks, taking my hand. That she will call if I don't want to is implied.

Should I have called Laura when he was found, given her the chance to stand beside me? I wonder if seeing was her right too, something denied her because I didn't think of it. Maybe we should always let family watch a resuscitation if they want, so they know how much everyone tries, how hard we fight to not let people unexpectedly go.

If she asks, I'll say I'm sorry. I *am* sorry. I'm sorry I didn't ask him to come sit with me this weekend. I'm sorry I didn't run up here first, I should have known this is where he'd be. I'm sorry that everything's fallen apart around me. I'm sorry I couldn't hold it all together.

With Daphne's arm around me and Jyothi watching on, I call Laura. I tell her words I never thought I'd have to find, and then I call my mother and find them again a second time. And then someone asks if there's anyone they can call for me, but there isn't because Shamsi's still in the middle of nowhere, and even though it *is* an emergency, I don't want to have to call his workplace and explain.

And so I stay in the room that smells of stale coffee and vomit and near-death, clutching my friends, waiting: for Andy to go down to ICU, for Laura to flee her clinic, for my parents to scream up the freeway.

'His intern said he was late to work.'

'His sister said she couldn't find him.'

'I was looking for him, but I didn't check the on-call room. I heard his ring tone.'

'We knocked but the door was locked. We kicked down the door. I called a code blue because, well, it was obvious I should.'

Snippets of the story waft through the air.

The police turn up in case he still dies. They take his phone and his bag, to be returned later. Someone hands me his letter. I fold it up and put it in my bra, where it won't fall out by accident. It's far too precious for a pocket.

'I called him,' I tell Vikram. 'After I spoke to you, *I* called him.'

'And I heard that awful ringtone because you called,' he replies.

We cling to each other and cry.

'I saw a box under the bed last week,' I tell the CEO.

Did I see what was in it?

No, I was searching for my bra, again, and it was a cardboard box. Nothing sinister, I thought.

'No, sir, I didn't open it. I simply noticed it when I dropped my pager.'

'What were you doing in the general surgery on-call room?'

No, I wasn't having sex with my boss.

'We don't have one allocated to our unit, and I knew it wouldn't be in use. I was killing time, waiting for a transfer. Usual day at work.'

'Did your brother tell you he had plans?'

Would I have let this happen if he'd told me?

'No, sir, no, he did not.'

'Do you want us to arrange a taxi to take you home?'

No, I don't need your fifteen fucking dollars.

'Thank you, I'll wait for my family.'

At last the ambulance service arrives, and Andy's transferred to their trolley and wheeled out of the room. And at last the crowd disperses, back to work, like nothing happened.

———

Nic finds me in the afternoon. After Andy's been cooled, his core temperature brought down to save as many brain cells as possible. After I sat with Laura, listening to Aidan's update.

As always, he started with the punchline, this time, 'He might not make it.' She clutched my hand, choking.

I went to buy Laura a coffee she wouldn't drink to escape the stifling air of the small 'family room' outside the ICU. On the sofa opposite was another family grieving.

'What happened to your loved one?' they ask.

'The unthinkable,' I say. Everything that brings people to ICU is unthinkable, until it happens. I don't ask, 'What about you?'

Nic finds me in the coffee queue, throws her arms around me. The line pauses, people unsure whether to leave us in our place, or move around us to order their double-shot macchiato with one sugar, please.

'He texted me last night,' she whispers in my ear. 'In fact, he texted me all weekend. He was eaten up by that patient.'

I round on her angrily. Why didn't she tell me? The coffee line looks uncomfortable. I push her behind a pillar.

'He said you weren't okay. That you and your husband had a fight. That he thought something else was wrong, but he didn't ask what. He didn't want to bother you.' Her eyes shine wet.

Shamsi must have called him. Damn it, Shamsi, you knew he was busy, studying, overwhelmed.

'The senior surgeons told him it was fine. But he didn't trust them because he thought they were covering for themselves too. The system closing in on itself. He didn't think that was right.'

Of course he didn't, I should have known that. Or maybe I should have tried harder to listen. All the time he spent telling me to eat lunch and leave clinic, order bloods tests rather than think, I thought he'd changed—become indifferent, resilient. I should have known that's not the doctor he could ever be. That those words weren't about him, they were to try to protect me.

'Laura told him that it wasn't his fault too. He didn't believe any of us, but I thought he might believe me, as a surgical peer.'

I'm angry she didn't tell us. He's a chapter in her life, a friend for the seasons they work together at the same hospital. She didn't—doesn't—know him like the rest of us. She should have made a MET call, sounded the alarm and brought in extra people who could stop the deterioration before it became a crisis, but they haven't written the criteria for this, they don't have a team on standby for this.

'He's been so cool, doing so well with his practice exams. I thought this was a small hiccough.' She pulls out her phone, and scrolls through the messages, dozens, that they exchanged over the weekend.

'He texted me last night to say he was thinking about quitting. I thought he was thinking about quitting surgery. I didn't think . . . I couldn't know . . .'

I want to be angry. I want to scream that she should have told me, told Laura, that we could have fixed this. But there's no point. It's too late.

A lifetime of wondering if we should have done something different will be punishment enough, for all of us.

———

Much, much later Daphne drives me home. After Dad asks me why Shamsi hasn't come to the hospital. After Mum's allowed to see her firstborn, hooked up to tubes and machines. After Laura's parents bring the babies even though they don't understand and can't go into the ICU.

We walk to the car park, and I wonder who'll come and get Andy's car. Will the hospital keep charging him the daily parking fee for it to sit here until someone can drive it home?

It's an irrationally sunny afternoon, the world full of people for whom nothing's changed. Young mothers pound the pavement, pushing their prams in their activewear. University students balance on their bicycles at the lights. The birds swoop in the sky. How is this possible?

We're almost home when Daphne pulls into a spot under a large tree. The filtered light falls in a dappled pattern across her skirt.

'I need you to know that this isn't on you,' she says, gently.

What am I supposed to say?

'I wasn't there for him this weekend, Daphne. He had to turn to someone else, someone who doesn't know him like me. Someone who couldn't protect him.'

'But you couldn't protect him. You don't need to tell me about what happened last week, but clearly something did. Did he know that too?'

A group of schoolchildren run past, one acting the clown. My eyes well up. That was Andy. Always funny, always loved.

'That's the thing, Em. Medicine drives wedges between us. Not because we aren't mostly good people, but because we're all beyond capacity in one way or another. Andy's had a typically crappy year with typically crappy bosses who don't think they're crappy but are, with a crappy exam and then a crappy patient outcome.'

This is all it's taken. Such small common things can accrue in exponential ways and make the centre fall apart. How will any of us survive?

'I noticed your husband wasn't called to visit his brother-in-law in hospital and drive you home,' Daphne observes.

'We had a fight, and now he's at a weekend work retreat, uncontactable.'

Daphne takes my hand. 'You know, Em, it's as hard for the partners, the family and friends, as it is for us. I've had plenty run away.'

All weekend I'd thought about what I needed to do to mend things with Shamsi, worried about how I'd find the energy, the time. How would I sustain being the perfect registrar, the perfect wife, maybe even a perfect mother for four more years? But today, I can't find any sympathy for these others that Daphne wants me to care about. They don't know how we work, how we live, how we might die.

'Emma. Andy lost his people, his supports. Practically living at work, stressed to his eyeballs from ticking other people's boxes about what it means to perform well. So when he needed help, he was alone. Too alone. And that'll happen to you too, if you're not careful. We can't go to work and have people die on us, yell at us, starve us, deprive us of sleep . . . and not have somewhere soft to land.'

'They should fucking change the system, so we don't need to land softly,' I say angrily.

'They can't change the system, Em. That's for us to do.'

———

Daphne doesn't want me to be alone, but I insist that she leaves. Maybe later I'll drive to Andy and Laura's—or is it Laura's now? If he dies, will she even be able to keep the house? Did he have insurance? Will it cover *this*?

She pushes a small note into my hands before she goes. I unfold it and read:

Lifeline 13 11 14.

If only someone had handed this to Andy.

I'm surprised to find the front door unlocked. I creak it open, wondering if this is how I left it this morning, and then startle at a shadow in the kitchen. And then I'm sobbing in Shamsi's arms.

'What's wrong?' he asks, repeatedly, until I find those words again.

'You should have called,' he says. 'I could have left. I would have come home.'

'I thought you were angry,' I reply, still lying to protect myself, still making it his fault even though he left flowers and a note and an apology, even though *I* haven't apologised and my sins have ended up far worse.

'I wasn't angry anymore,' he replies. And he holds me and strokes my hair, but all I can think of is another person who held me just the same. How will I face any of it, ever again?

Chapter Twenty-nine

All of them are at The Mount the next day. Vikram and Daphne and Aidan and Jyothi and Julia and Brayden and Maya and me. The resident who helped Vikram kick down the door and called the code blue. The medical registrar who cleared the room. The ICU nurse who jumped on his chest and then cleaned up my vomit. The dozens of eyes who watched.

They all come to work and walk these halls, knowing that one of our own is in ICU. Our world is off kilter. We aren't supposed to be the patient.

I come to work too, even though everyone tells me not to. I'd have to be here anyway and I'd rather take calls than merely sit in the stifling family room waiting, waiting. Steve reluctantly diverts his pager. Prof Bones calls Dad instead of me.

When Julia pages me I'm wary, but she says, 'Can you come and see a child with an elbow fracture.' I'm grateful she didn't ask about it without warning. I'm already tired of the tears that come unbidden. She takes me aside when I get there, the short walk to a quiet nook notice enough to compose myself. 'Are you okay to be at work, taking calls?'

Of course not, but I nod yes.

She knows what I'm doing and gives me a hug.

'How about you?' I ask, and she says yes too.

But no one stops me.

Because that's how we deal with things. We ask each other if we're okay and say yes when the answer is no. Because saying no is a failing. Because food and sleep are for the weak, and maybe grief and sorrow too.

There's no locum to replace Andy at first. No one in administration thought of it. His intern holds the phone for a couple of hours until Julia notices. She sends Brayden to cover general surgery until Brenda can find a replacement. There isn't a single spare surgical registrar on standby, not at The Mount, not anywhere in the state. There never is. An ED registrar isn't a general surgery registrar but it means a shell-shocked intern isn't alone.

This is also how we deal with things. By splitting ourselves and our teams into halves, into quarters, into eighths, into ever smaller and smaller pieces until there's nothing left of us and we disappear into the thin air forever.

I try not to think about what happens if Andy dies, about the inevitable autopsy. The bit where they cut out his internal organs and weigh them. Surgery is for the patients, not the surgeons, and never more is this true than when the incision is dry and bloodless, the parts still and silent. Heart: 291.4 grams. Brains: 1372.7 grams. As if their mass somehow indicates their capacity, or the magnitude of their loss.

Because this is how we're trained to deal with the unthinkable. We learn to close our eyes and our hearts and our minds to the brutal realities that surround us. But in not dealing with them, we press on, pretending we do.

Until we fail.

They will his heart to beat on, his neurons to awaken. So they can go back to pretending.

But Andy's my brother and the pretending is over for me.

———

Everyone tries to find reasons to go to ICU, to see the cardiac trace for themselves. Aidan locks the doors. Only those medical teams who have a patient in ICU are allowed in. The other family in the family room is puzzled. 'Why have they made it harder for us?' they ask. Laura stares at them. How do you start to explain?

We talk about his funeral, should it be needed. She suggests a suburban funeral parlour and my father objects.

'Andy wouldn't want you to waste money on a funeral, money that would support the girls,' she sobs.

'We'd do that too,' my father weeps.

I don't enter that conversation. Instead, I imagine a funeral in Government House, in the Cathedral, on a ship upon the wine dark sea. These are the funerals for Andy, not the dingy funeral parlour that the debt-laden half-widow of an almost-surgeon can afford.

The doctors, banned from the ICU, lurk outside, pretending they aren't lurking, worry written on their faces.

'So performative,' Nic says, but it's more than that. Andy taught Maya to suture, and Vikram to examine a surgical abdomen. One night when Steve was stuck with a patient he was worried about, it was Andy he called. I know this all now because they've told me in the days since Andy went to ICU. He had friends everywhere that I didn't know about. I wonder if *he* knew that by doing his job generously, he'd touched so many lives.

Some of them come to visit in the family room to tell Laura what Andy meant to them.

'He was so close to passing The Exam, finishing his training,' Nic says to Laura.

'We were so close,' Laura says back.

'He gave up so much for his career,' Prof Wilson says to Laura.

'You made us give up so much for his career,' Laura says back.

'I'm sorry this has happened,' the CEO says to Laura.

'You should be,' Laura says back.

Dad, back in his old stomping ground, tries to take charge. He borrows my ID tag to get into ICU but the stern nurse in charge shoos him back out and shows him the doorbell. He complains to the CEO but is mollified by the healthy food vending machines.

He calls the head of ICU directly for updates, and in this, at least, he gets his own way.

I rescue Andy's plant from the residents' room to take home. I'll give it back to him when he wakes up. We sit and tell stories of the Andy we loved. The man who played basketball despite being the shortest on the team, who drank little and drove everyone else home, who met his future wife in a library where she was studying with his sister, who calmly delivered their twins on the bathroom floor when they came too fast, the ambulance still screaming through the night towards them.

'He sounds like a good guy,' the other family tells us, overhearing.

'He is,' I smile.

My phone beeps. Another message that will go unanswered flashes up below the one before.

I hope you're okay. Thinking of you.

Not today, David. Not yet. Not now.

'Who was that?' Shamsi asks.

'A problem for another day.'

I text Steve that I can't work anymore and turn my phone off for the first time this year. Medicine will not find me.

———

The hours and then the days go by.

Shamsi and I offer to take the babies for a night but Laura refuses. She'd rather be exhausted than without them. They're all she has of him. When she holds them, feeds them, rocks them to sleep, she doesn't cry, can't cry. Nor can she fall into the exhausted sleep of worry and grief that we hope for her. Her GP prescribes her sleeping tablets but she doesn't go to the chemist. Her GP writes her a referral to a psychologist but she doesn't pick up the phone. Where I needed to see, she's determined to feel.

On the third day, Shamsi and I join Mum and Dad and Laura in the ICU family room. Inside, Aidan's tipping cold water into Andy's ears and shining lights into his eyes to see if essential parts of his brain still work. Dad's found a neurologist and made her drive across town, bullied admin into letting her come and assess him even though she doesn't work here. She'll zap his nerves with electricity, to see if his brain can feel it and respond. Dad paces and Mum clasps Laura's hand. We wait for the verdict, whether it's even worth trying to wake him up.

They tell us Andy's brain is responsive but we won't know how much until the next step, when the sedative drugs are turned down further and the breathing tube removed. Tomorrow morning they'll try.

That means that for today, he's still alive. Today, there's still hope.

———

Paul has to do an operating list on his own because I'm not at work.

'This is what I meant about your enthusiasm, Emma,' he calls to tell me. 'My wife was sick during my training and I didn't visit her in hospital every day. You have to learn to work despite the stuff in your life, not take time off because of it.'

I say sorry and hang up.

'You've made an enemy for life and he'll try to destroy you,' Nic warns me.

I don't care. Maybe he already has.

Shamsi's taken time off too, but *his* seniors are supportive. They don't understand the medicine, however, they understand the humanity.

Mum and Dad come and sit with Laura in the little family room. There are other families there and the room's too small for us all, so Shamsi and I go to the park across the road. The garden has lilies and the air has warm and cool currents mixing like we're in the ocean. We spot magpies in the trees and duck. It's swooping season.

Andy never got swooped on our grandparents' farm. He was the only one who escaped it. Maybe it's because he rescued a magpie chick and returned it to its nest. Maybe it's because he always fed them. They say magpies can remember people for years, know who's a friend.

The homeless woman waves from her post and I wave back. She shows me that she has crossed fingers and pumps the air in a sign of good luck. Shamsi asks who she is.

'Someone who knows everything.'

Aidan calls me, his number flashing up on my screen and startling the silence. Shamsi squeezes my hand and the magpies swirl overhead.

'He's awake, Emma. He can breathe, he can see, he can talk. He's properly awake.'

And then Shamsi holds me as I double over on the bench, gasping for air too.

———

My parents come to our house for dinner before driving back down the coast. That Andy will live is welcome but fills us with nervous energy. He's weak, he's confused, his memory is poor. But his cells are young, and Vikram and Maya did a good job getting blood to them. He'll make some sort of recovery.

We offer take-away but decide upon reheated sausage rolls. Shamsi and I made a huge batch, in case Andy died, in case there was a funeral and a wake, in case we had hordes to feed. It was so different from the twins' birthday, no jazz and scented tea. Finally, at 1 a.m., Shamsi took my hands to stop me filling pastry with mince, to stop me filling the freezer with food that no one was likely to eat. I didn't ask what he did with the leftover mince or defrosted pastry after I was put to bed.

'It's such a relief,' Shamsi says, laying frozen pastries onto a tray.

'It's been such a tragedy,' my father replies, wiping his eyes.

I'm suddenly filled with loathing. Everything I've been holding in, perhaps for years, rises to the surface.

'It's not a tragedy. This didn't happen because the problem was with Andy,' I snarl at him, focusing on the semantics. 'This was so predictable.' I shove the tray of sausage rolls in the oven and slam the door closed.

'What's that supposed to mean?' he asks.

Mum looks between us wary, bewildered. Today's supposed to be a good day. Andy's awake. I'm not supposed to be angry today. I'm definitely not supposed to be angry at my father who almost lost his only son. Except I am.

'What do you think it's like working at The Mount, doing your stupid fucking training program, studying for your dumb exam—'

'Emma, stop swearing.' Dad is stern.

'I'll fucking swear, Dad, because my brother almost died and it's your fucking fault.'

Pulling open the door of the fridge I grab a beer, while my husband and parents stare at me open-mouthed. It fizzes as it opens, beer streaming over my shaking hand and onto the floor.

Dad spreads his hands, distancing himself from this accusation.

I'll have none of it. 'It's *your* fucking fault, Dad. You and Prof Wilson and Prof Bones and even Prof Brown. All of you professors who made The Mount what it is, and then were so blind to what it is that you let your own kids go and work in it, without ever imagining one of them would succumb.'

'Emma, you don't mean that,' he says, softly.

I almost fling the can of beer across the room but don't. This time I stop myself.

'I do mean it, Dad. You never noticed the medical students who left medicine, the interns who fled the hospitals for *anything* else as soon as they could, the doctors who persist but struggle every day. You didn't care when any of them could have been Andy. You don't even notice that it could still be me.'

Shamsi puts his arm around me. Dad starts crying. He's wept softly in the last few days, but I've never seen him cry like this before. His shoulders shake, tears stream down his cheeks.

My mother, helpless beside him, beseeches me with her eyes to stop. I can't, I won't.

'I'm not okay. None of my friends are okay. *You* weren't okay.'

He slumps over the table, fingers gripping the edge to steady himself, his other hand over his eyes. His crying's louder now, moans that float through the pastry-scented kitchen.

'Medicine stole you, Dad,' I say more softly. 'And you thought that was normal. You thought that your fancy house and your farm and your aid work and your professorship was a good life. You were off making the world better while Mum picked up the pieces, thinking that your way was the only way. That there was no collateral damage on anyone, even on yourself.

'And you let it steal us too. You left us a broken miserable system that drives out everyone who isn't like you, without ever asking if what *you* are is actually excellent, if it's what patients need, what your colleagues need. And so, it's *you*—' I take a step forward and prod him in the chest, 'it's *you* who almost killed him.'

We stand in silence, a void gaping between us.

And then he opens his arms. I glower at him, but step into them, because he's my father and not just a surgeon, and he almost lost his son. 'This isn't forgiveness, Dad,' I tell him, and he holds me, his cheeks wet but his mouth silent.

Chapter Thirty

I don't go back to work after Andy wakes up. Instead, I take the two weeks of annual leave I was planning for the end of the year. Steve agrees to cover. Prof Bones doesn't argue. It's not like the hospital provides a replacement regardless of when I take my leave, so it makes no difference to anyone.

Andy's awake but he's not himself. He'll need a stint in rehabilitation before he can go home. My plan is to help Laura, but my mother intervenes. Laura's parents are still around and she can help too. After a long argument we agree that she'll stay in our house and I reluctantly fly away for a beach holiday with Shamsi. I'm worried about Andy, but they're all worried about me.

'It's not going to rain this week, is it?' I ask, draping a towel around my shoulders and wiggling my toes deeper into the hot sand.

'Hmm. No,' mutters Shamsi. He's face down on his towel, dozing.

I want to nap too, but sleep will not come. There's been so little of it for so long that the tropical sun is muted and dull, bearing little resemblance to the beach of my childhood holidays. When the biggest concern was who was going to collect the chips from the fish and chip shop to augment the cheese sandwiches brought from home, and whether the ice cream would melt over my fingers before it could be hastily licked off the cone. When my brother and I danced near naked in the waves and our father threw us in the air and handed us Fanta from the Esky. When my mother wore polka dots and built magnificent castles out of sand.

Shamsi groans and rolls over, dispensing a soft puff of beige from his beach towel. His skin glistens in the light and I find myself conducting a mole check in my mind. He refuses to wear sunscreen, claiming that the darker pigmented melanin acts as a natural defence to the sun's harmful rays. Biologically and statistically speaking he's right, but it's not he who has to tell people that they're about to die of a cancer they didn't know they had. I've long since stopped arguing the point. This is one of many things he can't possibly understand.

The sand dulls the blues and greens and pinks of his towel, and my exhaustion dulls the shimmering haze of the water beyond. Shamsi's now fast asleep on his side and snoring despite the safety of the left lateral position.

I want you to think back to a football stadium right before the national anthem is played, when eighty thousand people are standing silently. And I want you to tell me what you can't hear.

The sound of snoring always invokes the words of an emergency physician giving us a medical school tutorial. No one in our group knew the answer, to the annoyance of the emergency physician. I can't remember his name but it was probably John.

The seconds ticked by, the air heavy with John's disappointment. *Anyone? Anyone? Can't anyone tell me what they can't hear?*

I thought about all sorts of answers: frogs, rocket engines, someone singing Happy Birthday, but none of these were especially relevant to a medical school tutorial and would have made me sound like a smart arse. I'd already learned that people, especially men named John, didn't take well to being smart-arsed by young brunettes.

Breathing. You can't hear the sound of eighty thousand people breathing.

This tutorial on airway management started with the recognition that noisy breathing always means some sort of airway obstruction. Right now, this is another reason to worry. Wondering about Shamsi's obstructed airway, wondering whether the left lateral position is safe enough when he's snoring so loudly, wondering if I should perform a jaw thrust or even poke him awake. Worrying where the next medical emergency will follow me.

I have to escape my irrationality. Perhaps the salt of the water will wash me clean. I glance at the lifeguards as I shed my T-shirt and walk towards the surf. It's mid-week and we're the only ones here, but the sea is full of danger and they're still required to watch over this corner of the beach. The old one looks bored and the younger one fails to look interested.

The waves are gentle today. I float on my back, my stomach warming in the sun. I hope that this will remove the cold from my bones. The stinger nets aren't up yet but there's a risk of early season jellyfish with their giant tape-like tentacles, each containing thousands of pods of venom. Translucent, invisible until their prey swims innocently into their reach. But even among the jellyfish and crocodiles and Dengue-mosquitos and mangrove-bacteria, all I can think about is the danger at home, in a concrete building like many concrete buildings, full of men named David and women named Brenda and the sick and angry and hurt and dying.

I ran into David the day after Andy woke up. I went to buy Laura lunch and he pulled me aside in the lobby. At least he'd had the grace not to come to ICU.

'I know things have been awkward,' he started. 'I'm sorry that happened to your brother before we had a chance to talk about—'

And then I cut him off, no longer a polite registrar but an angry lover.

'What's there to talk about? It's simple. You pretended to mentor me and lured me to your bed.'

'Emma, you're being unfair,' he said, almost with a pout. 'I *did* mentor you, and I *do* want you to succeed.' He smiled.

My heart flipped lightly, unbidden. I willed it to be still. 'David. You're my boss. I'm on leave, but is there anything work-related that I can do for you?'

'Oh, Emma, I love a strong woman, and you're so brilliant. Can you blame me for adoring you?'

I studied him and saw how we fell together, mistaking professional respect and admiration for attraction, love, desire—the ease of academic discourse for genuine conversation and meaning. I'd even sat in my room that awful weekend and wondered if I married the wrong person, someone who couldn't make my blood run fast as we cut into flesh together, when the truth might be that he took advantage of me and I fell for it. But then, in his expression, is that—?

'We can talk about things again, some other time,' he said, tipping his head and wheeling his suitcase out of the hospital. I watched him go, remembering the feel of his broad shoulders under my hands and his hips against mine . . . Oh, David.

Now I finally have time to think about what happened, come up with my own resolution, but instead, I turn in the water and slowly swim to shore.

———

We walk hand in hand back to the house that Shamsi rented. I'm still wet and salty from the ocean, and Shamsi leaves sand sprinkled on the front doorstep. He gives me a peck on the cheek but I tiptoe away through the house, trying not to leave drips of water and sandy footprints on the clean boards.

I'm rummaging for clean clothes in the closet when Shamsi comes into the bedroom and sits on the bed.

'Hey, Em,' he says in that tone of voice.

I close my eyes. We haven't had sex since David, since long before David. I can't quite remember a time when it was easy and natural and spontaneous like I know it used to be.

'Yes, babe?' I ask without turning. I hear Shamsi stand up and then he's got his arms around me. He nestles his chin on top of my head so that I'm completely contained within his embrace. I wish my body would relax. Even I can feel how stiff and uninviting it is under his arms. I don't want to do this, but at some point, we have to. Otherwise, it might as well be over. We might as well part ways. Sex isn't reconciliation, but there's no reconciliation in a relationship without sex either.

'We don't have to, but . . .' Shamsi starts, reading my thoughts. I know why he hasn't finished the sentence. He knows I'd object to any reason he might give. I don't like him telling me it's been a long time, as if there's a required frequency that's part of the conjugal bargain. I don't even like him telling me he wants me or that I'm beautiful. Even though I'm sure he means it honestly, to me it feels contrived. I've told him I hate all these things, all I've left him is ellipses.

I turn around slowly. He loosens his embrace so that I can but doesn't entirely let me go. I tilt my head to look into his face. And there, I can see nothing but undeserved love.

'Can I?' he asks, his hand on the clip of my bikini top. I nod like it's the first time, inexplicably embarrassed again about showing my body to him. He fumbles the clip off and the bikini top falls to the floor leaving me exposed, vulnerable.

'I . . . can we get under the covers?' I ask, holding my arms over my chest. 'Can you maybe, not look?'

'Okay,' he nods and lets me lead him to the bed. I almost stop and complain that I'm wet and he's sandy, that the beautiful sheets will be ruined and they haven't left us a spare set to change them. If we do this we'll have to sleep in the grit tonight. But I don't say anything. I pull the sheets over me as quickly as I can.

He pulls my bikini bottoms down and then his own bathers. Our skin is damp and grainy as we press against each other, shifting our bodies slightly, small movements of our muscles until we fit together in a way that's unexpectedly familiar.

'Let's just kiss and then, if you want, we can go further. Okay, babe?' he asks.

I nod, still uncertain. I'm suddenly worried that maybe I'm diseased and should go get tested. How would I explain that? Because I've already decided that I'm never going to tell Shamsi what happened, if I can help it.

His lips are gentle and hesitant. I wait for his hands to wander but he keeps them on my cheek, on my waist. Maybe it's not just me. It's been so long that maybe he's shy too. We lie there almost paralysed, letting our lips do the work while our bodies pressed together, avoid each other.

And so, to break the impasse, knowing he's left it up to me, I sneak my hands lower and pull him onto me, into me. He buries his head in the pillow so that we're moving in unison but neither is looking at the other, right up until the end when he lifts his head up and his eyes are rolled back and I remember for a moment how we used to be.

———

'Was that okay?' he asks as we lay there, watching the room get darker. We should get up and shake the sand from the sheets, make dinner, wash the salt from my hair.

Yes, I nod.

'Emma, you know that we never talk. I understand you don't want to ruin the good days, but if we can't talk on the good days and it's impossible on the bad days . . .'

I roll over to face him, my cheek against his shoulder. 'What do you want to talk about?'

'You. Me. Us. The whole babies, houses, careers thing. Whether we're going to bow to this normal life we planned or if we're going to throw it all in and be revolutionaries and set mountains on fire. Or maybe live in a commune and grow our own vegetables. Or sail out to sea. What do you want anymore? I don't know. I don't think you do either.'

I take his hand and we lie together in the dark.

'How do you plan for the future when you can't ever see past the end of tomorrow?' I finally ask.

Chapter Thirty-one

Laura's exam is on Monday and she wants to sit it. She knows she might not pass, but if she does then *she'll* no longer be a trainee and can financially support their family.

'I'm so lucky,' she whispered, neither of us feeling at all lucky.

I glance at Andy, sitting quietly in the car beside me. The twins, strapped into their seats, have fallen asleep. After six weeks in rehab, he's only recently gone home. His short-term memory is still poor, but his physical strength is returning. The rehab physician is optimistic. Maybe in a year or so he'll be well enough to work. Whether or not that'll be as a surgeon remains to be seen.

Laura insisted I take his textbooks. She's emptied the house of everything that might remind him of medicine. His books, his notes, even his medical degree, never framed, waiting for a wall to be hung on once he was a specialist, have been packed into boxes and stored in our spare room.

I hope he'll open them again. He was such a good doctor, and so close to finishing. If not, Ava and Aurora might leaf through them one day, reading words he once absorbed and touching the pages he pored over, wondering why he ran from the beauty and intricacies of the human body. Even as I'm terrified my nieces will follow that path, it seems inevitable they will. Just as I can't leave no matter how much I think I should. What else would I do? My mother paints on canvas and moulds with clay, but we remove disease, rearrange life. How can any other job compare?

The day Andy got home, I took over the plant that he'd rescued and nursed back to health.

'What's this?' Laura asked as I handed it to him, resplendent with white flowers.

'My plant,' Andy smiled.

I turn off the freeway and onto a back road. Almost home.

I haven't come down all year. This is the house my parents bought the year I started school, the place I watched them eke out on weekends and holidays. They repaired the dilapidated weatherboard cottage, pruned eighty-year-old fruit trees, planted roses in the front and native flowers in the back. Andy helped sew curtains while I laid the stone path with Dad. Mum painted designs on the walls, no wallpaper for her, and then, most weekends, she filled the house with friends—other artists, writers, thinkers—while Dad carried a pager around, always ready to speed away.

Like Steve, I've taken a Friday off. Shamsi will join us tomorrow, and Laura has a long weekend to study in peace.

Andy smiles as we turn onto the dirt road, still lined with agapanthus, their purple and white heads bobbing in the wake of the car. Over the crest of the next hill we'll see the ocean, only a few kilometres away as the wedge-tailed eagles fly. There's a new gate over the end of the driveway but someone's already left it open.

Mum comes out to meet us, still in her painting apron, her hair tied up, her arms open. Andy stumbles from the car. He's often unsteady, especially after he's been sitting a while. My father, in her shadow says nothing, yet hastens to give him a hand. Perhaps he's learning to be gentle. Perhaps, this time, he'll let Andy walk before expecting him to run.

———

I'm in the garden watching the shadows lengthen. Today's been a good day. Last night, I slept long and well, for the first time in months, in the bedroom I used to share with Andy. For once there was no need to retreat to the cave with the pink sky. Today, I've read a book and napped in the hammock. Shamsi arrived early and brought pastries for morning tea. Despite the lengthening shadows, the colours seem brighter than they have in months.

I'm starting to suspect that our decline started even before this year. That over many years, we were inducted into a strange new normal so abnormal we stopped being able to notice. Perhaps Dad, in his own bizarre way, was trying to train us for this, to protect us long before we wanted or needed. Andy, in his turn, was trying to protect me.

Tucking my feet under me, I slowly sip the wine in my hand. The cold pinot gris makes the glass frost with condensation on this warm summer evening.

Across the patio Shamsi appears with a platter of bread and olive oil in one hand, and a large salad in the other. The rest of the family went to the beach today and had an early dinner. Now my mother's reading stories to the babies and my father's patiently playing checkers with Andy. It's just us under the wisteria, where Andy and I talked about how *I* would survive surgical training on the weekend my acceptance letter arrived, only a year or so ago.

'Are you okay today?' Shamsi asks, and I nod.

Yes, today I've had food and sleep and rest and sunshine. I've played with adoring babies and watched some of the light come back to my brother's eyes.

He places the food on the table, and sits opposite, handing me a napkin. I dip the bread into the oil, and as I bring it to my lips, a large drop falls on my chest. We laugh, and he leans over and wipes it away with his napkin, because that's what real lovers do. In the dim recesses of my mind, I feel that another story starts, or ends, this way. But I can't quite remember. And maybe it isn't important.

Because what I've realised since we got home from our holiday is that it isn't the patients that scare me. It's not they who have broken me. It's not the silver hair glinting in the sun that startles me, or the children on their trampolines or the motorcyclists riding too fast in the rain. These aren't the things that make my heart quicken and my brow bead with sweat. There's no terror to be found there.

Instead, it's the professors lurking in the darkness, and the administrators and Sarah with her bright red curls and Nic with her bright red lips. And David, oh, there's David with his brilliance, a problem I haven't yet fully solved even as I try to move on and mend things with Shamsi. We're back to strict professionalism, but then sometimes he'll say my name in that way and I'll wonder . . .

The fairy lights around the pergola twinkle. The salad is bland, if I'm honest, my palate so poisoned by salt and sugar and fat and ingredients made up of numbers and letters and not words. But it's a meal lovingly prepared, and my body could use the vegetables. I eat without complaint.

'Emma? Are you there?' Shamsi asks, pulling me from my thoughts about Coke and chips from the vending machine, and the last things I bought Andy, and if I applied enough first aid that day.

'Sorry . . .' I apologise, but Shamsi's smiling too.

'It's okay,' he says, and serves me more vegetables.

Maybe he's right. Maybe it's okay to admit that I started to fall apart. Maybe it's okay to ask that he wait until I start to pay attention again. Maybe I'll go see a psychologist, like Daphne suggested. Maybe I don't have to figure out everything on my own.

———

After Andy's gone to bed, after Shamsi's opened his laptop again, I pack up the checkers and take the box to Dad's study. He's redecorated since they moved here full time. The walls have been painted peacock blue, and beautiful wood shelves line one side.

I smile at a photo of my grandparents when they were young, with Dad and Uncle Bill as small children. Now that I've worked at The Mount, I see how far Dad's come from that scrawny kid. The encouragement of a country teacher, a full scholarship to a private boys' school in the city, a medical degree in that small window when university education was free, a job at The Mount and a house in the leafy inner suburbs. Andy and I didn't need scholarships to go to the best schools.

His bookshelves appear arranged by decade, documenting his myriad hobbies. Winemaking books from the brief time he planted grapevines, before he dug them back up and planted olive trees. Woodworking books from when he made the large dining table for sixteen that fills the front room. Computer books from when he decided he'd learn to manage his own network. Cookbooks from when he bought copper saucepans to make exquisite sauces and fought with Mum that it counted as 'housework' in the census.

I smile at the photos from Vietnam, Nepal, Vanuatu, taken with the surgeons he trained, but quickly turn away from the picture of him as an examiner for the College that almost killed my brother.

I hear a scuff in the hall and Dad pauses at the door.

'You came a long way to be the Head of Surgery at The Mount, didn't you?' I point to the photo of the old farm that my cousin Marty's taken over.

'It's why I always worried about you kids, especially after you decided to study medicine. I wished you were more like what I learned to be, rather than like your mother.'

'What do you mean, you "learned to be"?' I'd been convinced that he was born brilliant.

Dad moves close and studies the photo. 'The kids at school were awful, Em,' he sighs. 'I was the dirty country kid, not good enough at footy, much too good at maths.'

'Really?' Dad didn't speak much about his city school. All I know is that he didn't send Andy there.

'I had to learn to be like them. Served me well my whole career. Seems it didn't always serve everyone else well though,' he says, softly.

I feel the urge to tell him again about his failures, the ones looming larger than his successes. But for the first time, I know I don't need to. It seems that he's come to realise it for himself.

'Andy will be fine,' I tell him instead, repeating the words he once said to me.

'I know, darling, and you will be too.'

Chapter Thirty-two

Cheryl and I are having a cup of tea in her office. She's cracked the window open and summer sunlight pours in, spilling over her desk, a light breeze rustling the papers she's piled everywhere. Not many windows in the hospital open anymore. When the engineers came to this floor to seal them, she told each team that another had already done hers. She smiles in the telling.

On her bookshelf above, there's a photo of her, another woman and Joe Evans in front of a bright red London bus.

'Didn't you know that Joe trained here? I'm still good friends with his wife—she was a nurse at The Mount. If you want to spend time with him, let me know, Emma,' Cheryl says, pouring me more tea.

I hide a rueful smile. I could've just asked Cheryl for support to get that fellowship with Joe all along.

Nic sticks her head in the office doorway, her blonde waves glowing in the sun. 'Is she ready?' she asks.

Cheryl nods with a smile. 'Transport's arranged, they'll pick her up in an hour,' she says.

Nic pumps her arm in the air. This is a victory for all of us.

Jacqui's in her wheelchair packing a bag on the bed when Nic and I burst in.

Nic's brought a bunch of gerberas. 'Your favourite hospital flower, you won't get these out bush,' she says with a grin.

Dale doffs his hat at us.

'Emma! Nic!' Jacqui's bright and happy but still has a drain coming out of her groin, and her breathing is slightly laboured from having part of her lung removed. A plastic tube, extending almost to her heart, is taped securely to her chest. She'll have to travel to the local hospital for her weekly chemotherapy but she's going home, to the verandah that wraps around her house, to sit under the gum trees.

Eliza's checking out her discharge medications. Painkillers, sleeping tablets, nausea medication, enough for six weeks. My heart races at the sight of all those boxes of drugs and I demand it be quiet. I'm getting better at managing my feelings, letting myself cry at the right times, and not at the wrong ones. Today is Jacqui's day.

'I think we're set,' she says, looking around, and Dale smiles in agreement.

I crouch down to give her a clumsy hug around the wheelchair, and this time we laugh at my awkwardness.

'Jacqui, Nic and I will be moving on to other hospitals in a couple of months. They're going to manage your chemo closer to home, so by the time you come back here, there'll be a whole new team, apart from the Professor. So, I, we, wanted to say goodbye properly,' I explain.

Jacqui smiles, and gestures to Dale. 'Yes, I knew that,' she says, and takes a small bag from him. 'These are for you both, and Dr Daphne who came to see me all the time, and Dr Nathan the nice lung surgeon, and Dr Andy who was so kind to me the day you told me it had come back.'

Nic takes my hand quietly. We haven't told Jacqui about Andy, only that another team took over her care. I'm glad he'll be fondly remembered as part of her story, like he is in so many others. I'll tell him this, to remind him that he was a good doctor and, if he's able, could be again.

'Oh Jacqui, that's very kind,' says Nic, accepting the bag and saving me from speech. Inside, there are five individually wrapped boxes.

'It's nothing, not given what you've done and how wonderful you've all been. I'd like you to open yours, if that's okay? They're all the same.'

Nic hands me a box. I sit down on the bed and we open them together. Inside each is a small crystal angel with wings dipped in gold.

'I've felt so safe here . . . you're probably not religious, but I . . . I wanted to give you a small token, a wish and a hope that the angels are watching over you.'

I hug Jacqui a second time, but she doesn't know why my cheeks are wet.

Nic says she might visit Jacqui some time. She's leaving the city for the country too. When I asked her why, she was frank. 'I've watched too many people promised jobs only to be passed over for someone else—chosen for their personality, for playing the game better. Or, if they've been given the prestigious job, be forced to play that game forever. In the country I can get on with making a difference.'

I think back to Shamsi's question at the beach, one we agreed we'd leave for now. Here's Nic, showing another way. She gives me hope.

We wait until the transport ambulance arrives. They'll drive Jacqui to the local airstrip, where a small single engine plane will wing her to her nearest town. Then the local road ambulance will pick her up and bump her 'down the road' as they'll call it, a long straight path cutting across ancient song lines, to a small settlers' home like my grandparents'.

We all have something in common with each other. We just have to find it.

———

Daniel and Will are telling me about their plans for next year, both still in surgery, when Albert flags me down at the end of clinic.

'Mmm, Emma . . . come have a coffee with me,' he wheezes, thrusting a take-away cup from the café into my hand. David might be charming, but maybe I should stop judging Albert because his mannerisms are weird.

I take a sip and am surprised he's remembered my preferred coffee order.

'Aaah, I want to see if you are okay?'

I tell him that I am, and right now it's not a lie.

Albert leans against the wall of the clinic. 'Mmm, you know, your brother was, aaah, not unique here,' he says. 'Your father, mmm, he lost a friend once. They didn't get to him in time.'

I didn't know this and tell him so.

'Aaah, we all did, Emma. We must be honest. We've lost so many friends, brothers, sisters.'

The silence stretches. I'm unsure if he's supposed to be comforting me, or I'm supposed to be comforting him.

'Sometimes, in hospital, people die,' I say, to fill the void.

'Aaah, yes. But not all of them should.' Albert finishes his coffee and picks up his bag. 'Mmm, Emma—' He pauses.

'Yes, Albert?'

'You are, aaah, an excellent registrar. People . . . mmm . . . people won't understand you, and people will, aaah, try to make you who they want you to be. Do not, mmm, do not let them change you.'

———

Daphne is upstairs in the residents' room. I've decided it's okay to come up here again, to reclaim this space. For everything that unfolded here, there were also many good times—friends made, meals shared. The broken door on the on-call room's been removed, but not replaced. The sofa looks permanently in the wrong direction, and even the air hockey table's been angled away. I toss the puck at Daphne and she knocks it back. This seems like one of the few ways to move the air around in a room where, now, it's altogether too often still.

'When do you go to Boston?'

She smiles slightly. 'March. We're going to spend February on holiday, in bed.' Her smile widens slightly as she returns as hard as she can. She only told me last week that she and Vikram have been seeing each other, quietly, for months. His PhD, building an infectious disease model for Ebola, will be mostly done here, while Daphne spends a year at Harvard.

'Honestly, it's so long since we were both in long-term relationships that some distance at the start might save it.' She flicks the puck at me again and it sails into the goal. 'Sucker!' she shouts, both arms in the air.

I ask if she's made arrangements for her mother. After thirty years of being her carer, it's part of the reason Daphne's going overseas.

She grins at me and puts the puck away. 'Mum will be okay,' she says. 'I'm going to pay our neighbour to be her primary carer while I'm gone. We've drawn up a contract, but even without it, they've always been close. She cares about Mum—and she needs the money. It'll send me broke, but I need freedom more than savings.'

The afternoon sun sinks lower across the horizon, and glints off one of the tall glass buildings in the city, sending a shaft of light across the middle of the room.

'Hey, I have to go.' Shamsi and I have a date tonight and neither of us is allowed to cancel. And by neither of us, we mostly mean me. Tonight, we're having Japanese and visiting the Christmas windows. Whatever happens, we won't allow that distance between us again.

I toss her the box. 'Here's a present from Jacqui.'

Daphne opens it and lifts her crystal angel up high in the stream of reflected light. The photons split, little fragments shoot across the room in rainbow colours, brighter and purer than David's chandelier.

'I hope Jacqui gets all the good things,' Daphne exclaims, delightedly. 'I hope we all do.'

———

I give Steve a quick call on the way out and thank him for covering this evening. It was meant to be me on call, but we've rejigged the roster a little, adding a bit more flexibility where we can. His mother's not doing well and any day our situations might be reversed. The balance of life and death permeates everything.

Outside, I stop to chat to Gladys, the woman who has been homeless for years but finds refuge beside the Emergency doors. I give her ten dollars and a hug. I'm about to run across the street when someone calls my name.

Prof Bones is waving from the entrance. Damn it.

'I hear the sarcoma woman went home today,' he says, with an expression I've never before seen on his face. A smile. It sits oddly, like his facial muscles have long forgotten to pull in those directions.

I nod. This is worth a smile.

'Um, Emma, your father called me,' he continues. This is a surprise. 'We, um . . . well, the year's almost over and you'll leave us soon, but we want to make sure this sort of thing . . . it never happens again to anyone.'

'What, a doctor, like my brother, trying to suicide?'

He flinches, but like David, I hold my gaze. I won't let them hide behind weasel words anymore.

'You know, Professor Lyndhurst died in that building?' Bones points to the private hospital.

'Yes. I went to his funeral with Dad. I was only in high school.'

'He . . . Emma, he, uh, ended his own life. Had a patient die on the table. Cementing. Elective joint replacement. Took it badly.'

'It was probably more than that,' I correct him slowly. 'It was for Andy. He didn't take one thing badly, he had no capacity to take anything well. And he had no one to sit in the rubble with him when it all fell apart.'

Prof thinks on this and agrees, reluctantly. 'Ah, yes. Your father was quite angry, said the same things. Said it could be you next, if we didn't fix things. Said we'd been driving good people away, and worse, for years. Emma, are . . . are you okay?'

Lots of people have asked me this in the last few months, but none quite so uncomfortably. I'm sure he's never asked this before, of anyone. It's incongruous, coming from such an angry, old, self-absorbed man.

Does he actually want to know?

Does he notice that Paul's a bully but no one does anything about it? Does he want to hear about that whole confusing not-quite-resolved mess with David? Or that my only other poss-ible mentor hears bells and smells numbers? How much does he care that my brother's home though not yet himself? But the sun's out, Laura's passed her exam and Jacqui's gone home. And I'm still enthralled with the beauty and power of healing.

'What can we do, Emma? What should we do?'

I think about the small boxes in my satchel with Jacqui's angels inside, Andy's as yet unopened and heavy. He should have been there to get it from her himself.

I know what Andy would want, what he'd say if he were standing beside me. He'd tell me to remain silent, play the game, be a good girl, succeed in all I want. He'd say that in a broken system we should protect ourselves first.

But I know now that if we don't fight for everyone else, we aren't fighting for ourselves either. And for all the things he said, this was not how Andy lived.

'You could be nicer to everyone,' I suggest. Prof looks taken aback. 'We all could be, but you're at the top of the system. Anger's for us at the bottom. You could see people for what they have to offer, not what you think they do wrong. You could listen to *our* anger, for a change, and make things better.'

Prof goes slightly red but remains silent.

For once, I'm safe because I'm a Swann. I dig my angel out of the bag, and hold her, glinting, into the sun. 'You remember Jacqui?'

Prof shakes his head.

'You just asked about her. The woman with the femur sarcoma. You've been treating her for a year and you don't know her name. She's got two little kids and lives on a farm in the middle of nowhere. And she's going to die. You could also learn her name and get to know her as a person and not as a tumour after I move on.'

He purses his lips, but still says nothing.

'I'll see you next Wednesday?' I ask as I put the angel away.

He nods. 'See you Wednesday, Emma.'

And I skip out into the sunny evening.

Acknowledgements

This novel was written on the lands of the Wurundjeri people of the Kulin nation. I acknowledge that sovereignty was never ceded.

It's an honour to wield a pen as well as a scalpel. Sometimes I'm not sure which is sharper. Thank you, Kristine Ziwica, for handing me a pen, and for your ongoing encouragement and friendship. I'm so glad we had that coffee and you told me to write that thing. Thanks also to Georgie Dent, Tarla Lambert and Angela Priestley for their early support of this little hobby.

My eternal thanks also to:

Those family and friends who first read early drafts and convinced me that these words might have value: Julia George, Gowri Janakiramanan, Adele MacMillan, Trupti Prasad, Sara Townend.

Those who provided encouragement, stories, conversations, fact checking, confidence and friendship: Zanfina Ademi, Kate Barrett, Alistair Bishop, Stephanie Convery, Seamus Delaney, Astrid Edwards, Alys Gagnon, Kate Gregorevic, Cori Hodge, Vanida Na Ranong, Pearly Khaw, Jack Latimore, Isabelle Oderberg, Jamila Rizvi, Natalie Thurtle, Mariam Tokhi, Tara Whitaker.

Everyone in all the medical groups: the founders, the moderators and the participants, for holding spaces where we might feel less alone in our experiences.

The judges of the 2021 Victorian Premier's Literary Awards, and The Wheeler Centre, who shortlisted an early draft in the category of Unpublished Manuscript and provided such support after.

Melanie Ostell, thank you for your keen eye, sharp wit and being all and more than anyone could ask from an agent. I'm so grateful for all the ways you've helped me tell this story.

Jane Palfreyman, Ali Lavau, Christa Munns, and the whole team at Allen & Unwin, thank you for your attention, care, insight, clarity and faith. It's an honour and delight to work with you.

To my parents, Bhooma and Babu, my unending gratitude.

To my sister, Gowri, my unending love and thanks.

To my husband, Brad, and our children, I love you more than words can convey.

To those we've lost, you won't be forgotten.

———

If you're in need of crisis support, you can call Lifeline on 13 11 14 in Australia and 0800 543 354 in New Zealand at any time of day or night, or visit blackdoginstitute.org.au or beyondblue.org.au to access mental health tests, tools and support resources.